Josephine Jordin

Riding the Storm

STORM SERIES: BOOK TWO

Copyright © 2026 by Josephine Jordin
Cover design: Smoldering Rose Publications
Editor: Vallie O'hara

Smoldering Rose Publications
Okemos, MI

First edition 2026
ISBN: 9798234010834

For Sherry:
Thank you for attempting to fill a cavernous void.
You are nothing short of remarkable and sure know how to
leave a lasting impression—one lipstick kiss at a time.

__Dear Reader:__

For maximum enjoyment, please consider reading __Ready for a Storm__, the first in the Storm Series, before enjoying this book. Otherwise, you're simply shortchanging yourself. And let's be honest—you deserve better.

Prologue

His long fingers glided down the length of her exposed back, her moist skin smooth and beckoning to his insatiable hunger. His strong hands locked onto her hips and drew her back onto his aching shaft. His passion penetrated her, prompting a mounting pressure inside of him. Repeatedly, he thrust himself inside of her inviting body as she gasped with delightful shock. Long arms reached around her back to clutch her bouncing breasts before, with quickened breath, he erupted with soundless spasms.

Heart pounding at mission-critical speed, he plopped down on his back beside her. His long legs hung over the edge of the bed; the soles of his feet pressed against the maple-glazed floor. With a light moan, she snuggled up to his chest—their breathing in sync—and her fingers traced the beads of sweat from his glistening six-pack.

He glanced into her craving eyes as he brushed his full lips over hers. Her ebony pupils flowed into mahogany irises that, on this afternoon, seemed to contain the tiniest specks of gold. Those patient eyes had seen him through a myriad of trials and tribulations over the years—and they never once wavered with uncertainty.

"Marry me," he whispered, his heart and body held captive.

A skeptical expression swept across her face. Then, as she peered into his sable eyes, the depth of his heartfelt request seemed to register. Her smooth, round lips spread wide, followed by rapid-fire nods. The retired SEAL ran his hand over his shaved-smooth head, then kissed his bride-to-be.

Chapter One

Mace's grip on the leather leash tightened as his cherished mate tracked the abnormally large gray squirrel darting across the dew-covered London grass. Following a whimper, the one-hundred-seventy-pound Newfoundland abandoned its instinct and forged on alongside the retired commando.

Mace's eyes descended to his new oil-rubbed leather boots as they alternated into lead position, while he traversed the worn dirt path. Nature's creatures seemed to greet the spring day with more jubilance than usual, which he found lulling. Perhaps he didn't need to talk, after all.

"It's been about two months," the blonde beside him announced in her typical soft, albeit authoritative, tone.

Mace blew out his cheeks. "Yeah…" Anticipating his mate's curiosity, he wound the leash around his hand, eliminating the slack, when he spotted yet another bushy tail dart across their path.

"Would you like to talk about it?" She tucked a thick spiral of hair behind her ear as she relayed the empathy-laced inquiry.

"Nope."

"All right…"

They strolled along in silence once again, umbrellas at the ready as a blanket of gray draped across the London sky. Mace resumed his fixation with his boots. They had cost more than he intended to pay, but did not disappoint comfort-wise.

"Tell me about these dreams you mentioned on the phone," her soothing voice requested.

Mace threaded a hand through his recently sheared hair. He didn't really feel like talking, but knew he had to get it off his chest. With a gentle tug on the leash, he paused mid-stride, prompting Maximus to halt. The beautiful canine returned to Mace's flank, then sat on its haunches. Mace peered into the mossy-green eyes of his former therapist, her focus steadying him. Following a shallow breath, he mumbled, "My unit was in the midst of a heated CQB… I had no choice but to dispatch a threat…" He shuttered his eyes as he relived the vision from his subconscious. "I turned around to discover a young boy staring up at me…"

After a long silence, he heard Annie murmur, "Then what happened?"

He opened his eyes to find Annie's analyzing gaze upon him. Mace massaged his jaw with his free hand while the other remained glued to the leash. "The boy asked me why I killed his *baba*." Annie continued to study him. "That's when I wake up," he added with a shrug.

Mace resumed his slow pace, his obedient mate—along with his former therapist—matching his stride.

Annie untied the belt attached to her beige double-breasted peacoat and let the material fall against her thighs. "And you've had this same dream three times?" Her tone held a trace of solicitude.

Mace nodded. "Yep." His feet came to a rest as they approached the parking area, the Newfoundland pausing at his side.

"Oh, Mace." Annie craned her neck to peer up at him. "I'm so sorry you're dealing with this."

Mace dropped his chin to his chest and carried on with his appreciation for the contrast stitching on his new boots.

Annie tugged at the hem of her fuchsia V-neck sweater, which hung on her active frame, stretching it past her hips and revealing a peek of shallow, freckled cleavage. "I worry your operator syndrome is getting worse."

Mace shrugged, then crouched down beside Maximus. His hand glided across the dog's lustrous, soot-colored coat with ease, tracing an imaginary line from its head to its tail. With systematic strokes, his hand repeated the circuit on auto-repeat until interrupted by a loud sigh.

"Mace..." Annie crossed her arms over her chest.

The retired commando stood and met her gaze. "I'm okay, doc."

"Look," she clasped her hand over his. "What you've been doing with these veterans over the past few months is wonderful… but I do worry it's become a trigger point for you."

Mace's forehead puckered as he looked her square in the eyes. "I want to try to help them with their recovery."

"I know you do." Annie gave a gentle squeeze. "That's why I asked you to be involved with this new foundation. But I fear it's taken a toll on you." She fluffed her shoulder-length, dirty blonde hair—her thin, red lips pursing with the movement. "Perhaps we should resume regular sessions."

"I don't think that's necessary," Mace said, massaging his forehead.

Annie's fingers traveled to his forearm. "Mace, I want to be here for you—as a friend, not just a therapist." She flashed a sweet smile. "I trust you know that you can call me anytime. Day or night."

"I appreciate that." He rotated his wrist to glance at his titanium diver watch, the movement freeing him from her grasp. "Well, I'd better go get ready for my date."

Annie's smile faded. "All right, but let's get together soon." Following an acknowledgment from Mace, she added, "Preferably outside of the community center so we're free from distractions."

Issuing a quick pat on her shoulder, Mace mumbled, "Thanks, doc." Then he pivoted and strode towards his SUV, Maximus at his heel.

****

Freshly showered and shaved, his typical garment choices—black tactical pants and a form-fitting shirt—not because he chose to put his broad chest on display, but because he struggled to find shirts that accommodated his chiseled mass—clung to his frame. With an aggressive pace, he crossed into the sought-after hotel's dining area, pausing just long enough for the hostess to direct him. He'd been looking forward to this luncheon all week. With one eye glued to the panoramic view of the River Thames, he trekked along the designated route towards the southwest corner of the exclusive restaurant.

Despite the elegant restaurant bursting at the seams with guests, Mace spied his lunch date with ease—for she stood out in any crowd. She rose to greet him as he drew near, a delighted expression stretching over her face. She swept a strand of sandy blonde hair across her forehead before being swallowed up by his heavy arms, her head brushing against his solid chest.

After planting a quick peck on her cheek, she retreated to her fleur-de-lis embroidered chair. Clasping his hands over the high-back frame, Mace slid her forward, careful to halt a few inches from the table—her long legs disappearing from his view—then took his spot beside her. He tossed back a refreshing sip of his laced-with-lemon ice water and watched with curiosity as she reached into her ivory crocodile satchel. A small crimson envelope emerged, which she proceeded to slide in front of him.

A beautiful smile crossed her face. "Here—before I forget."

Chapter Two

Ava slipped the harness over her thighs, then secured it at her waist with a soft click. As instructed, she clipped the carabiner to the top pulley. Leaning back, she allowed her weight to test its hold. Satisfied, she clutched her hands around the nylon strap that hung in front of her. Tightening her grip, her right palm felt a sharp poke as the sizeable diamond ring attached to her left finger cut into the skin. She had hoped to be accustomed to it by now, but the precious jewel still felt foreign.

Disregarding her inner voice, she chanced a squinted peek over the hundred-foot-high ledge. A sea of green foliage varying in height—some crowns as high as the cliff she stood upon—greeted her glimpse. She drew in a long, deep breath, exhaled slowly, then launched herself off the edge of the summit.

The steel cable dipped, then tapered as Ava sailed across the magnificent mountainous Canadian landscape. Dark, diminutive forms grew into recognizable shapes as she approached the halfway point of the four-hundred-foot span. Her eyes fell upon her fiancé, his arms spread wide, and a beaming smile plastered on his face.

She braced for impact as she glided toward the landing. A moment later, her size seven hiking boots connected with solid ground, and she collided with Reed's outstretched arms—his muscular build failing to impede her momentum—sending the two of them to the ground. After exchanging laughing, loving smiles, Ava pressed her lips to his cheek.

"Cut!" The sound of their director's French-inflected voice bellowed from behind. "*Magnifique*!"

Ava stood and dusted off her shiny black leggings while the crew broke out in a round of applause.

"Great job, partner," Reed raised his large palm in the air.

Ava met it halfway, resulting in a satisfying clap. "Right back at ya."

Their director, Pierre, hurried toward them. "Ava, my dahling,"—he kissed her cheek—"you *never* disappoint." He swiveled to face Reed. "You don't *usually* disappoint," he said, patting the imposing actor on the back.

"Gee, thanks, Pierre," Reed said with a shake of his head that sent slight, jet-black strands swaying.

Pierre wrapped his arms around both of them. "Go—rest now. But be back on set at five am tomorrow, not a minute later!" he called out as he turned and marched off.

Ava's fingers worked to unfasten the multitude of clips that held her harness in place. She slid the elastic band from the nape of her neck and gave a toss of her long blonde locks.

"You forgot one." Reed's fingers grazed the fabric stretched over her toned stomach as he released the clip fastened to her waist, sending the harness coasting down her thighs.

"Thanks." Ava stepped out of the nylon and then handed the gear off to the designated crew member.

"Feel like grabbing a drink at the hotel before you head back to your cabin?" Reed asked, a hopeful glint in his silvery eyes.

"I'm exhausted, Reed." Ava met his gaze with pursed lips. "I'm sorry. Plus,"—she extended a one-shouldered shrug—"I promised Scotch we'd continue our action flick marathon tonight."

"Ahh… yes…" Reed cast a fleeting smile. "I'd almost forgotten."

"Besides,"—Ava tilted her head—"I'm sure your kiddos are excited to see you—even if it is only through a laptop screen."

"I suppose…"

"Good night, Reed," Ava murmured. "I'll see you first thing in the morning," she added as she pranced off to find her trusted bodyguard. Sifting through the bustling crew, she failed to spot the red-headed Scotsman. Then the sound of high-pitched giggles, echoing in unison, revealed his position. Wreathed by a crowd of broad-smiled female crew members—their hankering eyes affixed to him—Scotch stood, his head and shoulders exposed above the admiring swarm.

"Oh, Scotch, you're *so* funny!" Ava overheard one of them say as she approached. The young woman's hand rested on the Scotsman's bicep, while another hand—belonging to an entirely different woman—rested on his other bicep. *Oh dear.*

"Hey, Ava." Scotch tipped his head back when he caught sight of the actress.

"Hello," she cast an amused smile as the admirers stepped back from their coveted possession. "I'm ready whenever you are."

"Great. Let's make like a baker's truck and haul buns outta here," Scotch said, prompting yet another round of high-pitched giggles. "Ladies, it's been real." He flashed a two-finger salute, then fell in place beside Ava as she sauntered toward their rented Range Rover.

Their western route afforded them a spectacular view of the magenta horizon as the sun disappeared behind the rolling plains. Scotch maneuvered the luxury rental over the rocky gravel road that led to the resort's private vacation rentals. Ava appreciated the accommodation option, as she had grown tired of trailers and traditional hotel rooms. In the distance, a large two-story chalet materialized, its shape dark against the eastern sky. After rolling to a gentle stop, Scotch spun the knob into the park position before jumping out of the vehicle. He dashed across the front of the truck, then pried the passenger door open.

"Thanks, Scotch, but you really don't have to get my door *every* time," Ava said as she climbed out.

"It's all part of the service," Scotch said with a wink.

Side by side, the two of them roamed up the wooden front steps that led to the expansive covered porch of the cedar-sided log cabin. Her patience was tested as Scotch dug through multiple pockets in search of the key to the single-lock entry. At last, the door swung inward, revealing a vast murkiness. The darkness swallowed the Scotsman as he entered ahead of Ava, before a faint click bathed the sweeping great room in a soft glow.

"I'll get the popcorn started!" The retired sniper called out as he ambled across the generous space and headed toward the kitchen.

"All right… I'll be back down in a few minutes." Ava made her way to the glossy, exposed log staircase situated across the far end of the gourmet kitchen. At the top of the stairs, she minced past the russet-brown suede sofa and mission-style rocking chair that adorned the loft before crossing into the master suite. With a gentle push, she closed the door behind her and drew in a soothing breath. *Silence*. She took a moment to treasure the glorious sound of absolutely nothing. They were nearly three-quarters of the way through filming—which marked the twenty-first consecutive day of fourteen-plus hours on set—and exhausted didn't even begin to describe how she was feeling. The brutal schedule had never been an issue for her before, but—given that this was her third production in four short months—the commitment had begun to take its toll. *Just get through the next few weeks.*

She wandered over to the pine nightstand that rested beside the king-size bed. With a graceful slide, she removed the huge rock attached to her left finger and dropped it in the small acacia bowl next to the sleeping black bear that formed the base of the bedside lamp. The cabin's woodsy motif didn't appeal to her; she preferred a nautical décor, but she'd grown fond of the curled-up mama bear holding the soft LED light.

Ava slipped out of her clothes and tossed them on the oversized chair opposite the bed, while reminding herself to return them to her dressing room tomorrow. She threw on a pair of cotton pajama shorts and a coordinating pink tank before swiping her phone to life. A quick assessment revealed an overwhelming number of emails—but only one text.

"Popcorn's ready!" A Scottish voice boomed from below.

Ava swung open the pine door and responded with a resounding, "I'll be right down." She finished crafting her response, then, with an aching in her heart, tapped the *send* icon.

Chapter Three

Luke." Ava's voice held a steady hush. "Something feels off..." she whispered as she and Reed cautiously canvassed the dark, secret tunnels below the infamous hotel with stealth. Despite the warm spring temps, the abandoned sublevel space delivered a frosty dampness that chilled her to her core.

"I feel it too… We must be extra cautious." Reed's high-powered LED flashlight continued to sweep the path in front of them. "Here—take my hand," his bassy, melodic voice reverberated off the archaic masonry as he reached out for her.

Ava laced her fingers with his and stepped closer to him; her nostrils welcoming the spicy scent of his cologne. Reed's beam continued to probe the deteriorating concrete in front of them, unsteady in his shaky hand, until it landed on a crimson-colored stain. A shadow danced across their faces, disclosing their concerned exchange in silence.

A few hesitant steps later, Ava froze in place. "Luke—I think we just found our client!" she cried, concurrent with her rehearsed expression of horror, as the camera zoomed in on her face.

"Cut!" Pierre yelled. Her hand still clasped in Reed's, Ava waited with bated breath as the director spent a few moments studying his viewfinder. An anticipatory silence befell the crew, only to be broken by a booming, "*Superbe!*"

She felt Reed's grasp tighten around her as the overhead fluorescent lighting kicked back on. "We make quite the team, Ava."

Ava cast a bright smile and said, "I'm just glad you're not sick of me yet." She delivered a playful shove to her co-star, freeing herself from his embrace.

"Never." Reed briefly lidded one eye.

"I can't believe this is our fourth movie together… and I've only been with Homepoint for a little over two years…"

"What can I say? The fans love us!"

"It's true," Pierre announced as he appeared at their side. "Ava—the studio is even thinking of replacing your *Summer Squash Surprise* co-star with Reed for the sequel!"

Ava shook her head in disbelief, a fleeting smile escaping her lips.

"Now, you two go get ready." Pierre gestured toward the exit. "The *Mystery and Mayhem: More Mayhem* reception starts promptly at seven!"

✳✳✳✳

With her hand wound around Scotch's shredded forearm, the crisp cotton grazing her bare skin, Ava hesitated at the threshold of the sunken reception hall. She drew in a sharp breath as she surveyed the decadent space from three feet above. Silky gold draped across a multitude of Palladian windows. Opulent empire-style crystal chandeliers, strategically located, hung from the fourteen-foot ceiling. A Chamber orchestra harmonized from the southwest corner of the room, opposite a walnut hand-carved bar.

Their presence at the top of the six-step entrance lured admiring leers from every inch of the room.

"Damn, Ava," Scotch muttered. "I'm not used to this many people staring at me."

"Well, if you didn't look so *handsome.*" She cast a wink at the Scotsman.

"I *was* worried about that."

Ava delicately bit the inside of her cheek to keep from laughing. *Humility was not his strong suit.* Arm in arm, Scotch led her down the polished mahogany steps into the spacious hall. By the time they reached the base of the steps, most guests had directed their gaze elsewhere, though some eyes still lingered, roaming over Ava as she passed by.

"Mind if I make my way to the bar?" Scotch asked as they paraded toward the center of the capacious ballroom.

"Not at all," Ava said, relinquishing his muscular arm.

"Bloody great! What can I get ye?"

Ava smoothed her red, curve-hugging sequined gown over her hips. "I find myself in the mood for a mojito."

"Nice." Scotch bobbed his head. "Be right back," he said before scurrying off.

"Ava!" The familiar sound of Reed's voice called out from behind, prompting her to pivot in her red stilettos.

"Hi," she whispered as he maneuvered around the other guests to reach her side.

"My God." His eyes descended over her sparkling form. "You look absolutely stunning." He dipped his head and planted a soft kiss on her cheek.

Ava felt herself grow flush as she tucked a long, wavy golden lock behind her ear. "Thank you."

"Ah! There's my dynamic duo!" Pierre's voice resonated from across the room. "Ava! Reed!" the director motioned for them to approach. "Come. I'd like to introduce you to someone."

Ava exchanged a knowing glance with Reed. "And so it begins," she whispered in his ear.

Chapter Four

Scotch leaned against the veneered, oil-stained bar, his eyes scouring the extravagant space. He recognized a few faces as crew members, but wondered who the rest of the guests were. *Probably hoity-toity wealthy snobs.* He drummed his long fingers on the walnut counter while he waited for the rotund, past-his-prime bartender to make their mojitos.

"Would you like my cherry?" a soft voice from the opposite end of the bar inquired.

Scotch whipped his head in the direction of the sultry sound. His eyes fell upon a middle-aged woman staring at him. Long, sleek, dark locks trailed past her slender, olive-colored bare shoulders. Both of her elbows rested on the lustrous counter while a long, cherry-red nail traced mocha-painted lips. From her free hand, between delicate-looking fingers, dangled the stem of a maraschino cherry.

Scotch unbuttoned the cuffs of his new, white dress shirt, then rolled the sleeves back, unveiling his powerful forearms. He stepped around the corner of the bar, closing the distance between him and the temptress. His gaze traveled at a leisurely pace up her exposed legs—the shiny black fabric of her tight dress barely reaching her thighs—and hovered over the pronounced crease of her décolletage. Her dress—Scotch wasn't sure it even qualified as one—demanded attention, and he fell victim without the slightest resistance.

After a long moment, his jade eyes lifted to hers. "I never turn down a cherry," he said, extending his palm beneath the suspended fruit.

The woman's chocolate orbs studied him as she dropped the sweet, round fruit into his hand. "Shall I presume you're sleeping with that gorgeous *actrice?*"

Scotch inched closer to the French enchantress; the arousing scent of her perfume wafted up to him. "Nah. I'm just her bodyguard."

She arched a dark eyebrow. "Bodyguard, huh?"

Scotch nodded before biting the sweet fruit from its stem.

Her chocolate gaze rolled over his chest—twice. "What other services do you provide?"

Long-range threat elimination, explosive assault engineering, aerial surveillance… "Let's just say I take security very seriously." Scotch's eyes drifted down to the massive mounds of flesh peeking out from her black haltered neckline.

A muffled *ting* sounded as the bartender set two Collins glasses filled with clear liquid and adorned with mint leaves in front of him.

Scotch wrapped a large hand around one of the tall vessels and raised it to his chest. "Cheers," he said before downing half the glass.

"You seem thirsty," she whispered before teasing a sip from her own cocktail.

Scotch locked his gaze on her glistening mocha lips. "You have no idea." Then he grabbed the second highball from the bar and stalked off in search of Ava.

*****

"So, I go to jam the gun back into its holster, which is at the small of my back, right?" A crowd had gathered around the actors as Reed gestured behind his back. "Well, I miss—spectacularly, I might add—and shove the gun right into my pants!" Hearty chuckles surrounded her. "So, now Ava's supposed to grab the gun out of my holster, right?" Ava couldn't contain her laughing smile as Reed continued. "She's patting me all over trying to find the darn thing!" Infectious laughter spread amongst the guests.

"The question is…" a tall, well-dressed man standing beside their director spoke up. "Did she reach inside your pants to retrieve it?" His brandy-colored eyes held an impish gleam as he concluded his question.

"Well, a guy can dream," Reed replied with a wink in Ava's direction.

Ava felt a burst of searing heat pervade her cheeks. The sudden touch of a strong hand clasping hers took her by surprise; she pivoted to see Scotch standing next to her, and he thrust an ice-cold glass in her grasp. "Thank you," she whispered.

With their director at his side, the well-dressed man stepped closer. "Ava, Reed," Pierre indicated to the handsome stranger. "I'd like you to meet Pierson Levasque, the owner of the resort."

Ava studied the man who stood before her as he shook Reed's proffered hand. His expensive-looking black suit did little to hide his impressive physique. Thick, dark hair tossed to one side atop his head, and his chiseled, finely creased face featured a neatly trimmed circle beard with specks of silver.

Directing his attention to Ava, Pierson took hold of her hand and whisked it to his lips. "*Enchanté,*" he whispered before planting a light kiss. His voice held a deep but silky, French-inflected eminence. "I adore your films."

A sparkle pierced his captivating eyes as Ava canted her head and uttered, "*Merci beaucoup.*" She added, "It's lovely to meet you," as she withdrew her hand from his.

"And here I thought *I* was smooth," Scotch quipped.

As the owner's stare shifted to Scotch, Ava thought she detected a glint of annoyance. "Mr. Levasque,"—Ava swept her palm toward Scotch—"allow me to introduce my bodyguard, Mr. Scotchfeld."

"Nice to meet ye, mate," the Scotsman threw his hand out.

"Actually, it's *doctor* Levasque," the owner corrected.

Pierre's domed head bounced up and down. "Pierson also serves as the medical director for the resort."

Ava arched her brow. "Impressive."

"Just pursuing my passion." Dr. Levasque shrugged his shoulders. "My sister actually oversees the day-to-day operations of the resort." He perused the room. "Ah, there she is at the bar. *Excusez-moi* while I get her—I'd like to introduce you."

Ava noticed the Scotsman's posture stiffen as the doctor walked off. "Everything okay?" she asked under her breath. In lieu of a response, Scotch stroked the corners of his mouth.

"Ava—" Pierre clasped her forearm.

"Yes?" she replied, shifting her attention from Scotch.

The slightest of frowns manifested on the seasoned director's face. "I'd like to retake the zipline shot."

Ava flashed him a quizzical look. "I don't understand. You said you loved it?"

"You were *parfait,* but the camera operator crossed the line, and I don't want to use a buffer shot." He smiled at her. "We simply reshoot on Thursday."

Ava offered a reluctant nod. *Great, another half-day tacked onto the schedule.*

Encircling guests parted, and Dr. Levasque reappeared, a beautiful forty-something at his side. "Reed? Ava?" The doctor gestured to the woman beside him. "This is my sister, Julietta."

Reed proffered his hand first. Ava watched as the ebony-haired woman gave it a graceful shake before swiveling toward her. The doctor's sister stood a few inches below Ava, despite her five-inch stiletto heels. Her heart-shaped face revealed traces of well-nourished fine lines. She peered at Ava with deep, chocolate eyes that seemed to linger over every inch of her body, projecting an appreciative gleam. Ava's gaze unintentionally followed suit, skimming over her petite, barely sheathed frame, which featured a garish display of unnaturally large breasts. Ava forced a gracious smile. "Hello," she said as she clasped the woman's delicate hand in hers. "Your resort is beautiful."

"*Merci.*" She spoke with a sultry French accent, breathy and tantalizing. *If she offered an after-hours podcast on the art of seduction, she'd have like a billion followers.* At last, the woman's eyes departed from Ava's physique—and zeroed in on Scotch.

Ava again gestured to the imposing Scotsman. "May I introduce my bodyguard, Mr. Scotchfeld?"

Following an ostentatious once-over, Julietta extended her hand, which Scotch clutched in a hearty shake. "Rumor has it you're quite the *sécurité* expert."

Scotch shrugged. "I guess you could say that."

"*Fantastique*." A coquettish smile spread her lips wide. "Why don't you stop by my place tomorrow? I'm planning some *sécurité* upgrades and would like to get your thoughts."

"Aye." Scotch bobbed his head. "Be happy to," he said as he smoothed the tip of his ginger beard into a point.

Julietta reached into a small satin purse and withdrew a square business card. She stepped closer to the retired sniper, then slid the card into his chest pocket. "I look forward to it, *Monsieur* Scotchfeld."

"Feel free to call me Scotch."

"Feel free to call me *anytime*." Then, following a graceful one-eighty, Julietta sashayed into the crowd and disappeared amongst the gathered guests.

Chapter Five

Following the lavish reception, Ava—Scotch at her side—ventured out into the murky, misty April evening. Beside the valet stand, they paused while Scotch fished a slip of paper from the slanted pocket at his hip. He passed it off to the attendant—a young man whose height was the only indication he was old enough to operate a motor vehicle. While they waited for her Range Rover, Ava whispered, "Are you okay to drive?"

A look of contempt crept over the Scotsman's face. "Of course."

"Sorry." Ava imparted a reassuring smile. "I just wasn't sure how many mojitos found their way into your hands…"

"Only two," Scotch said with a waggle of his bushy red brows.

A piercing set of headlights and a subdued, protracted squeal announced the arrival of their vehicle in the circular drive. After coming to a stop alongside them, Scotch yanked open the passenger door to allow Ava's ingress before hurrying over to the driver's side. A comfortable silence settled over them as the Scotsman navigated the familiar route—the moonless night stealing their typical scenic view. Ava stared through her window into the dark void; an unrest stirred within her—one she couldn't seem to shake. She chalked it up to fatigue. She missed home—and everything that went along with it.

"I'll plan on swinging by Julietta's place tomorrow afternoon so I can be back on set before you wrap up for the day." The delightful Scottish accent dragged her back into the moment.

"Oh, Scotch." Ava studied his handsome face, veiled by the shadowy interior. "Please be careful with that woman. There's something about her I simply do not trust."

"Hey—careful's my middle name." As he veered into the drive, he reached across the center console and placed a reassuring hand over her forearm.

The driver and passenger door slammed synchronously—although she appreciated Scotch's chivalrous efforts, whether feigned or genuine, she grew tired of being waited on. With congruent strides, they ambled up the steps of the dark, empty cabin. Ava embraced the evening norm and waited while Scotch removed the metal key from his pocket. He grasped the round, satin-nickel handle and was about to insert the key when the door inched open.

He whipped his head toward Ava. "I'm sure I locked this."

Ava recalled their mad dash out the door that morning. "We left in such a hurry." She offered a consolatory smile. "I'm sure everything is fine."

With soundless movements, Scotch stepped inside and switched on the overhead light. All seemed still. Ava followed at a cautious pace as he inspected the first floor of the cabin. The great room and large, eat-in kitchen were exactly as they had left them—Scotch's breakfast plate and coffee mug still rested beside the sink. The retired sniper wandered down the short hall, which led to his bedroom and bathroom, Ava meandering behind. With a slap of his hand against the wall, his room awoke under a soft light. Two queen beds, one untouched, the other—its moose-print cover lumped into a mass of green and black—greeted them, along with a scattering of giant-sized clothing strewn about.

Ava made an earnest attempt to keep her brows from furrowing. "Is this how you left your room this morning?"

"Yep," Scotch said with a shrug. "All looks well."

A sigh fled her lips. "Well, that's a relief."

"I'd better go check your room." Scotch bounded toward the hall.

"No need." She waved a dismissive hand. "I'm sure it's fine."

The Scotsman did an about-face in the doorway. "You'd deny me my one responsibility?"

Ava released a delicate yawn. "Of course not… I just really want to get ready for bed."

Scotch's broad shoulders slumped. "What? No *Die Hard* tonight?"

Ava gave a gentle shake of her head. "Sorry, Scotch. I'm exhausted—and we need to be back on set by five in the morning." Ava watched as the Scotsman's bottom lip jutted out, so she followed up her statement with, "But we'll plan on tomorrow, okay?"

"Aye." Scotch's gem-like eyes reclaimed their familiar sparkle. "Counting on it, lass."

"Good night, Scotch." Ava spun on her heel, then called out, "Thank you for being here," as she sauntered toward the door. From the hall, she heard him return the sentiment.

She made her way back through the quiet house and up the stairs that led to her room, her petite feet silent over the polished oak. She crossed the threshold into the spacious suite, flipped on the light, then let out a startled scream.

Chapter Six

Ava's entire body tensed as she skimmed over the disconcerting damage. The luxurious, knotty-pine suite had been desecrated. Her belongings were scattered everywhere—clothes had been tossed across the floor and the king-size bed, while others spilled from the dresser's drawers. The thick, plaid comforter had been heaped into a lumpy pile next to the window while the elongated pillows lay askew near the bathroom entrance. Her laptop, which had rested atop the large wooden desk adjacent to the bed, now lay on the floor near the balcony. The desk's drawers had been emptied—their contents dispersed over the smooth wood surface and beneath it. Her eyes locked onto the mirror centered above the dresser as the thunderous pounding of footsteps bolting up the stairs journeyed to her ears.

Scotch materialized in the doorway. "Damn—and I thought my room was bad," he mumbled as he browsed the messy madness. Ava's head fell to her chest. He inched closer and said, "Sorry," before clamping his strong arms around her. His comforting embrace slowed her breathing, and after a long moment, he whispered, "You okay?"

She shrank from his grasp and offered a reluctant nod. Her shoulders sank as she pointed to the ornate mirror above the dresser, drawing Scotch's stare. Scribbled across the reflective surface with what appeared to be a red dry-erase marker were the words: *GO BACK TO CALIFORNIA!*

Ava shook off her angst, grabbed a cloth, and marched over to the mirror.

"Hold up," Scotch ordered, throwing up his palm. He extracted his phone from his back pocket and snapped a picture of the threatening message, then swiveled to capture a few of the disorderly room before gesturing for her to proceed.

To Ava's relief, the mirror wiped clean, leaving no traces of the threatening message. She went straight to work restoring her room to its previous state in silence.

"Can you tell if anything's missing?" The retired sniper asked as he gathered her garments from the varnished wood floor.

"It's hard to say at this point..." Ava surveyed the wreckage for the fourth time. "My laptop is the most important thing, and that's still here." She walked over to the nightstand and peeked in the small, wooden keepsake bowl that lay atop it. "And my jewelry seems to be accounted for..."

Scotch finished picking up the clothes from the floor and rested them in a pile on the bed. "Ava… any idea who might've done this?

The actress grew thoughtful. "No… I haven't encountered anyone who raised any red flags," she murmured. She powered up her laptop to make sure her files were secure, her eyes glued to the screen as she spoke. "There are so many people here… between the crew and guests… it could've been anyone." With a sigh of relief, Ava set her laptop on the nightstand, then marched toward the pine desk.

Scotch's hands balled into fists. "I never liked this cabin. The front door doesn't even have a dead bolt, for cryin' out loud! Might as well welcome the bad guys with drinks and hors d'oeuvres!" his adorable Scottish voice grumbled; his feet rooted in place. With an aggressive shake of his head, he continued, "I knew I shoulda installed some cameras and better locks when we first got here," he clenched his fists for the second time.

Ava offered a comforting smile. "Please don't beat yourself up. Security cameras and locks can only do so much."

He fixed his eyes on her. "You're right, but until we figure this out, you're either with Reed or me twenty-four-seven. Understood?" Ava slanted her head in acknowledgment as he began to pace the recently cleared, narrow path along the foot of the bed. The creases of his forehead bunched up as he halted mid-step. "We need to notify the police."

"No." Ava slammed her arms over her chest.

Scotch flung his head back. "Ava—you were just threatened!"

She turned her attention back to the cluttered desk. "Notifying the police will simply delay filming—let alone alert whoever did this." She pivoted to face Scotch. "Please, Scotch, I just want to wrap up this film and go home!" Her voice held the slightest shake. "Besides,"—she dabbed at the corners of her eyes—"it's not like this is the first time this has happened."

Emerald eyes challenged her. "That may be—but never on my watch."

Ava cleared her throat. "Nothing appears to have been taken, and no one was hurt," her velvety tone soothed. "Maybe some fetching young lady is just trying to scare me away so she can have you all to herself," she teased, lifting a shoulder to her cheek, prompting a flattered smile on behalf of the Scotsman. "Let's just stay vigilant and focus on finishing this project, Scotch," she blurted before pausing to catch her breath. "Please."

The retired sniper conceded with a loud sigh. "Fine, but we're bringing on more security."

Ava swept the remaining items that covered the desk into her arms, then dropped them into the center drawer. She glanced back at Scotch. "What do you propose?"

The Scotsman shifted his cleanup efforts to the oversized leather chair in the corner of the room, decorated with erratically placed intimate garments. He picked up a large satin bra and examined it before placing it on the bed, then moving on to its counterpart—a sage-green thong panty marked with ivory polka dots.

Ava rushed to his side. "I'll finish the clothes, Scotch." The Scotsman's lips curved downward. "Thank you, though."

Scotch stroked the tip of his ginger beard. "We need a presence at the house."

Ava tilted her chin and arched an eyebrow while she folded the pair of panties and secured them in the dresser's top drawer. "I don't know…"

Scotch's hands landed on his hips. "Ava—it's the only way."

With a soft touch, Ava glided the drawer closed, keeping her back to the Scotsman. "I know who you're referring to, and I don't want to be a bother…"

"Ava, look—I promised to keep you safe." Scotch's tone grew serious. "My life is literally tied to your well-being."

Ava turned to face him, her arms folded over her chest. "What makes you think he'd even be interested?"

A gleam penetrated Scotch's jade eyes. "Because I just talked to him the other day and he's bored out of his mind."

The last thing Ava wanted was to be an imposition, but when Scotch waggled his shaggy red brows, she couldn't resist the commando's request. "Okay, fine," she said with a gentle shake of her head and a hint of a smile. "Call him."

Chapter Seven

With Ava safe in the confines of Reed's arms on set, Scotch decided it'd be a good time to run a quick errand.

He parked Ava's luxury rental at the circular drive's mid-point, next to the silver Spyder—a black horse over a crested coat of arms decal attached to the center of the hood. Cloaked by the SUV's privacy glass, he let out a low whistle of appreciation as he scoped out the sprawling estate that lay before him. *Bloody incredible.*

The stone castle-like home spanned several hundred feet across and featured a multitude of gabled peaks offset by round two-story turrets positioned at either end. Scotch stepped from the truck and trekked across the cobblestone drive toward the front steps, where double glass doors trimmed with wrought iron scrolling greeted him. He glanced at the camera positioned in the upper-right corner of the alcove, its tiny green light prompting him to wave. He brushed the lint from his stretched-thin tactical shirt, then pressed the round, golden button next to the door.

Scotch detected a shadowy movement through the glass and, a moment later, the iron-lined door parted. A man with neatly trimmed espresso-colored hair dusted with silver and an athletic build manifested. Standing only an inch or two below his six-foot-three frame, the man fixed his wary amber eyes upon him. "Yes?" he inquired, his tone brusque and dry.

Scotch met his stare. "I'm here to see Ms. Levasque."

The man flashed an irritated look. "Do you have an appointment?"

Scotch swallowed his annoyance. "She told me to stop by today. *Anytime.*"

"I'll bet." The man mumbled before running his tongue over his teeth inside his mouth.

For a moment, the man remained still. Then, he swung the door wide and announced, "She's out back." With a jerk, he rotated one hundred eighty degrees, then strode toward the center of the estate. Scotch maintained a comfortable distance as he followed the butler across the marble-lined entrance hall and passed an elegant, curved staircase, its cherry-wood railing bestowing a radiant sheen, that led to a bowed balcony above. His eyes glanced skyward at the exposed gable beams, then to the right, where he drank in the details of a grand sitting room complete with a two-story stacked stone fireplace and concert grand piano. He continued to trail the butler into a cavernous kitchen lined with antique-white paneled cabinets topped with black quartz, before, at last, being led through a nine-foot French door and onto the patio.

The man gestured toward the pool, then turned and marched back inside the home. Scotch stepped down onto the stamped concrete and scanned his surroundings. Natural stone curved around a custom, kidney-shaped in-ground pool and hot tub, with a slate bridge connecting the two bodies of water. *Damn.*

A splash sounded a split second before a dripping wet head, ebony hair slicked back, emerged from the water. "Ah, *Monsieur* Scotchfeld." A glistening smile broke across Julietta's dewy lips. "*Bon après-midi.*"

Scotch inclined his head. His French was a little rusty. "*Bonjour.*"

Julietta submerged herself in the water and then swam toward the nearest ledge. After propping her elbows on the stone surface, she laced her thin fingers, then rested her chin on her overlaid hands. "Thank you for coming."

"My pleasure." Scotch smoothed his coarse beard. "Isn't it a bit chilly for a swim?"

Thick, dripping wet eyelashes fluttered. "We heat it all year."

Must be nice. "How can I help?"

Another smile. "I'm glad you asked." Glossy, cherry-red nails stroked her own skin. "I'd love to hear your thoughts on what my new security system should include. I want to make sure we have the most advanced *fonctionnalités*."

"Aye." Scotch bobbed his head as his eyes darted from side to side. "Your home is incredible."

Julietta smoothed her hand over her dark, dripping-wet hair. "*Merci*."

"This place could house an army." Scotch's brows knitted together. "Who all lives here—besides you and your uber-friendly butler?"

Julietta let out a light laugh. "My brother lives here as well—in the east wing."

"Wings, huh?" Scotch shook his head in disbelief. He had never seen anything like this in all his travels. This place made the Ellis estate look like a shack.

"Why don't you walk the terrain while I finish my swim?" She imparted a wide, beautiful smile. "Then we can discuss your suggestions."

"Sure thing." Scotch cast a two-finger salute, then trekked toward the south side of the property, where large slate slabs led up to the front of the house. Scotch noted the existing cameras—outfitted with thermal-imaging lenses—placed at every corner and entrance. He peered through the French casement windows that lined the first floor—each fitted with the latest sensors available. Dusk-sensitive flood lights were stationed throughout the property, and an eight-foot-high wrought iron fence lined the parcel. Aside from armed guards, suggestions for improvement escaped him.

Thirty minutes later, he found himself back beside the inviting in-ground pool. Failing to spot Julietta, he pivoted toward the patio door, catching a glimpse of her dark tresses along his rotation. Adjusting course, he aimed for the hot tub—her chocolate eyes locking onto him as he approached.

The stratus sky fostered the cooler-than-average April afternoon, and steam billowed from the effervescent whirlpool. Olive-tinted hips, sans tan lines, swayed with each step as Julietta emerged from the gurgling water. Eyeing the neatly folded stack of towels resting on a nearby chaise, Scotch grabbed one and then hurried beside the raven-haired beauty.

"*Merci*." Her moist lips gleamed with her broad smile. She patted the towel over her petite, voluptuous form, then tossed it aside.

The concept of a gentleman had never resided in Scotch's wheelhouse. He allowed his eyes to loiter over the wealthy resort owner as she positioned herself in the reclined chaise lounge beside him. Her olive skin, punctuated with intermittent freckles, shimmered with tiny droplets. A thin, red string stretched across the curve of her hips, connecting to a fragment of fabric that rested well below her belly button. His eyes traveled north over her taut stomach, coming to a rest at the generous mounds of flesh that escaped the tiny, triangular fabric.

"What are your thoughts?" her smooth voice inquired as she bent one leg at the knee.

Scotch strained the sinful notions from his mind. He crossed his arms over his hulking chest. "You've got this place on lockdown. Your current system has all the newest technology available on the market."

"Well, that is a relief," Julietta said, as she ran a long, acrylic nail back and forth across her lips.

"Quite honestly, I'm not even sure why you needed me to come over," Scotch said, failing to keep the irritation out of his tone.

"I'm sorry you feel that way." Julietta flashed a sultry smile. "The least I can do is offer you something for your time."

Scotch threw his hands in the air. "I don't want your money."

"*Non, non, Monsieur* Scotchfeld." Julietta swiveled in her chaise, her head waist high to the Scotsman. "That is not what I was referring to."

Few things surprised Scotch. The sudden tug on his zipper, however, did. He gaped as her fingers worked to free his swelling manhood; the delight dancing in her eyes conveyed her pleasure with the discovery. She wasted no time pulling him into her mouth, struggling to accommodate his length and girth. Scotch's fingers found the knot at the base of her neck and teased it free. His large hands massaged her bare, silicone-enhanced breasts, as her mouth undulated over his engorged shaft. His heart pounded erratically inside his chest, until—with a loud groan—his scaling excitement peaked. After a moment of bliss, he kneeled before her and pressed his lips to hers, savoring both the feel and taste. Eager to return the favor, he yanked the red fabric from her hips and spread her legs wide, then dove headfirst between her thighs. Her pleasure-filled moans progressed to loud gasps as his mouth feasted on her chlorine-glazed flesh, till she cried out with a shudder of ecstasy.

Chapter Eight

Muted creaks sounded at sporadic intervals from the Eastern White Pines as they rocked back and forth with the harsh breeze. Reed brushed a wisp of long blonde hair from Ava's face, then reached for her hand and, with an elegant sweep, lifted it to his lips.

"Leslie… I couldn't imagine doing any of this without you," Reed whispered.

Ava gazed into his shimmering, silvery-blue eyes. "Oh, Luke, I—"

The sound of a gunshot rang out in the distance. With a gasp, Ava raised her hand to her mouth, her eyes consumed with worry.

"Cut!" Pierre yelled. He stared into the director's viewfinder for a moment, then gave two thumbs up. "*Très beau!*"

Ava breathed a sigh of relief. She glanced at her watch: seven-fifteen in the evening, and they'd been on set since five that morning. She couldn't wait to get back to the cabin.

"Great job, once again, Ava," Reed's voice sounded from behind.

Ava smiled. "You, too, Reed." She removed the tiny microphone clipped to her angora sweater and slipped it to a crew member. Her eyes scanned the set in search of Scotch.

"Hey—you doin' okay?" Reed whispered, stepping close.

Ava met his gaze and nodded. "I am…"

Reed wiped the natural-colored lipstick from his lips. "You just seem a bit distracted…"

"I'm sorry," she said, her eyes shifting downward. "I'm afraid I was a bit overzealous with my commitment this year." She tucked her hair behind her ear. "This schedule is getting to me."

"Three films in four months is brutal for sure." He shook his head, his jet-black hair swaying with the movement. "Even I can't do that."

Ava imparted a fleeting smile as they moseyed back inside the cordoned-off area of the resort. She sidestepped a crew member pushing a large, wheeled cart and waved to her enthusiastic makeup artist, who called out, "See you at four a.m. tomorrow!"

With a jerk, Ava stopped and turned to face her co-star. "Reed?" She fixed her gaze on his stunning eyes as he planted his feet beside her. Of all the men she'd met during her career, he was the most trustworthy. Beyond that, she loved working with him; their alchemy was unparalleled amongst current actors. They'd become great friends over the past two years, and she knew she could confide in him.

"Yes?" his sincere eyes settled over her.

Ava cupped her neck in her hands. "I've been thinking a lot about the *Mystery and Mayhem* series…"

"Oh?" he said with a tilt of his head.

Ava caught a glimpse of Scotch near the buffet table. "I have an idea I'd like to get your thoughts on."

Reed smiled and said, "I'm all ears" as he stuffed his hands into the pockets of his jeans.

*****

Ava examined Scotch through a sideways glance as he weaved the high-end SUV around the potholes aggravated by last night's rain. The impressive Scotsman leaned one arm out the window, his shaggy, ginger-red hair dancing with the evening breeze. The gleaming smile he wore since stuffing his face on set with the remaining crab cakes was still plastered to his face.

Ava reached for the silver volume knob and spun it counterclockwise, reducing the rock music blaring through the speakers to a tolerable level.

Scotch's brows snapped together. "What, I thought you liked that song?"

"I do like it… But I enjoy it so much more when my ears aren't throbbing." Ava rested her hands in her lap.

"Sorry," Scotch mumbled, his beaming smile momentarily tapered.

"You seem to be in a good mood." Ava wasn't sure she wanted to know why.

"Oh, *yeah*... Today's been great."

Ava decided to leave well enough alone as they rounded the last bend before their cabin. She spotted the new rental in the drive—*a minivan?*—and a wave of energy roused within her. She hopped out of the vehicle before Scotch could open her door and dashed toward the entrance.

Greeted by the savory aroma of tomato-based pasta, Ava pranced across the welcoming great room and into the kitchen, where their newest addition stood over the stove, his back to her.

"Honey, I'm home!" Scotch bellowed out from the doorway, foiling her surprise attack.

Redge spun around—his eyes bright—and caught Ava in his colossal arms. She clung to the retired SEAL's six-foot-seven-inch frame; it felt wonderful to hold him after all this time, and her chest swelled with affection.

"How's married life?" she asked following their embrace.

He flashed a glowing grin. "Great."

"Hey, mate." Scotch pulled him into a one-armed hug. "Thanks for coming."

"Happy to." Redge projected a playful glare at Ava. "Just wish this little lady could stay outta trouble."

Ava released an exasperated sigh. "I'm sorry… Are you sure Angie doesn't mind your being away?"

Redge waved a dismissive hand. "Nah. Actually, her sisters are visiting for the next two weeks. You did me a *favor.*"

Ava let out a light laugh. "Glad I could help!" she said before excusing herself to freshen up before dinner.

"It'll be ready in fifteen," Redge called out as she sauntered toward the stairs. From the loft, she heard the retired SEAL's voice again—"I want your half of the room cleaned up. You're turning into a slob."

Alone in her room, she savored the momentary silence. She slid her phone from her pocket and swiped it to life. After trashing a ridiculous number of emails, she peeked at her texts. Only one was worth reading.

Chapter Nine

The pink moonlit morning illuminated the cabin's silhouette as he approached on foot. With each passing second, the melodic hum of the taxi's engine grew quieter as it faded into the abyss. He assumed the actress would be up by now, preparing for her day, yet the structure remained bathed in a swell of darkness. He zipped his fleece jacket; the crisp early morning air proved chillier than he expected. He reached the cabin's driveway, careful to maintain his stealth over the slippery gravel. He eyed the dark minivan with curiosity before—with measured steps—proceeding up the wooden porch steps. He traced the round satin-nickel door handle, shifting it the slightest degree clockwise, to make sure it was locked. *Just as I suspected.*

He reached into his inside pocket, removed his wallet, and selected a dispensable card. He slid it against the door jamb, wiggled it between the spring bolt lock and switch plate, then smiled when he heard a faint click.

At a sloth's pace, he turned the round knob and inched the fiberglass door open. His duffel bag dropped to the floor beside him with a muffled thud. His intent was to wait for his eyes to adjust to the dark space before making his way into the actress's bedroom—but the muscular arm that threatened to crush his windpipe convinced him otherwise.

Mace immediately tucked his chin as far down as the mammoth-sized arm would allow, then twisted his body to the side and pushed as hard as he could into his attacker—sending both of them crashing against the hardwood floor. The huge arm loosened its grip with the sudden impact, and a familiar body odor traveled up to his nostrils.

"Redge?!"

"Mace?!" Redge shouted at the same time.

Mace rolled off his behemoth-sized friend, sacked the complaint from his back, and climbed to his feet before extending a helping hand to Redge.

After a hearty laugh and brotherly embrace, Mace said, "Bloody hell, mate."

"Gee, it's great to see you, too." Redge flipped on the great room's overhead light.

"Sorry—I just expected Scotch." Mace threaded a hand through his shaggy crew cut.

"Why didn't you tell us you were coming?" The SEAL asked as he stretched out his back.

"I wanted to surprise Ava." Full of hope, the retired commando asked, "Is she still sleeping?"

"Sorry, man." Redge offered a one-shouldered shrug. "Her day started earlier than usual. She and Scotch left about half an hour ago."

Damn. Mace blew out his cheeks. "Okay… but why the hell are *you* here?"

****

Ava toyed with the prop engagement ring, sliding it on and off her third finger. It felt looser than usual, and she worried she'd inadvertently send it sailing across the room during filming.

"Ava,"—Pierre propped his slight form up on his tiptoes, his head oscillating as he scanned the private reception room that had been staged for the scene's dinner party—"where's your guy with the red hair?"

"Me?!" Scotch's eyes jutted out of his head. "What'd I do?" he asked as he leaned against the cordoned-off bar.

"You, yes, come here. Now." Pierre directed.

Ava watched with a curious eye as Scotch swaggered over to them.

"Apparently, my bartender has the stomach bug." Pierre stared at Scotch with discerning eyes, as if trying to talk himself into the idea. "How'd you like your first acting gig?"

Scotch's emerald eyes sparkled. "Absolutely."

"*Très bien*. You have one line." The French director held up one finger and shook it. "We rehearse today and film tomorrow—got it?"

"Yes, sir." Scotch nodded before bolting behind the bar.

A fleeting concern that Scotch might let the trivial role go to his head infiltrated Ava's mind. She watched the retired elite operative as he feverishly rearranged the variety of glass bottles lining the service well, stepped back to observe, then bobbed his head in silent approval of his work. Ava realized it was too late.

"Ava? Reed?" Pierre's voice summoned her focus. She moved into position next to the director, her co-star at her flank. Pierre placed a hand on each of them and took a deep breath. "This next scene must capture your profound stirrings of affection." Pierre lifted his chin to the ceiling, a dreamy look in his eyes, as he channeled his creative chakra. "Ava, you just realized that you're in love with him, but you're scared to tell him because you've been hurt so badly in the past."

"We get it, Pierre," Reed flashed a reassuring smile as he patted the director on the back.

Pierre continued, "This is the prelude to the pivotal bedroom scene next week!"

Ava nodded. *How could I forget?*

Chapter Ten

Swarms of butterflies fluttered in his stomach. Mace parked the burgundy minivan in the roped-off section of the southwest parking lot of the grand resort. He surveyed the incredible sight before him. None of the pictures Ava had sent captured its magnificence. Situated on high ground overlooking the beautiful French-Canadian city, the castle boasted numerous pinnacles and turrets surrounding a vast central tower evocative of medieval times.

He followed the sign marked *Crew Entrance* around back and slipped in undetected. Just as he'd expected, the set was bustling with activity. The flurry of movement awakened his anxiety, forcing him to take a deep, calming breath.

Mace wound his way toward the myriad cameras positioned in the center of the room, careful to step over cords and around crew members as they dashed about. He caught sight of Reed standing in the middle of the purposefully placed equipment, script in hand. Mace shuffled to the left, hoping for a better viewing angle, then his heart burst.

Ava stood beside Reed, a stack of white paper attached to her hand. Her eyes seemed to alternate between the document and her co-star as they ran through their scene. Golden hair descended in waves down the length of her back. A navy, off-the-shoulder cable-knit sweater clung tightly to her curvaceous frame, landing at her thighs. Snug jeans and brown, pointed-heel boots that stretched to her knees completed her camera-ready ensemble.

His heart ached to wrap her in his arms and pull her against his chest. Instead, he watched as another man did.

"It gets easier." He heard a hushed voice say from behind.

Mace turned to address the woman who snuck beside him. He was beginning to wonder whether his ears were failing him. "Excuse me?"

"Watching the two of them so close… it gets easier," she said with a pleasant smile.

I'm not sure I believe that. Mace must have failed to mask his doubtful expression, because the woman followed up with, "I promise." Mace offered a slow nod.

"Hi, I'm Stephanie," she said, extending her hand. "Reed's girlfriend."

Girlfriend? Mace took hold of her hand and reciprocated the firm shake. "I'm Mace, Ava's—"

"Oh, I *know*," she said with a chuckle. "Ava talks about you *all* the time." Her bright, honey-hued eyes emitted a playful roll.

She does?! His heart leapt inside his chest, his body temperature spiking. *Funny, Reed never mentioned you...* "How long have you and Reed been together?" Mace asked as the warmth waned from his cheeks.

"Since just before Christmas. I'm sorry we haven't had a chance to meet earlier." She removed her ponytail and tossed her long, caramel hair. "But I wasn't able to join Reed till the second half of their last film."

Mace jammed his thumbs in the pockets of his black tactical pants. "And I was only here for the first half of"—he struggled to even get the words out—"*Lavender Love: More Lavender*."

"Ugh." Stephanie's lips curved downward. "That schedule was brutal!" With an incline of her head, her brows lifting in sync, she added, "And that's coming from a fashion model." She sighed as she tightened her green duster around her athletic frame. "The network hadn't even planned on filming that this year, but crammed it into the schedule because the first one was such a hit."

Mace swallowed the sinking feeling in his stomach. "Oh, I remember..." He crossed his arms over his shredded chest. "That's how I ended up in London—alone."

"Oh." A surprised expression surfaced before she could squelch it. With a tilt of her head, Stephanie offered a consoling smile and said, "Well, I guess that explains why we haven't met sooner." She flung her fingers toward the bar. "Is that why you asked the Scottish guy to stay here?"

"Yeah." Mace wrung his hands in front of his chest as he watched Scotch play bartender. *After what happened last fall…* "I wanted someone I could trust to look after her while I was in England."

"I understand you joined Ava for the filming of *Summer Squash Surprise* earlier this year?"

"Yeah." Mace massaged his temples as he recalled the details of the autumn romance Ava starred in just after the new year.

"Well, now they're talking about replacing that guy with Reed for the sequel—if you can believe that." Stephanie's eyes grew wide, her forehead puckering. "The fans sure love these two."

"So it would seem." He gestured toward Ava and her co-star as they stared into each other's eyes—Reed's arms draped around her in a loving hold. "This… doesn't bother you?"

Stephanie lifted her chin and fixed her honey-tinted eyes on him. "Reed and Ava are very passionate people—which is what makes them so amazing at what they do." Her eyes flickered downward for a moment before again meeting his. "I'd be lying if I said it didn't take some getting used to… But it *does* get easier—I assure you."

Chapter Eleven

Extras, elegantly clad and masquerading as dinner guests, danced across the glossy wooden floor, maintaining a minimum distance from the actors as directed.

Camera one zoomed in on Ava, a large microphone attached to its side boom. She closed her eyes, then allowed them to flutter open. She studied Reed's handsome face: the silver-tinted hue of his blue eyes, and the fine scores of lines that accentuated them, as he held her close. His clean-shaven skin and lips—courtesy of the natural lip color his makeup artist just applied—looked baby soft.

"Luke—" she began before sweeping her head toward her shoulder.

"Leslie, being with you here—playing the part of husband and wife…" Reed whispered with a stroke of her cheek. "It's been incredible."

As Ava lifted her head to meet Reed's stare, a familiar face in the distance stole her gaze—and she found her inspiration. "There's no one I'd rather be here with," she whispered with a raw sincerity. She shifted her eyes from Reed's to the man standing just beyond her reach as her co-star rested his forehead against hers. "You transform me, and—" the corners of her eyes dampened as she continued— "my heart craves you."

"Oh, Leslie!" Reed cried out. He pulled her closer, her breasts tight against his chest. "I've fallen in love with you." He tilted his head to one side and leaned toward her glossed lips.

"Cut!" Pierre yelled with a beaming smile spread across his lips.

Ava stepped back from Reed and smoothed her sweater as Pierre ran over. "Ava—that was *très magnifique!*" He kissed her on both cheeks. "You adding that '*my heart craves you*' line was genius!"

"How'd I do?" Reed asked, tossing his jet-black hair.

"Oh, you were great—of course." Pierre tapped him on the back. "Now, you two take five while we get ready for the next scene." Ava heard him say as she weaved through the crew members, her eyes locked on her target.

She zigzagged left then right to avoid a collision, then sprinted into the arms of the man her heart *actually* craved.

Mace's strong arms swallowed her whole—her soul instantly nourished. She raised herself on her tiptoes, despite her four-inch heels, and pressed her lips to his on auto-repeat, alternating with a loving smile.

"I missed you," his husky voice whispered. His British accent proved too much, and her lips were again upon his.

"Ava! Your *makeup!*" The shrill voice of her stylist scolded.

With difficulty, she pulled her lips from his. "Sorry!" she called out; Mace's wide, crooked grin didn't help curb her laughing smile.

"Ready in five!" echoed from behind as Mace clasped her hands.

"I'd better get back," she whispered, gazing into his watery, steel-blue eyes. "But—I'm looking forward to tonight." Following a repetitive arch of her brows and a kiss on his cheek, she swiveled from his grasp.

Before she could flee his long reach, Mace's hands found her hips; a delighted gasp escaped her lips as he spun her back around. He delivered one last kiss before mumbling, "You have no idea, sweet angel," in her ear.

Chapter Twelve

The cabin's dark silhouette projected a picturesque glow courtesy of the great room's windows, even while cloaked. Mace pulled up to the vacation rental and shifted the people hauler into park before his rugged hands gripped the black leather wheel at the twelve o'clock position. He rested his forehead upon them, then cast his eyes at the actress. The minivan's night-mode illumination provided perfect viewing: her long hair cascaded down her shoulders, and her expectant, sapphire eyes emitted a loving gleam. Incredible didn't even begin to describe her, which made this much harder for him.

"Ava," Mace started, his husky tone serious. "Why didn't you tell me you were threatened?"

Her shoulders slumped in conjunction with a hushed sigh. "I didn't want you to worry..."

Mace's forehead creased. "Would you rather have me *not* worry?" He reached for her hand—thankful she'd removed the prop diamond ring she had to wear for her role—and squeezed.

"Of course not… It's just—" She turned toward the window; her misty eyes fixed on the black void that lay beyond.

Mace lowered his lips to the top of her hand. "Just what?" he whispered. It pained him to see her struggle with being vulnerable.

Ava ran her fingers over the gold chain that hung from her neck. After a long moment, she turned back toward him. "I don't want you thinking I'm some helpless woman who has to be rescued all the time," she uttered.

"Ava," Mace stroked her cheek and leaned in close, willing her to grasp his sincerity. "You're the bravest woman I know."

The actress arched a skeptical eyebrow.

"I'm serious. The way you handled the situation last fall…" Mace gave a gentle shake of his head. "You were terrified, but you willingly put yourself in harm's way and kept your cool like a commando. You were bloody incredible."

Ava rendered a fleeting smile. "That was only because you were beside me."

Mace pulled her to his lips. After planting a lingering kiss, he whispered, "No… you've got grit, Ms. Ellis, and that's not something that can be taught."

"*Uh-huh*." Ava pressed her back against the captain's seat. "That's why you *insisted* Scotch stay with me while you went back to London?"

"Ava—you're the most precious thing in the world to me." He fixed his focus on her as he clasped her hand. "The only thing I have to offer you is my protection. And if I couldn't be here with you, I had to send someone I could trust. Besides,"—his eyes grew wide as he inclined his head—"based on what happened the other night—I obviously made the right call."

Ava gave a gentle shake of her head. "Stuff like that happens all the time in my industry… it was probably just some disgruntled fan or some wannabe influencer trying to drum up followers. I'm sure it's nothing to worry about." The look in her eyes suggested she was trying to convince herself.

Mace scoffed. "You can't be so naïve."

Ava stretched her body across the center console. She glided her cheek against his before her soft lips grazed the delicate skin of his neck; the warm, moist tip of her tongue making an occasional emergence. "It's a moot point anyway… I have my trio back," she murmured.

Mace's yearning swelled with her so close. He ran a thumb over her lips and lifted her chin to meet his gaze. "You look tired." Then, with a waggle of his brows, he said, "Maybe I should take you to bed."

Ava's eyes spiked with desire. "You absolutely should."

Hand in hand, they made their way into the luxurious cabin, their stride in perfect sync. They discovered Redge lounging on the maroon leather couch, his long, heavy legs propped upon the cocktail table. He greeted them with a nod.

"How's it going, mate?" Mace asked, tossing him the keys to his minivan.

"Great," the retired SEAL paused the television before answering. "The trails out back are incredible. I love this place."

Ava's naturally gorgeous smile appeared. "I'm so glad to hear that."

Mace surveyed the living space. "Where's Scotch?"

Redge lowered his chin to his chest. "Where he's been all night… in the bedroom rehearsing for his big scene tomorrow."

Ava let out a light laugh. "He's only got one line."

"Don't tell him that." Redge's eyes did a three-sixty. "He's convinced he's on the brink of stardom."

Mace wrapped a powerful arm around Ava's waist. "We're gonna get ready for bed."

"I figured." Redge issued a puckish grin.

Ava's sapphire eyes imparted a playful scolding. "Good night, Redge."

Mace's hand maintained its position on her hip as he trailed her up the long, straight gilded log steps. After entering the master suite, he slid the door closed behind them, then gathered her into his arms. His passion mounted exponentially as she clung to his chest, her lips molded to his.

After a moment, she parted from him and whispered, "Let me just freshen up real quick."

Mace raked his fingers through his chestnut hair, then mumbled, "Of course."

The second she closed the bathroom door, Mace darted over to his duffel bag, secured his toothbrush and toothpaste, and dashed out of the room. He bolted down the slippery wooden steps and across the smooth ceramic tile that defined the kitchen and into the main floor bathroom just as Redge's bassy voice called out, *"What the—?"* behind him.

He brushed his teeth in record time, used the bathroom, and washed his hands—taking a split second to appreciate the peach-scented hand soap—before making a mad dash back across the kitchen and up the stairs, three steps at a time. He stripped off his clothes, leaving only his boxer briefs, then climbed beneath the heavy navy and green plaid comforter that coated the bed, just as the bathroom door swung open.

The cause of the hammering in his heart transitioned from physical exertion to affectionate arousal the instant Ava emerged from the ensuite. A thin white tank stretched across her chest, accentuating her voluptuous breasts, and extended to the top of her blush pink panties.

Mace couldn't curb the beaming grin attached to his face as she slipped beneath the covers and snuggled up to his chest. He wasted no time lowering his lips to her luminous, makeup-free face, kissing the soft skin of her cheeks and neck. His finger traced the top hem of her tank, then tugged it downward—his lips tickling her generous cleavage—before landing on her mouth with a passionate kiss. Her body rocked with ramping desire as her pink, pouty lips cried out for more.

He reached his large, strong hands under the thin cotton that veiled her chest as she maneuvered her body on top of his, straddling him at the waist, her fingers tracing the definitions of his broad, bare chest. A light whimper escaped her lips as his rock-hard mast pressed against her. He slid his fingers inside her panties just as the sound of heavy footsteps sprinting up the stairs debuted.

With shocking speed, Ava rolled off of him and pulled the comforter up to her chin. A second later, Scotch burst through the door, Redge at his heels.

"Ava!" Desperation filled the Scotsman's eyes. "I'm struggling with my line!"

"Mate!" Mace yelled, shooting daggers at his Scottish friend, as his mast slowly capsized.

Redge threw his hands out wide. "Hey, I tried running interference."

"But, this is *important!*" Scotch countered.

Mace let out a harsh sigh. His fingertips flew to his forehead, where they proceeded to knead it in a semi-circular fashion.

Ava sat up in bed, careful to ensure the plaid drape covered her braless chest. "Okay, Scotch. Let me hear you say your line."

Scotch stood at the foot of the king-size bed, took a deep breath, then said, "*What* can I get you?"—his usual delectable accent sounding coarse and unnatural.

Ava nibbled on her lower lip. "Try not emphasizing the word *what*," she suggested.

Scotch's chest expanded with another harsh breath, contracted as he exhaled slowly, then he blurted, "What can I get *you?*"

Oh, for the love of God.

Ava's nibbling continued. She glanced at Mace with a look of disbelief that mirrored his.

Scotch paced the length of the room, fingers teasing his unruly red beard, repeating the phrase. "What *can* I get you? What can I get *ya?* What can I get *ye?...*"

Redge shook his head and crossed his arms over his hulking chest.

Scotch must have noticed the disapproving gesture, because he turned to Redge and shouted, "Well, if it's *so* easy, let's hear you say it!"

Redge met his sniper friend's stare. "What can I get you?" he uttered in perfect fashion.

"Ugh!" Scotch tossed out his arms, a look of complete despair seizing his face.

Mace watched as Ava attempted to suppress a yawn. Not seeing her for the past eight weeks had just about killed him, and all he wanted to do was cradle her in his arms and make sweet love to her. But now he had to compete with this madness.

Ava patted the bed in front of her. "Scotch, come here."

Scotch jumped onto the fourteen-inch mattress and positioned himself in front of Ava—hope speckling his emerald eyes. She took hold of his large, milky-white hands. "This is something we actors refer to as the *Magic If*," she began before instructing him to take a deep, calming breath. "Now, close your eyes." The Scotsman squeezed his eyes shut. "Envision the room we'll be filming in. The soft lighting… the cognac leather stools surrounding the beautiful walnut bar…"

Ava's inherent silken voice may have pacified Scotch, but it was getting Mace worked up—again.

"You twist a frosted glass bottle so the label is displayed perfectly… Then, you remove a soft, white cloth from your back pocket and polish the dark wood into an exquisite sheen… a well-dressed gentleman approaches… what do you say to him?"

Scotch whispered, "What can I get you?"

Ava squeezed his hands. "That was perfect."

Scotch's eyes popped open, and a beaming grin commandeered his face. He wrapped an arm around her. "Thanks, Ava—I knew I could count on you," he said before somersaulting off the bed. He made his way toward the loft, Redge at his flank.

Ava lay her head against the pillow and snuggled up to Mace's chest. He wrapped her in his arms and planted a soft kiss on her forehead.

Scotch turned with a jerk in the doorway, his expression growing thoughtful. "Hey,"—his hands rested on his hips—"do you think I should arrange for a professional headshot?"

Redge's mouth fell open.

"I mean, people may want my autograph." Scotch shrugged.

Clenching his fist, Mace shot him the eyes. "Scotch," he said through tight lips, "*do ya bloody mind?*"

"Oh," Scotch said, glancing at Mace as he lay beside a curled-up Ava; the circumstances appearing to at last register. "Sorry for the interruption, mate." He flashed a mischievous grin. "I'll let you get back to whatever you were doing," he said before strutting out the door.

"Have a good night, you two." Redge pulled the door closed behind him.

Mace expelled the air from his lungs in one sharp movement. He lowered his chin to gaze at the masterpiece resting in the crook of his arm before imparting a tender kiss on her lidded eye. Her rhythmic breathing soothed his soul, leaving him with a throbbing in his chest and between his legs.

Chapter Thirteen

"What can I get you?" Scotch asked—his unique tone smooth and natural—as he stood behind the antiquated bar, polishing cloth in hand.

"Vodka, on the rocks." Reed propped his elbow on the bar. He fingered his onyx cufflink as his eyes darted about the room before locking onto his mark.

Camera two zoomed in on Ava as she approached. She wore a slinky, black cocktail dress that revealed the slightest crease of décolletage and several inches of thigh. She sauntered up to Reed with a radiant smile.

Back to camera one. Reed wrapped an arm around the small of her back. "Boy, are you a sight for sore eyes." He peered into her sapphire gems and brushed a lock of hair from her cheek.

Mace watched with a sick-to-his-stomach feeling.

"Cut!" Pierre yelled. The crew broke into a frenzy of movement. Ava and Reed appeared to congratulate Scotch, then Pierre put his arms around both of them—the smile pasted to his face suggested it was a one-and-done shot. Mace crossed his fingers.

Mace hung in the back of the spacious room, trying not to hinder the dedicated crew as they hustled. He spotted Reed's girlfriend, Stephanie, in the adjacent corner, appearing to do the same. He glanced at his titanium diver watch: almost fourteen hundred hours. He'd heard whispers of wrapping up before dinner this evening, which he hoped to high heaven were true. He pined to spend a nice, quiet evening alone with Ava.

A young man wearing a crisp white shirt under a juniper-ottoman-trim vest strode past Mace, carrying a massive bouquet of multicolored roses. *He's about to make someone's day.*

"Miss Ava Ellis?" the young man shouted as he ventured farther into the flurry of activity.

Mace's jaw went slack. He heard Reed's voice call out, "Over here!"

Mace marched closer, dodging personnel along his route. He spied the young man hand the bouquet off to Pierre's assistant. "Oooh! Ava, you lucky girl!"

Mace felt an arm brush against his, and he turned to see Stephanie standing next to him. "Wow," she said. "You sure know how to make a statement."

Mace felt a flash of irritation. "They're not from me," he muttered before stalking off toward Ava.

"Oh my…" Ava boasted a gracious smile as the woman handed her the overstuffed vase. Her sparkling eyes met Mace's as he appeared in her line of sight. His heart sank as she reached for the card; on the brink of discovering the flowers weren't from him. He watched as her joyful expression transitioned to bewilderment.

Mace inched closer, his curiosity getting the best of him. "Who are they from?" he asked, not convinced he wanted to hear the answer.

"I'm not sure…" Ava whispered, her brows knitted together. She held the small, rectangular card out for him to see. Mace plucked it from her delicate hand and read the glossy note in silence:

My dear Ava,
Your talent and beauty have no equal.
I have a once-in-a-lifetime opportunity to discuss with you.
Would you do me the honor of joining me for dinner this evening?
Seven o'clock in the resort's patio restaurant.
I do hope to see you there.

****

Mace rolled back his cuffs, exposing his shredded forearms. "I don't like this." He peered into Ava's unsuspecting eyes, wondering if he should've pushed back harder against this mad idea. *Honestly, who the bloody hell sends five dozen roses? A stalker, that's who. A deranged lunatic who's been watching from the shadows, waiting to make their move at a seemingly innocent dinner.* He adored her trusting nature, but it required his infinite vigilance.

With a sunny smile, Ava reassured, "It'll be okay." She raised herself on her tiptoes and planted a long, tender kiss on his stubbled cheek as they stood near the entrance to the restaurant. "Besides,"—she lifted one shoulder in a half shrug—"shouldn't I at least *hear* about this opportunity before I turn it down?"

Mace couldn't shake the vexation in his gut. She wrapped her silk-covered arm around his, signaling her readiness to cross the threshold into the unknown. He was thankful she'd at least changed out of that slinky black dress into something more modest for whoever awaited them.

Enclosed on three sides by a mix of arborvitae and ornamental hardwoods, the resort's patio restaurant offered a casual upscale vibe. Mace ducked through the doorway as they stepped onto the exposed aggregate concrete, then rolled his shoulders back. A quick stop at the hostess stand had them following a petite young woman with a long auburn braid that swung like a pendulum across her back. She led them along a curvy path through a labyrinth of tables before coming to a stop in the rear corner. Lobed green leaves canopied above the secluded setting, and another massive vase of flowers—a variety of spring blooms—rested in the center, cloaking the guest from their view. Standing six-foot-five inches high, however, had its advantages, and Mace caught a glimpse of short, sun-kissed brown hair as he peered over the top of the bouquet. Split-second disbelief was soon replaced with a churning anger.

Ava halted a few feet from the table as a tall, athletic form rose from a dove-white wooden chair. Her fingers flew to her mouth as the man's lips stretched across bright white teeth, forming a wide, beaming smile.

Mace felt Ava's shoulders sink as they grazed against his; an expression of shock overtaking her flawless face. "Kent?!"

"Hello, Ava," his smooth voice replied. "It's so lovely to see you."

His annoying smile loitered, and Mace fought the intrinsic urge to pound it off his face. He locked his steely gaze onto her ex-fiancé. "You've got some nerve."

"Ah,"—Kent canted his head toward Mace—"I see you brought the new bodyguard-slash-boyfriend," he said, a sly gleam in his eye. "Your reputation precedes you, my friend." He extended his hand to Mace, who made no effort to receive it. If Mace's spurn bothered him, Kent didn't show it. He gestured to the solitary chair across from him. "Ava, please join me." He flashed another grandiose smile. "I took the liberty of ordering all of your favorites."

Mace's chest heaved with anger. He stepped closer to the pompous producer. "She's not bloody interested in your *selections* or your *opportunity.*"

"Mason, I—"

Mace whipped his head around to confront Ava. A dissonance clouded her glistening eyes—and it spoke loud and clear. "Unbelievable," he mumbled as he stared at the alluring actress.

With a delicate touch, Ava smoothed her manicured hand over his engorged bicep. "I feel like I should at least hear him out," her satiny voice uttered with a hushed tone.

Normally, he'd find her caressing touch healing. At the moment, however, he was too annoyed to enjoy it. "Fine," he said through clenched teeth. He pivoted one hundred eighty degrees and snagged an empty slat-back chair from the table behind them—leaving the guests with mouths ajar and eyes wide.

A smug smile slid over Kent's lips. He unbuttoned his navy sports coat, then tucked his hands in the slanted pockets at his hips. "I was rather hoping to speak with Ava in private."

Ava crossed her arms over her chest and directed her attention to the producer. "I don't think that's a good—"

"No chance, mate." Mace slammed the stolen chair down on its legs with a loud thud, prompting stares from neighboring guests.

"Mace—calming breath!" a booming, European-laced voice ordered from behind.

Mace's entire body went stiff as Ava whisked her head in the direction of the foreign sound. *I knew this was a bad idea.*

A moment later, Annie appeared on Mace's flank. She placed a hand on his forearm. "I hate to see you so worked up," she said in a calm voice.

Ava's eyes narrowed, her posture straightening.

Annie twisted toward Ava. "I don't believe we've met," she extended her hand toward the actress.

Mace waited with bated breath as Ava gave it a brusque shake, forgoing her usual radiant introductory smile. He spied a gleam of delight in Kent's eyes as the producer observed this unexpected development.

Ava produced a forced smile. "Well, it seems this evening is full of surprises."

Just then, a handsome young waiter approached carrying a large tray filled with appetizers.

"Ava, please," Kent said, gesturing to her chair. "All I ask is for one hour of your time."

Ava's sapphire eyes frosted with a glacial glaze. She glared at Kent and—with an authority Mace hadn't heard since selection—said, "You've got one hour." Then, despite her four-inch heels, she lifted herself on her tiptoes and whispered in Mace's ear, "And you've got one hour to figure out why the hell she's here," before planting a kiss on his cheek, then swiveling back toward Kent.

Mace swallowed the lump in his throat as he witnessed his sweet angel seat herself at the intimately set table across from her ex-fiancé. *There's no possible way this is going to end well. Bloody hell.*

Chapter Fourteen

Redge pushed the six-foot-wide bi-fold doors open and stared at the glossy white machine in front of him. The unit's back displayed a multitude of digital options. Redge ran his large hand over his smooth, shaved head. He missed Carolyn. *How did I end up on laundry duty?*

His ears picked up an out-of-tune humming, and he turned to see Scotch enter the spacious kitchen. Redge studied his sniper friend as he pranced from the fridge to the island, then back to the fridge. Removing a silver can from the stainless-steel appliance, Scotch popped the tab before taking a long pull.

"I know that look."

"What look?" Scotch asked, a smile reaching his jade eyes.

Redge leaned his six-foot-seven-inch frame against the dark granite. "Who's the girl?"

Scotch's tongue poked around inside his mouth for a moment. Then, with vivacious eyes, he whispered, "Julietta."

Crossing his arms over his enormous chest, Redge rendered a lengthy shake of his head.

"What, a guy can't find love?" Scotch dropped his can onto the counter, producing a muted *ting*.

Following a pronounced eye roll, the retired SEAL countered, "You don't find love, Scotch—you find sex."

Scotch waggled his brows. "What's wrong with starting with the best part?"

Redge extracted a bulbous ceramic mug from the hickory cabinet and switched on the electric tea kettle. "Maybe you should ask your two ex-wives."

Scotch shot him the eyes. "Hey, mate, military marriages are hard. You know that better than anyone."

Redge dispensed a dismissive shrug. "So, things are serious between you and this filthy rich resort owner, huh?"

Scotch projected a salacious smirk. "Serious enough that she wants me to stop back over tomorrow."

"Uh-huh…" Redge bobbed his head, opting to bite his tongue.

Scotch took another long pull from the condensating can. "What? You think I have nothing to offer her because she's so bloody rich?"

"Oh, I definitely think you have something she wants…" Redge massaged his chin between his thumb and forefinger as he stared at his friend. "In the short term, anyway."

Scotch tugged on the tip of his beard. "Well—as usual—your support's over the top, mate."

"Look, I'm sorry." Redge threw out his hands. "Just don't want to see you be disappointed. Again."

"Don't ye worry 'bout me, big guy." Scotch rammed his fingers against his chest. "Besides,"—Scotch thrust out his chin—"it worked out for Mace and Ava."

Redge splayed his hands over the island's shiny black countertop and met his friend's wild-eyed stare. "Mace and Ava found *love* first—the fun stuff came after."

Scotch gestured with praying hands. "I'll be sure to keep that in mind, pops," before storming out of the kitchen.

****

"Mace, let's take a walk." Annie's voice sounded from behind.

Mace squeezed his eyes shut for a split second and took a shallow breath. Then he turned on his heel and—ignoring his gut—left Ava alone with her ex-fiancé. He trailed his former therapist as she weaved around the seated guests and toward the garden exit. They embarked on a wide, flagstone path that meandered through a rainbow array of blooming perennials.

Three steps in, the silver solar-powered stake lights switched on as dusk encroached. Mace stole a sideways glance at Annie. "I can't believe you're here."

Annie's lips curved up into a half smile. "I'm sorry… I didn't plan to announce my presence in that way."

Mace's brow furrowed. "I gotta ask…"

"I know…." She thrust her fingers into the pockets of her blue jeans. "Why am I here?" Her pace slowed as she continued, "I was very worried about you after our last conversation."

Mace channeled the memory of their last meeting. "I appreciate that…"—his head tilted to the side—"but, three thousand miles is a *long* way to travel to check in on a former patient."

Annie spouted a light chuckle. "True." Her loose curls brushed over her shoulders with each step along the uneven path. "I stopped by the Embassy to say 'ello, and they told me you were here—on location with Ava." Her tone expressed her shock as she continued, "And, well, I remembered how difficult it had been for you to watch her film the sequel to *Lavender Love* earlier this year."

Mace tucked his chin to his chest. He'd forgotten he shared that with her while they were remodeling the community center.

"Anyway," she continued. "I thought maybe you could use a friend… You know, someone who just *happens* to have special training in that arena." She flashed a coy smile.

Mace grinned. "Still…"—he thumbed his belt loops—"it's a long way to come."

Annie waved a dismissive hand. "Turns out I have family a few hours from here, so I get to kill two birds with one stone," she delivered a playful wink. "Plus, I could really use some time off."

Mace wrung his hands in front of his chest. "Well, I guess if you and your husband get to make a holiday out of it…"

"Mace," Annie scoffed, "my divorce was finalized before Christmas." She flashed a sour expression as she leaned back at the waist. "You're normally such a stickler for details—I must say, I'm rather surprised you didn't notice that I haven't worn my wedding ring in months!"

"Sorry." Mace offered a one-shouldered shrug. "How long are you planning to stay?"

Her sunny smile returned. "As long as you'd like me to."

Chapter Fifteen

Ava glowered at the annoyingly handsome man sitting opposite her. She leaned back against the wooden slats of her chair, crossed her arms under her breasts, and said, "Feel free to wipe that smug smile off your face."

The smile instead grew wider. She hadn't seen Kent since she left California, and she'd assumed she'd never again have to. She stared into the gleaming hazel eyes she once thought she'd wake up to every morning and felt… nothing. No anger. No longing. No remorse. In fact—wait, she did feel something—a growing sense of gratitude. Because if Kent hadn't turned out to be such a self-centered, self-serving bastard, she never would have met Mace.

He tipped the bottle of Cabernet Sauvignon into the stemmed glass resting before her, then filled his own. "Cheers." He inclined his head as he raised his half-full glass of maroon liquid and took a test sip. "You look absolutely incredible, Ava."

Ava gave in to the temptation to taste the bold, dark-berry wine. "Why are you here, Kent?"

Another smile as he stroked his pronounced jawline. His sun-kissed hair darkened with dusk's arrival. "I hate the way things ended between us."

Ava's finger traced the etched crystal of her glass. Her eyes drifted to the linen-wrapped surface where an array of appetizers rested, untouched. "My question stands," she whispered.

Kent let out a sigh. "I've been keeping tabs on your career, and it warms my heart to see how well you've done for yourself. Your network is damn lucky to have you." He propped his elbows on the table. "I meant what I said—your talent is without equal. Your talent and your beauty, Ava."

Ava's chest heaved with a deep breath. "That *still* doesn't answer my question."

Kent ran a hand through his perfectly formed hair. "Fair enough." A puckish grin appeared as he plucked a garlic butter-glazed snail from the plate in front of her. "I'm here because the studio wants you back."

Her breathing pinched. "What?" she muttered.

Kent locked his gleaming eyes onto her. "The sequel for *Studio Nine Eleven* is all planned out, but they'll only give it the green light if you sign on."

Well-manicured fingers cupped her mouth. Fearing Kent might perceive her negligible, albeit conflicted, interest, she shifted her gaze away from his.

"They're willing to double your salary from the first film." Kent leaned back in his chair and crossed an ankle over his knee. Negotiating had always been his forte, and he appeared right at home. "Although,"—a confident smile materialized—"I think I can talk them into tripling it."

"I- I'm not even sure what to say," Ava stammered. After receiving the unexpected invitation this afternoon, she'd been certain she wouldn't be interested in any opportunities. Now, that certainty waned.

"Please don't say anything now." Kent placed his hand over hers. "Take some time and think about it. I'm not leaving anytime soon."

His comments shored up the memory of her ransacked room. "You're not leaving anytime soon..." she murmured.

Kent nodded before downing another sip of his wine.

The glossy leaves hovering above their table trembled as a gentle breeze swept across the patio. Ava slipped her hand out from under his and drew her silky sleeves over her wrists. "But when did you arrive?"

"Yesterday." He arched a quizzical brow. "Why?"

Ava propped her elbows on the table and rested her cheek against her clasped hands. "Can you prove it?"

With his eyes fastened to her, Kent reached into the pocket of his khaki pants and removed his phone. A few swipes later, the screen displayed an image of his boarding pass. "Why does it matter?" he asked, his tone tainted with concern.

Ava tucked her chin against her shoulder, avoiding his stare.

"You were threatened, weren't you?"

Chapter Sixteen

So, she just happened to be at the *exact* same restaurant, at the *exact* same time?" Ava withdrew her fingers from Mace's and shoved them between her thighs. She studied his expression as he sat behind the wheel of her Range Rover rental; the fine creases that wreathed his captivating steel-blue eyes seemed more pronounced than usual. His elbow remained on the black leather console between them, just as it had a moment before when it held her hand—but his eyes flickered with sadness.

"Apparently," he mumbled with a shrug.

Ava scoffed. "And you *buy* that?"

Mace's eyes locked onto her. "She was worried about me."

Irritation swept through her. *It's my responsibility to worry about you, not hers.* "Why would *she* be worried about you?"

Mace massaged his temples. "She just knew how stressful it was last time I was on location with you, and…"

"And what?" Her mind instructed her leg to stop bouncing, but it refused to listen.

Mace's chin fell to his chest.

"Please talk to me," she whispered, her eyes moist. Her heart ached with his admission that the *Lavender Love* sequel had been difficult for him. She suspected that was the case, but he'd always denied it.

His thumb and forefinger stroked the corners of his mouth. After a long moment, he turned his gaze back toward her. "I've just been dealing with… some bad dreams again."

An acute pain stung her chest. "Oh, Mason, I'm sorry." She reached for his hand and gave it a gentle squeeze. "I thought those had stopped?"

A half smile emerged on his gorgeous, weathered face. "That's because I never have them when I'm with you."

Ava raised his sturdy palm to her lips and sealed it with a tender kiss. "I wish you had told me."

Mace bobbed his head. "What, during our five-minute conversations, when you can fit me in?" He extracted his hand from hers. "Or maybe I shoulda said something while replying to one of your bloody texts at zero-three-hundred hours."

Ava's heart sank. She worried this third film would take its toll on their relationship, but he had insisted she honor her commitment. "That's not fair." She willed away her tears. "You're the one who encouraged me to take this role," she whispered. "Besides, you haven't exactly been the easiest to get a hold of either…"

"Oh, gee, I'm sorry." Mace whipped his head toward her. "I've only been helping to establish a new community center for veterans."

"Oh, that's right—a new center that your *friend*"—her fingers made air quotes—"Annie, just happened to ask *you* to help with, hmmm…" She tapped her chin with a long, glossy fingernail.

"Yes, friend—nothing more." His husky tone rang deeper than usual.

"Oh, *please*. Now who's being naïve?" Ava grabbed the door handle, pushed it open, and climbed out of the sleek, late-model vehicle.

"So, I guess we're done?" she heard Mace say before she swung the door closed. A second later, she heard the driver's side creak open, then close with a loud *thunk*.

She made a beeline for the front steps and reached the entrance to the cabin just as his heavy steps sounded behind her.

"Ava—" She felt his strong hand upon her arm as he continued, "I'm sorry I said that."

Ava swiveled to face him. Under the harsh orange glow of the porch light, his beautiful blue eyes, veiled with sadness, appeared gray. "But it doesn't change the fact that it's true," she whispered, tears welling in her eyes.

Mace set free a heavy sigh. He inched back and leaned against the cedar-stained wood railing. "I just miss you," he mumbled, a shrug momentarily lifting his strong shoulders.

"I miss you, too…" Ava inched closer to him. "So very much." She glided her finger along the gold chain that dangled from her neck. "I recognize this year has gotten off to a challenging start, but we're at the tail end of filming."

"I know." Mace massaged the back of his neck as his head fell earthward. "I just miss the way things were before you started filming again…" Following a fleeting smile, he added, "When I had you all to myself." He threaded a rugged hand through his tousled chestnut hair. "I know that sounds selfish…"

Ava pressed her body against his chiseled, comforting chest. At once, his strong arms enveloped her—his intoxicating scent smothering her—and she cherished her fix. "I love you," she whispered.

He lifted her chin and gazed into her eyes. "I love you, sweet angel." Lowering his mouth to hers, he imparted a fervent kiss. Their passion mounting, he muttered, "At least we figured out who ransacked your room," in between the magnetizing of their lips.

Ava shrank back from his embrace. "What do you mean?"

Mace pulled her back against him, a trace of confusion in his stare. "It was obviously Kent."

With a gentle shake of her head, Ava stated, "No, it wasn't." She took a step backwards, forcing him to loosen his loving grip. "He showed me his boarding pass—and it was dated yesterday."

Mace's brows stitched together. "Ava, the guy's filthy rich; he could have easily bought two tickets to give himself an alibi." He crossed his arms over his hulking chest. "Or he arranged to have someone else ransack your room."

Her head shook in defiance. "No… he wouldn't do that."

"Are you bloody kidding me?" The whites of Mace's eyes grew more pronounced despite the dim light. "The guy tried to ruin your career!"

"Mason—I'm telling you—it wasn't him." Ava's hands flew to her hips. "At this point, I'm thinking your little therapist *friend* had a hand in it!"

Mace slashed the air with his palms. "Ava, there's no way."

"Well, did you ask her what day she arrived?"

"No, but—"

"How convenient!" Ava spun on her heel and threw open the front door. She burst into the living room in time to spy Redge and Scotch jump back from the blind-shrouded window, shocked expressions plastered on their faces. "I didn't take you two for the busybody type," she mumbled as she stalked toward the staircase.

"I told you we should mind our own business!" She heard Redge mutter when her foot connected with the first step. Then the sound of Mace's boots stomping in the doorway, and the sweep of the entry door as it retreated over the hardwood floor.

By the time she reached the bedroom door, she was surprised to discover Mace had caught up with her. She paused at the threshold. "Look, I have another ridiculously early morning," she said, tucking a long, golden lock behind her ear. "We'll have to finish this later."

Mace bobbed his head. "That's fine," he said through tight lips. "It'll be just like every other conversation we've had over the past two months."

Ava scoffed. "You're unbelievable." She whipped around and bolted into the bedroom only to return a moment later, arms heaped with blankets and a pillow.

"Guess this means I'm supposed to sleep on the couch." Mace wrung his hands in front of his strapping chest.

She shrugged. "You're welcome to bunk with one of your *mates*."

"No, he's not, Ava!" Scotch called out from below, prompting her to render a dramatic eyeroll.

Mace tossed his hands out wide. "Hey, not a problem— I've slept on more than my fair share of couches."

"Good—then you'll be nice and comfortable!" She dropped the armful of linens onto the carpet at her feet, then marched into the bedroom, slamming the door behind her.

****

Mace watched as the *Love is Patient* plaque that clung to the wall beside the door crashed to the floor. He blew out his cheeks, then retrieved the pillow and blankets along with the etched wood sign.

He picked up the decorative square pillow that rested in the corner of the brown leather sofa, complete with a mama black bear and two cubs stitched into the front of it, and tossed it on the floor.

"*Die Hard with a Vengeance* or *Terminator*?" He heard Redge ask from the living room below.

"Definitely *Die Hard*, mate." Scotch's response traveled up to his ears.

He folded one of the blankets in half lengthwise and laid it across the couch, then propped the plaid flannel-covered pillow against the rolled arm. He slid his long-sleeve shirt over his torso before folding it neatly and resting it on the rocking chair adjacent to the couch. After stepping out of his tactical pants, which he also folded and laid over the mission-style chair, he switched off the light and climbed under the blanket just as the sound of a bomb detonating through the telly pierced his ears.

So much for a nice, quiet evening with Ava.

Chapter Seventeen

Mace awoke to discover the loft bathed in darkness, the entire cabin still. He glanced at his titanium diver watch: oh-five-hundred hours. His ears listened for signs of life but found none. He folded the blanket back and jolted upright. His fingers massaged his obliques. His back was killing him. If Ava booted him from her bed again tonight, he was going to drive to the nearest store and pick up an air mattress because this couch was bloody dreadful.

He tiptoed into her bedroom—*please still be here*—only to discover the king-size bed empty. He made a mental note to have his hearing checked when he got back to London. His eyes canvassed the nightstands—nothing. He hurried to the large radius window at the front of the room: no minivan, but her black Range Rover remained. Then he returned to the loft and gave his makeshift sleeping quarters a once-over—desperately hoping for a note of some kind. *I can't believe she left without so much as a goodbye.* He felt crestfallen. Last night, he'd let his festering frustration out in the worst possible way.

He grabbed a fresh change of clothes—black tactical pants and an athletic-fit, charcoal-gray tee—because he felt like mixing things up—from his duffel bag, then wandered into her bathroom. He set his garments down on the pine bench across from the dual-sink counter before stripping off his boxers. With a pivot, he caught a glimpse of himself in the mirror that hung above the sinks. Smack-dab in the middle of his forehead lay a perfectly defined, glossy pink lip imprint. A warmth coursed through his veins as he watched a broad grin appear on his face. *So she did say goodbye.*

Showered, shaved, and dressed, Mace bounded down the slippery wooden steps into the kitchen to discover Scotch stuffing a breakfast burrito into his mouth. "Mornin."

"Mornin', chief," Scotch replied, a clump of creamy green pepper mixed with something falling to the floor.

The scent of fresh-brewed arabica filled the room, and Mace made a beeline for the half-filled carafe on display in the corner of the counter. "I take it Redge went to the set with Ava this morning?" He tilted the glass carafe and caught the steaming liquid with his moose-print mug.

"Yep." Scotch polished off the remainder of the burrito.

Mace pulled open a drawer in search of a spoon, but only found cooking utensils. He moved on to the next— found the measuring cups. His third attempt proved successful. "I can't believe I didn't hear them leave."

"Mate, you were out," Scotch said as he scoured the fridge. "Ava said you were even snoring."

"You were awake when they left?" Mace's forehead puckered.

"I was still horizontal in bed,"—Scotch splashed orange juice into a glass—"but I could hear her and Redge talking."

Mace nodded. "Did she sound okay?"

Scotch shrugged. "From what I heard, yeah…" Then, with a smirk, Scotch asked, "How uncomfortable was that couch?"

Mace set his coffee mug on the granite and stretched out his back, then laced his fingers behind his head. "I can't say I'm proud of the way I handled things."

"Look, I get it. This schedule is brutal."

"Yeah, that's an understatement. And being in different time zones doesn't help matters." Mace lifted the mug to his lips. "I can count on one hand how many times we've talked for more than a few minutes over the past two months."

Scotch nodded as he extracted a stool from underneath the counter. "Mate, you just need some quality alone time with her. You two will be right as rain."

"Yeah, but that's not gonna happen before this film wraps up… which is another two weeks."

Scotch shrugged. "Sorry, mate." He downed the rest of his juice, then set his glass against the granite with a heavy thud. "So—what's the deal with your therapist following you here?"

Mace winced. "It's not like I'm an official patient. She was just worried about me—as a friend." He studied the Scotsman's unconvinced eyes. "Before I left, I confided in her that I was"—his fingers kneaded his forehead—"having some... bad dreams again."

Scotch combed his hand through his scraggly ginger-red beard. "That's a long way to travel for a follow-up appointment."

Mace released an extended sigh. "I realize it looks bad, but she just knows my history." The expression on Scotch's face suggested he remained skeptical. "She helped me through a lot of difficult times over the years... And... she knew how hard it was for me to watch Ava on set with Reed earlier this year..."

"I remember..." the Scotsman affirmed. "Look, I'm the *last* person who should talk about relationship boundaries, but her coming here even raises some serious red flags for me."

Mace walked over to the sink and placed his mug against the stainless steel. He grew thoughtful as he peered out the window at the heavily wooded perimeter. Massive, mature trees outlined the cabin's parcel. *Is it possible I'm being naïve? I've known Annie for over ten years... She's always been completely professional, as far as I could tell, anyway. Then again, she was recently divorced. Maybe she was craving a new man in her life. Plus, she did seem upset that I didn't realize she was single...*

"Mate," Scotch's voice boomed throughout the kitchen, pulling Mace back into the moment, and he turned to face his sniper friend. "As I said, you just need some quality time with Ava."

"That's *precisely* what I need… but I don't know how to make it happen." Mace shoved his thumbs in his belt loops. "She starts her day before oh five hundred and who the bloody hell knows when she'll finish—it's different each day, which makes it impossible to plan anything."

"I'll give you that, but,"—a sly gleam manifested in the Scotsman's eyes—"what's the one constant her schedule does provide?"

Mace searched his mind for a split second. "Her lunch break."

"Exactly," Scotch added with a waggle of his bushy brows.

Chapter Eighteen

Automatic doors parted, and Mace crossed into the resort's grandiose lobby, his heavy tactical boots squeaking with each step across the slick marble floor. A variety of heads turned his way—sour expressions conveying their annoyance with the intermittent reminder of his presence.

He headed straight towards the registration desk, Scotch—his footwear kosher—at his flank. Behind the forty-inch-high walnut barrier stood a trim twenty-something, wearing a green ottoman vest over a white blouse, her copper-brown hair pulled back into a tight bun. She flashed a welcoming smile as they approached the desk. "*Bonjour et bienvenue.*"

"I got this, mate," Scotch murmured as he spun toward their greeter. "*Bonjour, ma dame.*"

A tinge of pink splashed across her alabaster cheeks. With a flutter of her lashes, she said, "How might I help you?"

Scotch propped a beefy arm upon the desk, ensuring the young woman was afforded a proper view. "So, listen, I'm part of the *Mystery and Mayhem* crew."

"Oh!" Her dark eyes lit up. "How exciting!"

"Yeah," Scotch bobbed his head. "I actually have a small part in the film."

"Oh!" A beaming smile. "I may need to get your *autographe*!" she said, lifting her shoulders.

Oh, good Lord. Mace ran a hand back and forth over his mouth, struggling to rein in his flaring eyes.

"Anytime, *ma belle*," Scotch said with a wink. "So, my mate here,"—he jerked his thumb toward Mace—"needs a room for a few hours to… prepare his equipment."

My equipment? That's the best you could come up with?

"Oh… we do not do that sort of thing… we are not *that* kind of hotel," she said, her lips curving downward.

"I know…" With a charming smile, Scotch flexed his arm and leaned in close. Then, in a hushed tone, he said, "But I was hoping you might be able to make an exception…"

The young lady appeared conflicted. She tapped the pen in her hands against the polished wood. "I'll go get my manager." She scurried through a doorway off the adjacent wall, then returned a few moments later with a stocky, mature-looking man on her heels. The man wore a stolid expression that made Mace consider throwing in the towel.

"These gentlemen need to reserve a room for a few hours." Scotch's newfound friend quickly brought her manager up to speed.

The man glared at Scotch. "Sir,"—his strained voice boomed throughout the lobby—"we are not *that* kind of resort."

Mace rolled his eyes. He tapped Scotch's shoulder, then cocked his head toward the exit.

Scotch held up his palm and flashed a look that said, *Gimme a sec.* "Look, I'm with the *Mystery and Mayhem* crew, and Pierre himself sent me up here to handle this."

The look on the manager's face softened. "I see… Unfortunately, sir, given the number of rooms your production has already required, I have none available."

Scotch blew out his cheeks in dramatic fashion. "That's just great. Do you have any idea how upset he's going to be?" He shook his head and forced a sad expression. "I'd hate for him to tell all of his industry contacts that he was disappointed in this place." With slow, measured movements, Scotch turned to leave.

"Sir, please,"—the manager gestured for him to stay—"let me see what I can do." Mace watched as his hands swept across the keyboard in front of him. "Hmm… I have a guest who will not arrive until late this evening… I could give you his room for half the day, but would need you out in time for housekeeping to clean it well before he is scheduled to arrive."

"Perfect," Scotch said, turning toward Mace with a gloating smile.

Mace breathed a sigh of relief. He'd gotten the room; now he just needed the actress.

"That'll be $1,298," the manager said.

Scotch's eyes blinked in rapid succession. "No—we only want to pay the half-day rate."

The manager tucked his chin to his chest and fixed his coal-like eyes on Scotch. "Sir, that *is* the half-day rate."

Mace attempted to calculate the Euro exchange amount in his head as he stepped up to the desk. He extracted his platinum credit card from his leather wallet and slid it across the polished wood. Then he crossed his fingers and hoped it went through.

Chapter Nineteen

Mace advanced across the long hall that led from the lobby toward the guest rooms, feeling certain any passersby would be thankful it was carpeted so they didn't have to hear his boots announce his squeaky existence. A long line of guests extended from the elevator bank off the lobby, prompting him to tread inward, in search of the stairs.

Wide, ivory-paneled halls created a welcoming path, lit by antique gold-plated sconces. He spotted a sign that read *Escaliers* and was about to push open the door when he heard a woman's voice, with an accent similar to his own, call out his name behind him.

He rotated to find Annie scampering toward him. "Top of the morning!" she called out as she drew closer, her short, dirty-blonde curls bouncing over her shoulders with each step. She wore a powder-blue trench-style windbreaker over her active frame and a smile of pleasant surprise across her face.

She halted beside Mace as he stood next to the stairway entrance. "I was just heading to the set to try to find you!"

"Oh?" Mace crammed his hands inside his black fleece jacket. "Well, I guess I saved you a trip."

Annie tilted her head toward her shoulder. "I thought you were staying in one of the vacation properties?"

"We are..." *But how would you know that?* Mace zeroed in on her seemingly innocent mossy-green eyes, plagued by a yellow tinge under the golden lighting. He cleared his throat. "So, how are you enjoying the hotel?" He asked, careful to keep the suspicion from his tone. "Was this your first night here?"

"Yes, I arrived early yesterday morning." She inspected her short, glossy vermilion fingernails. "Why?"

A wave of relief rolled over him. "Just curious."

"Anyway,"—she touched her hand to his fleece-covered forearm—"I have something for you." Mace watched with curiosity as she dug through the beige, crescent-shaped bag that slung over her shoulder. "Ah, here it is." Her hand reappeared, fragments of black peeking out from between her fingers. With a rotation of her wrist, she revealed the object: a small, black foam blob in the shape of a Newfoundland.

Mace removed his hand from his pocket and plucked it from her palm. The soft, pliable object felt foreign in his grasp. "Thanks," he said.

Annie cast a proud smile. "I thought it might help when you feel yourself getting anxious on set. I know how hard it is for you to watch Ava be so close with another man…"

Mace's chest heaved with the imagery.

"Anyway, it's scented with jasmine and sandalwood to promote relaxation," she added with a boastful smile as she tossed her short, muddy blonde hair. "Plus, I thought you'd get a kick out of the Newfoundland because I'm sure you miss Maximus."

Mace squeezed the small, black dog in his hands, then let his muscles relax as the spongy material expanded. "I do, but Ava's family loves having him at the Embassy. They spoil him rotten."

Annie offered a slight nod. "What brings you to this part of the hotel?"

Mace's eyes darted to the right. "Just felt like… exploring." He watched a young couple, their arms wound around each other, pass by wearing broad, loving smiles. He couldn't wait to get up to the room.

"Would you like company?"

"Um…" Mace gave the Newfoundland another squeeze.

Annie's lips pursed to the side for a brief moment before mumbling, "That's okay." She toyed with the diamond attached to her earlobe, said, "Look, I plan to just hang around the set as often as possible," before her palm again found his forearm. "That way, I'm here whenever you need me."

"Thanks, Annie."

"Now—go enjoy some quality alone time." She flashed a sunny smile, then whirled around and headed toward the lobby. "Cheerio!"

I'm hoping to… just not alone. Mace rammed the steel door that led to the stairs and bolted up them two at a time. By the sixth landing, his pace had slowed to a jog. One more flight before a large painted seven opened into view. He stopped to catch his breath before pushing the heavy door open.

A taupe, rectangular plaque adhered to the wall directed him to the right based on his room number. He traversed another long, ivory paneled corridor, passing by several doors, their spacing well beyond that of a typical resort, before spying the number he sought. He removed the plastic room card from his chest pocket and let it hover over the electronic handle. One green light and a grinding click later, the door swung inward, aided by a gentle nudge from his tactical boot.

A wave of natural light, tinted gray from the overcast sky, washed over him as he ambled into the corner suite. Windows, stretching from floor to ceiling, parted to accommodate a set of French doors, which summoned him. As he stepped out onto the stone base of the cantilevered balcony, a harsh breeze swept over him. He took a moment to appreciate the impressive view of the emerald lake-outlined city below, before his stare shifted to the cumulonimbus clouds that skated across the horizon. He wandered back inside to settle into the luxurious space. A king-size bed covered in feathery pillows and wrapped in white, its edges tucked under the mattress, sat opposite the splendid view. An elegant desk, its ornate legs suggesting it was handcrafted, rested in one corner, and a gray tufted Meridian chaise in another. A stately, marble-lined fireplace took up half of the adjacent wall. He dropped his black tactical bag on the floor near the hearth, then turned the dial positioned next to the mantle. With an explosive *whoosh*, an orange flame billowed over the ceramic log set. *So this is how the other half lives.*

****

Ava heaped a pile of strawberry spinach salad onto her plate after ensuring as many pecans as the large wooden spoon could scoop were included. She reached for a fork and a napkin just as Pierre appeared beside her.

"Ava," he whispered as he walked alongside, carrying his own plate filled with strips of fried chicken.

Ava cast a sideways glance at the seasoned director. "Yes?"

With his free hand, he guided her by the elbow toward a secluded section of the bustling set. Ava felt her pulse race as her mind computed the myriad follow-up statements. *Your last performance was subpar... We have to retake another scene... The Network is cancelling the series...*

He stopped beside a black, curtained-off partition and leaned in close. Ava studied Pierre's well-preserved face as he locked his indigo eyes onto her. "Reed shared your idea with me for the future of the series."

"Oh?" Ava tried to mask her surprise. *We were supposed to do it together.*

"My dear, Ava,"—Pierre slid his black frames higher over the bridge of his nose—"it's not like that. Reed was quite vague—said he wanted to wait till the two of you were together—but I'm intrigued." He smoothed the patch of silver hair above his ear. "I'm hoping to wrap up by seven this evening so the three of us can discuss over dinner," he said with a tug on his shirt collar.

Her heart sank. She so desperately hoped to spend some time with Mace this evening. "May I bring a guest?"

A knowing smile manifested. "The bodyguard boyfriend?" Following Ava's nod, he continued, "Of course. Now *excusez-moi.*" He kissed both of her cheeks, then called out, "Tell Reed to bring his lady friend as well," as he scurried off.

Ava stabbed her fork into the pile of spinach leaves amassed on her plate and lifted it to her mouth. She was starving. "Ava!" she heard her stylist call out. "Be *super* careful with your makeup while you eat! I won't have much time to touch it up before the next scene!" Ava nodded, then slid the fork against the side of the plate, removing half of its load.

She raised it to her salivating mouth again just as a strong hand squeezed her shoulder from behind.

With a startled gasp, the entire plate, fork included, tumbled to the tile floor. She spun to see Scotch, his jewel-like eyes wide. "Ava, I've been looking all over for you!"

"What's wrong?" she asked, her breath quickening.

"Nothing,"—Scotch reached for her hand—"but I need you to come with me," he said, spinning around.

"Where?" Ava scrunched up her face. "I'm due back on set in like twenty minutes…"

Scotch's pace teetered on a jog. "Never mind that. I just need to show you something." Ava tailed him across the cordoned-off area and through the crew's resort entrance. They hurried along the golden paisley carpeted halls; Scotch's skilled navigation suggested he'd recently taken the route. He led her to the hotel's northern elevator bank, dashed into a closing set of doors, and punched the number seven button.

Ava couldn't help but chuckle. "What in the world are you up to?"

With a mischievous glint in his eye, he said, "You'll see."

A moment later, the polished-nickel doors slid open, revealing another long and inviting hall. He gestured for her to follow as he trotted down the extended corridor before coming to an abrupt stop beside a recessed alcove.

Ava read the plaque on the wall beside the paneled door: 723. She arched a quizzical eyebrow. "Scotch, please tell me what's going on."

He wrapped his arms around her and imparted a quick peck on her pink cheek. "Have fun," he said with a wink, then shoved a plastic key card into her hand.

Chapter Twenty

Mace glanced at his titanium diver as he paced the length of the room: twelve-fifteen-hundred hours. *Where was she? Maybe she was still mad. Maybe Scotch couldn't convince her to come—nah, he's pretty convincing. Maybe Pierre revoked lunch privileges today because they had to retake a scene. Maybe she was encased in Reed's arms…* He raked his hand through his tousled hair. Then, worried he messed it up, he stalked into the bathroom and peeked in the mirror. His fingers combed his thick chestnut strands back to satisfactory condition.

Another peek at his titanium diver. The room now felt like it was eighty degrees, and he wished he had waited to turn on the fireplace. He peeled off his fleece jacket, tossed it over the desk chair, then roamed over to the French doors and swung them open. His forearms found a place over the wrought iron railing. He grew pensive as he peered out at the horizon. Towering, thunderhead clouds closed the distance, suggesting a storm was imminent. Although an incredible sight, despite the ominous skyline, the view paled in comparison to Ava's northern Michigan waterfront property, which he sorely missed. Last fall, they'd spent every day—and night—together, every moment blissful, creating a hoard of treasured memories. All that changed with the start of the new year, when her schedule exploded. Shards of rain began to fall at an angle, dimpling the surface of the beautiful emerald lake. The sight lulled him, easing his intrusive thoughts.

A faint click sounded behind him, and he pivoted to discover another breathtaking view: his sweet angel standing in the doorway. She wore a silky navy-blue gown that flowed across her curves like liquid. He worried his heart might explode inside his chest. With a nibble of her pink, pouty, bottom lip, she took a hesitant step into the room, her sapphire eyes filled with uncertainty. Then, she kicked off her silver stilettos and sprinted into his strong, craving arms.

Mace's grin stretched from ear to ear as she kissed his lips, his forehead, his smooth-shaven cheeks, before repeating the circuit. "I'm sorry," she uttered.

"I'm sorry, too. I—" He managed to say before the tip of her tongue teased his. She tugged his charcoal-gray fitted shirt from his belted waist and slid it over his head, her fingers caressing his carved chest along the route. Mace pulled her tighter against his bare skin. His hungry lips traced the curve of her neck, eliciting a soft whimper of desire, before descending along the plunging neckline of her dress. His hands fumbled with the zipper over her back, finally got it, freeing her from the silky acetate blend as it cascaded to her petite feet.

He felt his belt give before a yank at his waistline revealed his steely mast. Every ounce of him tingled under her tender touch, and he feared he might detonate before they even reached the bed. With a pinch of his fingers, he unclasped her bra, her plump breasts falling against his chest. An airy moan escaped her lips as he lifted her body—her toned legs wrapping around the small of his back—shuffled over to the bed, and draped her across the Egyptian cotton.

Beneath him, longing, loving eyes locked onto his. He ran his rugged hand over the curve of her hips, hooking the edge of her ivory satin panties along the way. His lips cleared their path, sliding them down her smooth thighs, over the arc of her knees, and along her tibia, before flinging them to the floor. His hungry lips traveled the same route back up her body, slowing their pace as he reached her inner thighs. She parted her legs; her body quivering against his, as her long nails dipped into the flesh that covered his back. With breezy breaths, she murmured his name, beckoning him to her mouth. Her spread legs summoned his faithful manhood as their lips, woven together, conveyed what words could not. His passion permeated her strong yet delicate body with each loving thrust. His lips parted with hers to enjoy the succulent mounds of her breasts before his strong hand took their place, caressing her voluptuous flesh. Their pleasure-filled moans harmonized as his thrusts escalated; his mounting love erupting from his trembling body.

He distributed his weight across her goddess-like frame, then planted a lingering kiss on her soft lips. She gazed at him with satisfied eyes. But he wasn't done trying to satisfy her. His long finger replaced his manhood, penetrating her to peak passion until her melodious gasps grew so loud his lips had to stifle them, her body shuddering in his strong, tender embrace.

Her fingers swept through his hair while he rested his head against her heaving bosom. "You transform me, Mr. Storm."

He lifted his head to peer into her soulful eyes. "Does this mean I don't have to sleep on the couch tonight?" he said with a crooked grin.

A radiant smile broke across her stunning face before she delivered a playful poke to his obliques.

"I'm sorry about last night," he whispered as he stroked her cheek.

"I am, too." Her eyes misted as she traced the contours of his chest. "It's certainly not how I expected the evening to go."

"I don't suppose you'll be done early tonight?" he asked with bated breath.

"Yes," her lips curved downward, "but I have a dinner engagement with Reed and Pierre."

"Oh." He maneuvered off her and onto his side.

"I'd love for you to join me," she said with a waggle of her precision-groomed brows.

He hated dinner parties almost as much as he hated dancing before Ava came into his life. "I don't know…"

Ava positioned her body on top of him, her golden locks trailing down his torso as she lowered her chest to his. Her soft lips found his earlobe and gave it a gentle nibble.

"No fair." He grinned. "You know that drives me crazy."

She pressed her lips to his neck. "I love having you by my side," she whispered between soft kisses. "Please join me."

And I love being by your side. She raised her body at the waist, straddling him. Mace's hands instinctively locked onto her hips. "What were we talking about again?" he asked with a mischievous gleam in his eye, prompting Ava to tilt her head, eyebrow arched. As his steel-blue eyes appraised the priceless treasure resting upon him, his heart swelled with gratitude. "It's impossible for me to say no to you…"

"Yay!" Her eyes lit up as she patted her hands in front of her, her breasts threshing with the movement. Mace's grip roamed skyward, over her toned stomach, landing on her chest. He sat up, pressed himself to her, and pulled her to his lips. His mast was ready to set sail once again.

"Darling, I've gotta go," Ava whispered, freeing her lips from his. She glanced at her diamond-encrusted watch. "Oh my gosh! I've *really* got to go!" She leapt from the bed, gathered her clothes, and ran to the bathroom.

It took Mace all of sixty seconds to get dressed. He grabbed his tactical bag and extinguished the fire. A moment later, Ava rushed out of the bathroom, her eyes loaded with worry.

"I'm sorry—I should've paid more attention to the time." Mace interlaced his fingers with hers.

She imparted a tender kiss on his mouth. "I love that you did this for me."

Hand in hand, they hurried out of the room. As Mace pulled the door to a close behind them, a thought entered his mind: *this was the best twelve hundred dollars I've ever spent.*

After a mad dash back to the cordoned-off set, Mace kissed her cheek, whispered "Good luck," then watched as Ava slipped the fake diamond back on her finger and traipsed toward the cameras.

"Ava—thank God—we've been looking all over for you!" Reed's worry-plagued voice echoed throughout the room. "Where have you been?!"

"Sorry!" he heard her reply as the distance between them grew. "I... ran into someone."

"Oh, Ava!" he heard her stylist yell. "What on *earth* happened to your hair?"

"Sorry, Nikki. It's really windy outside."

"And *why* is your makeup all *smudged?*"

Mace choked back his mirth.

Chapter Twenty-One

Scotch whipped Ava's Range Rover through the open, twelve-foot, wrought iron gate, its tires connecting with the cobblestone that followed. The castle-size estate magnified as he sped up the path, then slowed to a stop next to the exotic silver coupe on display.

Wasting no time, Scotch jumped out of the driver's seat and bounced up the sidewalk toward the front door. With a knowing glance, he flashed a half smile at the monitoring camera. Attempting to restrain his soaring excitement, he drew in a long, deep breath. When he had texted Julietta after his first visit, her immediate response yielded the permanent smile he couldn't seem to curb. The outreach resulted in several subsequent texts that redefined the term 'naughty'. He hadn't been able to get this woman off his mind. She clearly wanted for nothing—aside from a vigorous young man to make her feel safe and satisfy her sexual desires—and Scotch fit the bill to a tee. He could spend the rest of his life protecting her and fulfilling her every yearning.

He pressed the illuminated round button next to the door and heard the chime echo inside. He smoothed his tight long-sleeve shirt over his chest, stopping at his waist. He dared not venture any further, for the swelling between his legs was already uncomfortably pronounced. His favorite instrument was ready for deployment—and if Julietta herself answered, he just might have to pleasure her right there in the doorway.

He again admired the etched glass against the wrought-iron scrolling as he waited. He leaned an ear toward the door; no sounds revealed themselves. He pressed the round button a second time. Another few moments of impatience yielded no response. Scotch jerked his head toward the driveway. Her car was here—surrounded by patches of blue, as the storm clouds traveled east. *She must be in the pool.*

He strode back down the front walkway, then ventured west toward the back of the home. His boots trekked over the wide, slate steps as they descended toward the showstopping in-ground pool and hot tub, then transitioned to the sprawling flagstone patio that surrounded the fresh water.

His eyes scoured the crystal blue lough in search of his goal. Nothing. *I don't get it… She told me to stop by this afternoon… She said she'd be home all day.* Scotch continued past the pool. Floor-to-ceiling windows stretched across the back of the palatial structure, affording a great view of the interior. His jade eyes peered into the expansive, deserted kitchen as he strolled by. A break between windows shrouded his view for a fleeting moment, then his eyes skimmed over the capacious parlor that also appeared to be empty. *Maybe she was upstairs.* He continued past the edge of the window, his view of the interior again obscured by the fieldstone façade. He approached another large window accented with white grilles. He spied a floor-to-ceiling wall of bookcases, before a dark, espresso-colored executive desk opened into view. The desk was nothing noteworthy—in stark contrast to what rested upon it.

He had found Julietta: positioned upright on the desk—arms propped behind her to support her weight—legs splayed wide. He could make out the sight of one breast as it writhed up and down at breakneck speed. Scotch watched in horror as she caught sight of him outside the window—her eyes filling with a gamey gleam. A lewd smile spread across her olive-colored face as her stare held fast to his. Her mouth widened with moans silent to his ears, as the naked man standing between her legs bore himself into her repeatedly.

Chapter Twenty-Two

Scotch's heart crumbled inside his chest as her butler's pale backside continued to pulsate between her thighs. With trembling legs, he backed away from the window, one hesitant step at a time, catching sight of his own appalled reflection in the glass. After an about-face, he darted up the slate steps toward Ava's SUV.

Shaking hands gripped the steering wheel to ground him. *What the bloody hell was that? I knew she had an insatiable appetite for sex, but her butler? On top of knowing I'd be stopping by today! Why didn't she just wait for me?*

Confrontation had never fazed him; in fact, he often thrived on it, regardless of the result. He closed his eyes and embraced reality as it settled over him: Julietta had simply been toying with him this entire time. She had no interest in anything beyond carnal acts. His hopes of fulfilling her needs in a meaningful, long-term capacity were shattered. *Redge was right.*

With the push of a button, the luxury vehicle roared to life. Scotch punched the accelerator, wanting to put as much distance between himself and the deceitful temptress as quickly as possible.

****

Redge's gravity-driven hands yanked on his zipper, exposing his sculpted, tank-covered chest. His stride slowed momentarily with the movement before resuming its fast pace. He sprinted along the narrow, sandy path—one of several that weaved through the heavily wooded hills that outlined their cabin. He'd become intimately familiar with these trails over the last few days as they proved to be his primary source of entertainment, aside from this morning's jaunt to the studio. The chaos on set overwhelmed him. Fortunately, Mace took point for the afternoon, allowing him to retreat to their secluded hilltop haven. After Scotch called the other day and shared the news of Ava's ransacked room, Redge jumped at the chance to come up here and watch over the property. The refuge of nature soothed the perpetual noise of everyday life in the city. The fact that his request overlapped with Angie's sisters' visit was simply divine intervention. They drove him crazy, and he often wondered how they were even related to his beloved wife. Nonetheless, he was starting to miss his baby.

A loud chime sounded from his pocket. He halted to extract his cell. With a swipe, he pulled up the video feed of the doorbell camera he installed near the front entrance. He watched as an Eastern Gray squirrel darted across the wooden porch railing. Redge shoved his phone back in his pocket before his strong legs picked up speed.

His broad shoulders brushed against the deciduous leaves that clung to the encroaching branches. Meager sunlight penetrated the arborous overhead curtain. He focused on the ground before him, careful to avoid the occasional branches and stumps that cluttered the private path. His eyes could still make out his own footprints from days past—the only signs of activity along the trail—save for the addition of five-inch elongated heart-shaped prints, the tell-tale sign of a developing buck.

He approached the end of the two-mile trail, and the rear of the cabin opened into view. He could make out the balcony and sliding glass door that served the master suite, the red-stained cedar shimmering under the sun's spotlight. He hurdled the wide, dead tree trunk that blocked his path for the third consecutive day—his old track coach would be proud. The buck's trail disappeared into the trees, but a new set of tracks debuted. Chest heaving from exertion, Redge stopped to bend down for a closer look. The prints were small compared to his size sixteen running shoes, with a well-defined hiking tread. He followed their route, which led to the forest's edge, coming to a stop just before the exposed backyard of their chalet. Redge studied the tree branches to the left and right of the last print. Careful to tread lightly, he entered the woods to the left of the trail and followed the bent and broken leaves and branches at a snail's pace. He spied a half-print on a large rock and continued west through the thick woods, before a small clearing opened to reveal tire tracks. The non-aggressive tread suggested an all-season tire, not something found on an SUV designed for this environment. *Probably a rental.* A spec of silver caught his eye, and he reached for a discarded gum wrapper that rested beside the last print. Then, he followed the same route back towards the cabin.

Chapter Twenty-Three

Mace tugged at the cuffs of his new white shirt. Normally, he had to special order his dress shirts—given that his arms were three times as muscular as the average man—but, as luck would have it, discovered this one, along with a navy sports coat, in the resort's upscale shopping strip. The jacket was snug and barely reached his wrists, but at least now he'd meet the restaurant's dress code. He hoped it didn't look as awkward as it felt.

Boasting a perfect blend of historical elegance and modern design trends, the restaurant did not disappoint. A wall of windows stretched along the perimeter, offering a beautiful vista of the city below. Inside, rich walnut panels adorned the ten-foot-high walls, and gilded vintage sconces cast a warm, inviting glow.

An angelic vision, Ava wore an amethyst cashmere sweater dress that hugged her luxurious frame. The V-cut neckline teased with a touch of porcelain cleavage, and long, golden curls spilled over her shoulders in waves. With his sweet angel on his arm, they had arrived at the exclusive restaurant just as Pierre, looking dapper in a full suit, was seated at a large round table tucked into a secluded corner. Reed stepped into view, wearing a classic black dress shirt that accentuated his model-like hair and silvery blue eyes. His girlfriend's long caramel locks were tied back in a sleek, low ponytail. Ava smiled in amusement as she eyed Stephanie's wardrobe choice, for the fashion model wore a similarly styled black sweater dress, suggesting she and Reed coordinated their look. Mace regretted not choosing the purple-hued version of his dress shirt, so he and Ava could've coordinated, too.

Pierre explained that the restaurant was well-known for its cutting-edge cuisine as their server, a tall, broad-shouldered young man with dark hair cropped close to his skull, arrived. He wore the usual garb: a green ottoman vest over a white shirt, accented by a coordinating bow tie. The young man took their drink order—Mace opted for an old-fashioned in addition to Pierre's request for six bottles of wine, a mix of red and white—before hurrying off. His professionalism proved top-notch; either he wasn't familiar with the celebrities, or policy didn't allow him to engage.

With impressive speed, their server returned with a large round tray holding several amber bottles, along with Mace's lone glass of honey-colored liquid, stained by two bright-red stemmed cherries. Their waiter uncorked each bottle one at a time, poured a trace amount into separate glasses in front of Pierre, then waited, hands clasped at the small of his back, while the director nodded in approval after each sip.

Following the beverage formality, the waiter inquired about dinner selections. He explained that the restaurant specialized in exquisite culinary pairings designed for sharing as he distributed menus. Pierre waved a dismissive hand when a colorful laminated list was placed in front of him. "No need for menus. We'll simply have one of everything."

Mace almost choked on his brandied cherry.

"Very good, sir." Their waiter nodded. If he was at all surprised by Pierre's request, he didn't show it. "I'll get that right in for you," he said, then spun on his heel and marched off.

Pierre gestured for them to choose their intoxicant, then raised his crystal-stemmed glass above his head. "Here's to my two favorite actors in the world. Thank you for making me look so good!" Mace caught himself on the brink of an eyeroll, squashed it just in time, as the five of them smiled and clinked glasses.

"Now," Pierre dropped his vessel to the white linen, his indigo eyes shifting between his beloved stars. "Tell me about your idea." Reed and Ava proceeded to share their thoughts on how to enhance the *Mystery and Mayhem* series by taking it in a new direction. There was a long pause after their rehearsed statement, and Mace watched as Reed and Ava exchanged a nervous glance.

Pierre appeared thoughtful as he drummed the crystal in front of him. "I'm not sure I follow…" He stared at Ava with a quizzical expression slapped over his face, then inclined his head toward Reed. "You two basically want to write yourselves out of a job?"

Ava propped her cashmere-covered elbows on the table and laced her long, smooth fingers. "I see it as expanding our creative attributes, Pierre," she countered.

"Ava's right," Reed chimed in. "Screenwriting is a newly discovered passion of ours, and it'll only enhance our acting chops."

"Exactly," Ava said, with a graceful splaying of her hands. "As actors, we rarely get to be intimately involved with the *creation* of our character, which, to me, is the most fascinating aspect." She lifted her shoulders and clasped her hands against her ivory cheek. "This will allow us to explore that avenue through the mindset of an actor."

Pierre tipped his stemmed glass filled with golden wine into his mouth. "Don't get me wrong—I love the changes you two made to this film—they're brilliant." He slid his black-framed glasses up the bridge of his nose. "But the fans have such a strong connection to you both. They *love* you,"—he tossed his hands out wide—"which is literally why we're here at this very moment. Fan demand is what caused

Homepoint to squeeze this film into production in such a hurry!"

"We recognize that," Reed said as Stephanie plucked a piece of lint from the arm of his black dress shirt. "But *Mystery and Mayhem* was intended to be a stand-alone." Reed's forehead puckered under wisps of jet-black hair that had fallen out of place. "A sequel was never part of the original story."

"Pierre," Ava's smooth voice soothed, "if we're being honest—this film is great, but, in my humble opinion, very much lacks the magic the first one captured." Mace gazed into her sparkling eyes as she addressed her director. *How in the world did I get so lucky?*

Pierre grew quiet. "You're right," he whispered, following a heavy sigh. "As much as I hate to admit it."

"So, what's next—a lackluster third? By that time, ratings will be down, and we run the risk of ruining the entire franchise." Reed filled his and Stephanie's glass with a maroon blend for the second time. "I say we take it in a new direction—where we can truly let these characters shine." Reed flashed a bright grin.

Ava swiped a long curl from her shoulder and imparted an affectionate glance at Mace before turning her attention back to Pierre. "Furthermore, our most recent market analysis indicated that viewers are increasingly drawn to that demographic. They find that age range more relatable."

Pierre leaned back in his chair and laced his fingers behind his balding head. "All right. I'll go to bat for you two." His nose crinkled as he lowered his chin to his chest. "Just put in a good word for me so I get to direct the new, older versions of you two."

Ava's glossy pink lips spread into a joyful smile, and Mace couldn't resist the urge to kiss them. He loved seeing her happy. At first, he was confused by the suggestion, too, but the thought of her life not being consumed by filming sounded bloody amazing. However, a small part of him wondered if she wanted to free up her schedule with Homepoint so she could pursue the *Studio Nine Eleven* sequel. No matter, he'd worry about that later—he was still on cloud nine following their afternoon together.

Following a kiss from Reed, Stephanie announced, "Here's to two of the most beautiful and creative people I know!" She held up her drink. "Cheers to an amazing life *onscreen* and *off*!" The five of them again clinked glasses around the table set for eight, before Stephanie's eyes shifted toward the entrance and lit up like a light bulb. "Oh my gosh!" She leaned closer to Reed. "That's Kent Kincaid! He's a top producer!"

Chapter Twenty-Four

Mace caught sight of Ava's wince as Reed's girlfriend waved an emphatic arm in the air. His steady hand sought hers beneath the table as Stephanie's voice boomed throughout the restaurant, "Mr. Kincaid!"

Kent's attention transferred to them, an enamored smile appearing on his handsome face the moment he laid eyes on Ava. He strode over to their corner and, with a charming nod, extended a greeting. "Good evening, Ava,"—his eyes rolled over the other guests—"and Ava's companions."

Stephanie released a sophomoric giggle. She wasted no time kicking off the introductions, starting with herself—careful to point out that she's a fashion model—and Reed, adding that he's Ava's *Mystery and Mayhem* co-star. Pierre was introduced as a genius director, before she gestured to Mace, who apparently had nothing noteworthy to include after his name. Stephanie then pointed to Ava. "Though it appears you already know Ms. Ellis."

"I do, indeed." Kent emitted a charismatic smile.

Ava's chest rose and fell with a long, deep breath. She inclined her head at the producer, then grasped Mace's hand beneath the table, as if needing its strength to steady her.

"Mr. Kincaid, please join us!" Stephanie insisted, pointing to one of the three vacant chairs next to Mace.

Kent fastened his gaze to Ava, seemingly studying her expression. "I wouldn't want to impose."

"Oh, goodness, it's no imposition!" Stephanie cried out with a wave of her hand. Reed whispered something into her ear, and the broad smile on her face ebbed to the slightest degree.

"I'm not certain Ms. Ellis would agree," Kent said, his tone soft but steady.

"Oh," Stephanie whispered, her nose crinkling.

Kent's gaze held fast to Ava as a silence ensued. *At least he had the decency to seek her permission.* Mace skimmed the faces of their guests: their eyes were glued to Ava.

Ava stole a glance at Mace. The thought of her ex-fiancé sitting next to him was unbearable, but he gave the slightest nod of his head. He didn't want to make a scene for her sake. He was already so far out of his element; why not just push him over the edge?

"Kent, you're more than welcome to join us," Ava said, her tone lukewarm at best.

His eyebrows shot up. "You're sure?"

Ava gestured toward the vacant chairs. "Please," she said, adding a dash of graciousness.

Mace took a swig of his Old Fashioned as Kent positioned himself in the middle of the three open chairs. He was thankful the guy had the sense to leave an open spot between them. *Where the bloody hell was their server?* He needed to have his second whiskey on standby.

His desperate vibe must have summoned him, because the young man reemerged from behind a large column, an accomplice on his heel, and the two of them proceeded to present the gourmet works of art. The abundantly-sized selections—lobster, oysters, escargot, caviar, shrimp, kobe beef, foie gras, stuffed mushrooms, and calamari—filled every inch of available table space.

Mace and Ava reached for the calamari as the others delighted in the gluttonous variety. He brushed a wavy lock over her shoulder, then leaned close. "You doin' okay?" he whispered into her ear. She issued a beautiful, albeit slight smile, before planting a lingering kiss on his cheek. Mace felt a warmth spread throughout his face, then caught a glimpse of Kent just as the producer averted his eyes.

Stephanie, in particular, seemed to enjoy Kent's presence, and Mace got the distinct sense she had been longing to transition from modeling to acting. Regardless, he was thankful that she and Pierre were content to monopolize the conversation, as it took the pressure off him.

"Actually, Kent," Pierre started. "I'd like to get your thoughts on the idea Ava and Reed just presented."

"Oh?" he asked, a sparkle in his eye as he looked at Ava.

Mace shoved a bacon-wrapped shrimp in his mouth as he glared at the producer while Pierre relayed their earlier conversation.

"Screenwriting, huh?" Kent's thick brows drew together. "Interesting. Though,"—he thumbed his strong chin—"perhaps, it'll free up Ava's time to pursue… other projects."

I can't stand this guy.

Kent leaned back in his chair and unbuttoned his black sports coat. "Ava's right, Pierre—recent studies indicate viewing trends are evolving." He steepled his hands in front of him. "Actors in that age range are far more desirable now than they were ten years ago."

Stephanie rested a hand on Reed's chest. "But I do hope you'll take some time off when you wrap up this film in two weeks." Her bright-red bottom lip jutted out over its top in a puppy-dog pout. "I'd like to steal you away for a bit before you throw yourself to the screenwriting wolves."

Mace reached his arm around Ava and pulled her against his chest. "My sentiments exactly."

"We're actually running ahead of schedule, Stephanie," Pierre said before he sucked a snail from its shell with a loud slurp. "Thanks to your onscreen chemistry,"—he glanced at Ava and Reed—"I expect to wrap up by mid-next week."

Reed lifted his wine glass and nodded to Ava. "That's because she's the queen of the first take." He imparted an admiring smile.

"She's always been," Kent added, his hazel eyes locked onto Ava as her porcelain cheeks converted to crimson.

Mace snatched his ice-cold water—considered tossing it over his face—settled instead for a refreshing swig.

"Queen is certainly an apt description, my dear," Pierre chimed in as he reached for another bottle of wine. "You're the most beautiful thing on television."

Ava rested her chin in her palm. "There's always someone younger and more attractive waiting in the wings."

"That may be true." Kent dabbed his lips with his white linen napkin, then dropped it in his lap. "But you bring a magic to the screen Hollywood hasn't seen in decades."

Soon, industry-related stories surfaced, and the guests found themselves engrossed with entertaining tales of mischief and mishaps.

"That's nothing," Kent said after Pierre shared an amusing story about a snake sneaking onto a set. He tossed a mushroom into his mouth. "When Ava filmed the first *Studio Nine Eleven*, her co-star thought it would be fun to bring his pet tarantula to the set one day."

"Kent—" Ava imparted a cautionary glare.

"Lo and behold, it gets loose," Kent continued, ignoring her passive plea. "The entire crew spent half a day searching for the damn thing." Light laughter from the other side of the table. "Guess where it shows up?" Kent paused to scan everyone's expressions. "On Ava!" Hearty chuckles broke out across from them. "The hairy thing snuck into her dress, and when she went to put it on, it crawled up her back and over her shoulder—then planted itself on her breast!" Kent planted a palm over his right pec to create a visual; his green eyes exhibited a mischievous glint. "You gave everyone quite a show that day as Chris tried to wrangle it off you."

An explosion of pink broke out across Ava's cheeks for the second time. She issued a demure smile while two-thirds of the guests roared with laughter. Mace jolted as a surge of anger coursed through him, his knee ramming against the underside of the table with a loud thud. *I'm really starting to hate this guy.* He downed his entire glass of water, then dropped the crystal to the table and wrung his hands in front of his broad chest. Ava's soothing sapphire gaze whispered, *It's okay,* in silence, as she ran her hand over his thigh in calming strokes.

"You never mentioned that!" Reed proclaimed as the mirth waned, the corners of his eyes still crinkled.

"Gee, I wonder why," Ava spouted a playful eyeroll.

"Kent, you said the first *Studio Nine Eleven*... does that mean there's going to be a sequel?" Stephanie held up two sets of crossed fingers as her athletic frame bounced up and down in the chair.

"That depends on Ava." He weaved a hand through his perfect golden-brown hair. "The opportunity is there if she wants it," Kent added, casting a charming wink in Ava's direction.

"Wow, Ava,"—Reed's eyes grew wide—"that's incredible!"

"Oh, how exciting!" Stephanie beamed.

Mace glided his hand over Ava's back with loving strokes, monitoring the pensive expression that spread over her radiant face. Until his peripheral vision picked up a familiar shape. He twisted his head to discover Annie, dressed from head to toe in cherry-red, as she marched toward their secluded corner. Mace swallowed the lump that sprouted in his throat.

Chapter Twenty-Five

In dire need of a drink, Mace launched his hand toward his whiskey but overshot his target and sent Ava's stemmed glass toppling to its side. Thankfully, it was nearly empty, and only a trace of burgundy liquid trickled over the white cloth. He returned it to its upright position as Ava discharged a look that said, *Are you okay?* A moment later, her eyes flickered with irritation as they registered the approaching guest.

"Ah, there you are!" Annie announced with a cheery tone as she closed in. Her hands cupped the velvet back of the unoccupied chair that served as a barrier between Mace and Kent, her eyes scanning over the faces at the table. Then, she canted her head toward Mace and asked, "I was just curious to see if what I gave you earlier has been helpful?"

Ava craned her neck toward Mace, her gem-like eyes narrowed to slits. "And what—pray tell—might that be?" she asked. Her tone held its usual sweetness, but her expression suggested he was dangerously close to sleeping on the couch again tonight.

Mace propped his elbows on the table, his clasped hands partially covering his mouth. He mumbled, "It's just a little trinket."

Two small creases between her brows grew more pronounced as Ava continued to study him. Mace tugged at his collar.

"What was that?" Kent asked, leaning closer.

"Go ahead and show them," Annie encouraged with a wide smile.

Mace jammed his fist into his pocket and wrapped his fingers around the Newfoundland-shaped therapy ball. Then, with a sharp inhalation, he withdrew his hand and held it up to the group. "She gave me this."

"A stress ball, huh?" Kent flashed an impish gleam, the corners of his mouth teetering on a smirk.

One punch is all it would take.

Words seemed to evade Ava as she stared at the polyurethane dog. He suspected she might inform him that he'd be sleeping in the Range Rover tonight.

"Isn't the Newfoundland *adorable?*" With proud eyes, Annie searched the group for affirmation; seemed pleased when Stephanie offered an enthusiastic nod. With a slant of her head, Annie rested her hand on Mace's shoulder. "Is it helping?" she asked, her tone laced with concern.

He slid it back inside his pocket and squeezed it beneath the cloak of his tactical pants. He felt the muscles in his hand relax as it expanded. He looked at Kent. *Nope—still want to punch his face in.*

Mace realized everyone was staring at him, awaiting his response. "Yeah… a little."

"Oh, good!" Annie's eyes rolled over the two vacant settings at the table. "Well… I suppose I'll let you get back to your dinner…"

"Why don't you join us?" Kent asked, gesturing to the empty chair beside him.

Mace felt a crushing force over his knee courtesy of Ava's deceivingly delicate hand. Annie glanced at him, awaiting his permission—which he had no intention of giving—but had no idea how to proceed. He'd never been to a dinner party that included his girlfriend, *her* ex-fiancé, and *his* former therapist.

Fortunately, Ava came to his rescue. "Annie, you're welcome to stay," she said through tight lips.

"Brilliant!" She wasted no time sliding out, then slipping into the red velvet chair positioned between Kent and Mace.

At once, the waiter reappeared as if watching the entire scene unfold, filled her glass with crystal clear water, then, much to Mace's relief, topped his off along with the others. Mace pressed the chilled glass to his beaded-with-sweat forehead and hoped no one noticed.

"We were just discussing the onscreen chemistry between Reed and Ava,"—Kent flashed a mischievous smile—"and how the fans want to see more of them together."

Mace squeezed the Newfoundland inside his pocket.

"I can certainly see why," Annie said, reaching for an oyster. "Honestly, your chemistry is palpable in person—not just in front of the camera."

Who the bloody hell turned up the thermostat in here?

Pierre wrapped his arms around Reed and Ava and pulled them close. "You two are a match made in filming heaven!"

Mace caught sight of Stephanie's expression as she sat opposite him. Her my-heart-is-sinking look mirrored his feelings.

"I don't know, Ava..." Reed delivered an exaggerated headshake. "Maybe we should ride this franchise out as long as we can!"

The saliva evaporated from Mace's mouth. He hadn't sweated this much since his time in the Sahara. A fleeting image of Ava and Reed locking lips on set commandeered his mind. Mace tugged at his shirt collar, forced the image into hiding, then glowered at Reed. "Unless they kill your character off," he mumbled before downing the remaining whiskey his lowball glass offered. Six heads, mouths agape, whipped in his direction. *Oh crap, did I just say that out loud?*

A deafening silence rang out. Then Kent leaned back in his chair and crossed his arms over his athletic chest. "I like the way you think, Mace!" he chortled.

Roaring laughter broke out, relieving the rising tension. Ava planted a tender kiss on his cheek, her eyes projecting a promise of something wonderful to come.

Annie tossed her dirty blonde curls and then helped herself to a glass of Bordeaux. "In all seriousness,"—she raised her drink to bright red lips—"I worry Ava and Reed's intimate connection may be difficult for their partners to digest."

Mace felt certain his blood had reached its boiling point. His heart battered the inside of his chest. He unbuttoned his shirt collar as his eyes darted around the restaurant, trying to locate an AED unit, just in case. The crushing pain in his knee was back in full force.

Ava opened her mouth to speak, but Stephanie beat her to it. "It definitely took some getting used to," she whispered as she raked her fingers through Reed's glossy hair. "Ava and Reed do have a special connection, which is what makes them so believable on screen." She rendered a fleeting smile. "But Ava has done a beautiful job of maintaining healthy boundaries, and I've never felt threatened."

Ava inclined her head at Reed's girlfriend. "Thank you, Stephanie. I truly appreciate your saying that."

The sensation in Mace's knee started to come back.

Annie propped her arm over the velvety back of her chair and twisted toward Mace and Ava. "I'm certainly glad to hear that, but given Mace's past, even *seemingly insignificant* stressors can have detrimental effects."

Seemingly insignificant stressors like the one happening at this very moment. Mace swapped his empty glass of whiskey for his water, downed it in one crude gulp, but still felt parched. He could feel the beads of sweat crawling from his forehead to his cheeks. He reached for Ava's water just as a pulverizing pressure again overtook his knee.

Daggers danced in Ava's eyes as she zeroed in on Annie. "I'm well aware of the signs and symptoms of PTSD, as well as the triggers Mace has faced in the past." Ava rested her elbows on the linen tablecloth and tented her hands in front of her. "Rest assured, should I notice any signs of psycho-motor agitation, I'll see that it's addressed."

Annie folded her arms over her chest. "The only way to address it would be to resume regular sessions with his doctor, AKA me,"—Annie stuck her beak-like nose in the air—"where we could focus on cognitive behavioral therapy."

Mace pressed two fingers against his carotid artery.

With a measured pace, Ava laced her beautiful, manicured fingers; the graceful maneuver belied the icy glaze that permeated her sapphire eyes. Mace hadn't been this scared since Afghanistan. "That's rather disappointing to hear," she began, her tone cool and confident. "Given that current research indicates hypnotherapy in conjunction with CBT is *far* more beneficial in treating veterans with PTSD."

Annie drew in a sharp breath, her eyes spiking with disdain. "Well,"—she flashed a forced smile—"it would seem Mace is in good hands."

Mace put his arm around Ava's waist and pulled her as close as the velour chair would allow.

Ava planted her hand over his erratically beating heart. "Yes—*Mason*—most certainly is."

Chapter Twenty-Six

Kent ambled through the shiny, smudge-free elevator doors. He tapped the number thirty-two, then watched as the bronzed prancing horse shrank with each passing second. Only its head remained in his line of sight when an arm, coated in red, reached through the narrowing gap. The closing doors reversed course, and a woman stepped in. After raising a finger to the numbered options, she leaned against the opposite wall, clasped her hands in front of her, then locked her eyes onto him.

"It appears you and I may have an aligned agenda," Kent declared.

An iniquitous smile spread across Annie's lips. "So it would seem."

Kent held her gaze with an impassive expression as the elevator lifted in smooth transit. She stood about five feet seven inches, with loose curls of dirty blonde hair that grazed across her shoulders. Her sleek-fit red pantsuit—cut a tad longer than it should have been—clung to her average-size frame, revealing the pointed toes of coordinating ballet flats.

"Perhaps we should discuss over a nightcap." Her mossy-green eyes, marked with yellowish flecks, projected an appetite that dinner hadn't satisfied.

Kent continued to study her as he tried to decide whether he wanted to take her up on the offer. Her double-breasted top overlapped below the slightest of creases, displaying her freckled, sunbaked skin. Although a far cry from the glamorous women who typically sought his attention, she held a precarious appeal that intrigued him.

Kent glanced at the blue LED digits displayed above the door: twenty-one. "What's your poison?"

*****

Scotch rolled over on his back, his pupils struggling to absorb the traces of light that infiltrated the dark bedroom. He adjusted the band of his boxer briefs. They were feeling the slightest bit snug. Maybe he should lay off the carbs. His fingers dug through his coarse ginger beard to address an itch on his chin. Then, with a loud sigh, he laced his fingers behind his head.

"Redge?" he whispered. Silence.

Scotch squeezed his eyes shut. His mind had been racing since he left Julietta's estate this afternoon, and, despite the late hour, sleep continued to evade him. "Redge?" he abandoned his whisper.

"What?" the retired SEAL mumbled.

Scotch craned his neck toward the sound, his healthy eyes making out the faint outline of a large being resting on the neighboring bed. "You awake?"

"I am now," his gravelly voice confirmed.

"I can't sleep," Scotch said, propping himself on his elbows.

"That's obvious."

"You were right."

The mattress complained as Redge shifted his weight. "About what?"

"Julietta… I think she was just using me for my incredible body."

Redge ejected a loud sigh. "Dude, you're not twenty-something anymore. You gotta grow up."

"I can't help it. Women and reckless adventure are my two favorite things."

"I get it—but you can't expect to have a meaningful relationship at this point in your life when you're banging two minutes after being introduced."

Ugh… Redge was starting to sound like his mum. "Listen, mate—for the record—I didn't *bang* her. She just blew me, and I returned the favor."

"Oh, well, that changes *everything.*"

Chapter Twenty-Seven

With a piercing grating sound, Mace latched the gunmetal-gray locker door filled with his gear. He tightened the bright white cotton towel around his chiseled waist, then moseyed across the slick slate floor toward the exit. He held the door for whom he assumed was a father and his toddler son as they approached, wearing matching green swim shorts splattered with blue hammerhead sharks, then fell in line behind them.

The slate transitioned to one-inch glazed ceramic squares as he crossed into the resort's aquatic center. He passed the Olympic-size pool and the raised hot tub, which was larger than his entire condo back in London. A wall of windows separated the aquamarine water from a brick terrace featuring private cabanas. The adjacent wall, marked by a wide, arched-paneled entrance, bore a sign reading: *Spa, Steam Bath, and Centre de Fitness*. Mace trudged along in his rubber flip-flops and pulled open the door marked *Bain de Vapeur*.

Beige tiles of varying shapes, sizes, and shades covered every square inch of the capacious space. Mace's eyes scanned the room in search of other guests. It appeared he had the sedating space to himself. *Brilliant.* He maneuvered around the cozy, circular whirlpool and headed toward the wide alcove that lay beyond. A tiled bench stretched along the perimeter of the nook, with thin, oval rocks formed into pyramids displayed in the corners. He removed his towel, folded it neatly—his mum would be proud—then set it on the bench near an inside corner, and sat on it.

Mace closed his eyes and hung his head. Beads of sweat formed over his rock-solid frame, freeing his mind and body from the toxins within—filling him with a stillness for the first time since he'd arrived. Between the constant racket on set and the noise that occupied his brain, he cherished the sound of absolutely nothing.

Pacifying thoughts permeated his mind. His soul flourished with Ava's presence in his life; his entire concept of happiness reimagined. But this lifestyle… proved to be an adjustment to say the least. Her demanding schedule often teetered on the side of overwhelming. Let alone having to watch her pretend to be in love with other men. He had no experience in this industry, and the notion of separating Ava, the love of his life—from Ava, the actress—proved exceedingly difficult. Now this opportunity for her to return to Hollywood… it was his worst fear, aside from something happening to her, which he worried about more with each passing day. The ransacking of her room was bothersome enough, but with the addition of Redge's discovery on the trails behind her cabin yesterday, he couldn't shake the unsettling feeling in his chest. He opted not to tell Ava about the footprints. She seemed convinced her room incident was of little concern, and he feared that knowing a real threat existed might cause her to lose focus. He needed her to finish this bloody film so he could get her as far away from this place—and the past—as fast as possible. Then, they could move on with their lives—together.

With a gentle shake, he banished those thoughts from his mind. He was grateful that Redge offered to take point on set this morning. Keeping his eyes closed, he leaned his head back against the tile. He embraced the pervading placidity and soon found himself in a trance-like state.

The hushed creak of the door opening registered in the back of his mind, but he was too relaxed to investigate the newcomer. His thoughts wandered to Ava. He couldn't wait to hold her in his arms after she wrapped up tonight. He didn't care how late it was; he just needed her healing energy.

Through hooded eyes, he sensed a presence before him. His lids cracked open to discover sun-bronzed athletic thighs—a pale, flaccid penis surrounded by groomed chestnut brown hair—dangling between them.

Mace's eyes shot open, and he instinctively recoiled, slamming his head against the sandstone tile behind him.

He stifled an *ouch* as he raised a massaging hand to the back of his noggin.

Traces of a smirk appeared on Kent's face as he took a painfully long time to fold his towel before sitting his bare arse down on it. Mace's body temperature skyrocketed, and it wasn't due to the steam room's heat. His glacial stare served two purposes: one, to make Kent as uncomfortable as possible; two, to assess the physique of the man who once pleasured Ava. He had a smooth, broad chest with well-defined biceps, which had probably never lifted anything outside a gym. Manicured hands looked smooth and callus-free, a far cry from his rugged hands. It pained him to admit, but the guy was beautiful in a pampered, never-worked-a-day-in-his-life sort of way.

Satisfied that at least *two* of his body parts—one of them being his chest—were bigger than Kent's, Mace stood, snatched his towel, and fastened it around his sculpted waist before aiming toward the exit. One meter into his journey, Kent called him out.

"Is there a problem?" he asked, his tone spiked with pretentiousness.

Mace whipped his head around to face the pompous producer. "Yeah—I don't really care to see your naked arse."

Kent ran a well-cared-for hand through his damp hair, thrusting out his chin. "Well, Ava sure seemed to enjoy it."

It took Mace all of two-tenths of a second to respond. He cupped his large hands over the producer's knees and squeezed. Inches from Kent's frightened face, Mace felt his heart rate and breathing slow as he delivered his death glare. "Ava couldn't even remember your name after she and I were together."

Despite the hundred-plus degree temperature, Kent's face went ashen. "Get your hands off me!" he cried, his voice trembling.

"Gladly." Mace pivoted on his heel and stomped off as fast as his rubber flip-flops would allow.

Chapter Twenty-Eight

Scotch shoved a ripe strawberry in his mouth. The set seemed quieter than usual this morning as the crew prepared for the next scene, which was to be filmed outdoors. His eyes skimmed over the lustrous walnut bar where he played bartender. He'd thought maybe that critical role would lead to other opportunities, but nothing yet. No matter, he'd cherish his five minutes—literally—of fame forever.

He spied Redge near Reed and Ava as they read through the scene. Normally, Redge preferred to stay at the house while they were on set, but when they were getting ready during the wee hours of the morning, Mace decided it would be best if he tagged along. Something about his gut feeling. And if Scotch had mastered nothing else from his time with the Royal Marines, he'd learned the importance of always trusting your gut.

Scotch wandered down the gilded paisley hall that led back toward the hotel. He had no particular destination in mind; he just felt like exploring. He sidestepped a housekeeping cart as it rested unattended in the middle of the hall. A few meters ahead, a door swung open and a diaper-clad toddler, no doubt driven by the taste of freedom, bolted down the hall.

"Benny, no!" a voice called out as a woman emerged from the doorway just as Scotch approached. Her arms were full, holding an infant, and a look of terror spread over her youthful face as she watched the boy book it down the hall.

Scotch leapt into action. He caught up with the miniature fugitive in no time, swooping the boy into his strong arms. At first, the boy protested, then found delightful entertainment by tugging on Scotch's unruly red beard.

"Oh, thank you!" The woman beamed as Scotch delivered the toddler.

"My pleasure." Scotch nodded and watched as the mother, a baby on each hip, disappeared into the room, the heavy door latching with a loud click. A second later, the sound of the dead bolt engaging echoed through his ears.

Following an about-face, Scotch discovered Julietta emerge from a doorway marked *Exécutive* and advance toward him. She wore an expensive-looking fitted pencil dress with cap sleeves, the hem stretching just below her knees. The black fabric appeared custom-cut for her curves. Her long black hair was pulled back from her face, and she carried a leather-wrapped tablet in one hand.

The steady beat of his heart picked up its tempo.

"Ah, *Monsieur* Scotchfeld! *Bonjour.*" Her chocolate eyes sparkled as she strutted toward him.

The Scotsman braced himself against the ivory paneled wall and crossed his arms over his shredded chest. "*Bonjour?* That's all you have to say?" He made no attempt to hide his irritation.

Julietta slowed to a stop in front of him, the top of her head parallel to his chin. Scotch drank in the sight of her close up; her flawless olive face, red, juicy lips, and swollen chest peeking from her neckline tempered his aggravation.

She rested a manicured hand on his chest, between his engorged pecs. "*S'il vous plaît*, forgive me... I have a voracious *appétit.*"

Scotch fixed his hardened gaze on her. "Yeah, well, so do I. But I was waiting for *you.*"

"You were?" Julietta asked with a flutter of her thick, dark lashes.

"Yeah." Scotch bobbed his head. "But apparently your butler has quite the benefits package."

Julietta ran her hand over Scotch's bicep. Even furious with this beautiful woman, he still reveled in her touch. "You must understand, Geoffrey and I..."—her hand dropped to his belt buckle—"he knows how to take care of me."

Okay, the hand on my bicep was one thing. "Well, *I* was hoping to take care of you." With a brusque touch, Scotch pushed her hand away from his belt.

"*Non?* You do not like that?" Julietta asked with a seductive smile.

They stared at each other in silence as the housekeeping cart rolled by at sloth speed.

"Yeah, I like it," Scotch muttered. "But I'm still mad at you."

Julietta stepped closer, her buxom chest pressing against his. "Oh, *s'il vous plaît*, do not be mad." Her warm, chocolate eyes flickered with affection. Her hand cupped the center of his belt again, inches from his ever-at-the-ready armament. "Allow me to make it up to you," she purred, resting her chin against his chest and peering up at him.

Scotch examined her brown eyes—determined them to be sincere. "I don't know," he mumbled. He jailed his hands in the pockets of his cargo pants to keep them from ravaging her body right there in the hall.

"Join me for a massage tomorrow at one o'clock." With the feel of her warm breath upon his neck, he shoved his hands farther into his pockets.

"I don't want a bloody massage."

"*Non, non.*" Julietta emitted a coy smile. "I send my masseur away, and *you* massage every inch of my body."

He hated that he no longer *wanted* to push her hand from his belt. Scotch arched a skeptical eyebrow. "They're just gonna let us have the room to ourselves? I find that hard to believe."

Julietta lifted a shoulder against her cheek. "Are you forgetting that I own the spa, too?"

Scotch smoothed the tip of his beard as he studied the femme fatale before him; her beauty enhanced by the fine lines that danced across her forehead, and the barely discernible trident of creases that stretched from the corner of her gleaming eyes. Every microbe in his gut told him to walk away from this woman. "I don't know… I'll think about it."

She laced her fingers behind his neck and ushered his head closer, then pressed her plump lips to his cheek. "I must go now." She swiveled back around. "But I cannot wait to see you tomorrow!" she said as she headed down the hall in the opposite direction, her firm derriere waving goodbye.

"I said I'd *think* about it!" Scotch called out. *Oh, who am I kidding? I'll be there.*

Chapter Twenty-Nine

Ava stared out into the horizon; her nerves comforted by the serenity of the cloudless, baby-blue sky intermittently lanced by massive Eastern White Pines standing over a hundred feet tall. She focused on the tiny figures across the thick canopy of hardwoods that cloaked the earth below, separating the two plateaus. Cameras one through three were strategically placed to capture their respective viewing angle. She hoped operator one would get it right this time.

"All right, Ms. Ellis—just like last time," a modulated voice instructed.

Ava cast a glance at Hartley, the zip line operator, as her thin fingers yanked on the red nylon of the harness, twisting it into position. Ava slid the zipper of her periwinkle fleece shirt up her neck, then stepped into the gear. She fastened each carabiner at the waist and chest, just as she had before, under Hartley's supervising eyes.

The young woman then clipped the nylon cable to the line's top pulley. "Have fun!" she called out as she bounded down from the platform.

Ava knew the cameras would be zoomed in on her at this moment. She forced a beautiful, excited smile for their benefit, but couldn't shake the strange apprehension in her stomach. She'd done this before—why was she so nervous? *Hartley was the best in the business, and she'd checked all of the gear earlier this afternoon. There was absolutely nothing to worry about. Save for the thought of Mace watching as she flew into Reed's welcoming arms.* She hated that he struggled on set more than he admitted. His mouth said he didn't, but his eyes disclosed the truth. *Just get through this scene, and with any luck, Pierre will let us wrap early.* The thought of Mace's powerful body against hers in bed this evening pervaded her mind; the radiant smile across her lips no longer forced.

She shuffled to the edge of the platform. Gripping the heavy-gauge nylon that clipped from her belt to the pulley above, she leaned back, testing her weight. With the subtle descent of her eyelids, she drew in a deep, calming breath, then launched her body off the side of the cliff.

At once, the line caught and dipped with her weight, sending her zipping across the dense, spring foliage below. The gradual angle of decline provided the perfect steady speed for the cameras and granted her a spectacular panoramic vista. She spotted Reed, a bright smile plastered on his face as he waited for her. *Was it genuine, or was he simply playing his part perfectly?* At times, she wondered whether his feelings for her emulated those of his character. Her gaze traveled beyond him and discovered Mace, Redge, and Scotch. *How wonderful to have my trio back!*

She glided along the four-hundred-foot span seamlessly. She held her legs, crossed at the ankles, out in front of her, parallel to the ground, because she knew it made for a great shot. Reaching the midpoint, she felt the slightest slump. Her eyes descended to the nylon strap that attached to the carabiner on her harness. The bottom edge of the textile's threads was no longer woven together. Instead, the bright red thread stretched straight, thinning with each passing second.

Fear clawed through every organ in her body. Instinct took over, and her gloved hands gripped higher on the nylon cable, bracing for the sudden jerk of her weight. Her trio grew larger, their details becoming clearer as she approached. A few more seconds and she'd reach land. *Please hold on!* she willed the thread. She kept her eyes trained on Mace—her goal—as he watched her approach, his lips displaying his signature crooked grin. She treasured that grin.

One hundred feet from her prize, the thread gave, and her legs fell out from under her. A scream escaped her lips, and she watched as Mace swapped his smile for an expression of horror. She clutched the nylon with all her might, somewhat confident that her strength could support her weight for the remaining distance. But the smooth fabric offered no grip, and she felt her hands descend the length of the cable, inch by inch.

Please God, just twenty more feet! Either her estimation was off, or her prayer was heard a second too late, but her hands ran out of cable before reaching solid ground. She watched as Mace's jaw went slack; his outstretched hands cupped the side of his head. Then her entire world went dark as her pointed toes pierced the mantle of green.

Chapter Thirty

Mace's heart hammered inside his chest as he watched Ava's beautiful form free-fall from coffin height. Gasps of shock befell the crew. In an instant, Mace reached the edge of the cliff and peered into the green abyss that swallowed Ava. He spotted her insertion point, marked by the disruption of branches.

"Ava!" his resonant voice called out. "Ava!"

"Mace!" The faint sound of her trembling voice was music to his ears, and his heart leapt with hope.

After an appreciative glance at the just judge in the sky, Mace yelled, "Ava, hold on—I'm coming!"

He searched his mind for a plan. The plateau stood at twenty meters. He could free climb that if he had to, but had no way of knowing what condition Ava might be in. He pivoted back around to discover Redge and Scotch beside him, awaiting their orders. Mace's eyes scoured the environment for anything useful as the entire crew—Reed included—stood paralyzed in place. He spied a pile of prop cable from Reed's pretend encounter with the zipline heaped off to the side of the camera equipment. A glance at Redge and Scotch indicated they needed no further instruction, and the trio rushed to sift through the pile. With impressive speed, Redge wove one end between his powerful legs and over his shoulders, then anchored it to his waist using a bowline knot. Scotch positioned himself a few feet in front of the SEAL titan, securing the cable over his broad shoulder, then crouching into position, as Mace fashioned a body rappel post haste. He wrapped the double cable around his leg, pulled it over his torso and around his back, his strong hand gripping the end of the line. Following a nod to his mates, he dropped backwards off the side of the cliff.

A few meters down, he was swallowed by the dense foliage of Mother Nature. He called out to Ava as he rappelled at a measured pace, his keen eyes alert for signs of her path. No response. "Ava!" his husky voice echoed through the compact forest. A multitude of branches extended like a labyrinth around him, making his descent difficult. His ears detected the slightest whimper, and he paused against the peeling white bark of a massive birch tree to investigate.

"Ava!" he called again, stretching his neck from side to side.

"Please hurry!" Her quivering, fatigued voice traveled up to his ears. She sounded close, but he couldn't spy any signs of her path. He continued his descent, his ears and eyes functioning at their peak.

After another few meters, he detected the telltale sign of her route: a swath of depressed leaves and several snapped branches, their edges moist and jagged. Then he spotted it—a splash of gold amongst a canvas of green.

He relaxed the line, letting his body drop another meter, before stopping with a jerk as his heart exploded with grateful relief. Just outside of his reach, his eyes captured his jungle queen—veiled by the six-inch five-lobed leaves of the massive maple tree she dangled from. Her forearms encased a large branch while the tips of her boots rested against a much smaller one, unnaturally bent with the weight of her frame—appearing as if it might give at any moment. Wild, wind-blown hair adorned with leaves framed her head. A small branch skewered her fleece top, and her lustrous leggings exposed bits of scraped flesh through torn fabric. Her gorgeous face, pale and marked with fear, rendered the tiniest trace of a smile as her eyes registered Mace in his makeshift harness.

"Mason, please hurry!" Her whisper held an urgent distress.

Mace defied his intrinsic instinct to simply kick off against the side of the rocky surface and swing her to safety, but he had to be smart about how he did this. After all, he only had one chance.

"Ava,"—he modulated his voice—"I can't let go of the harness, so I've only got one free arm." He fixed his eyes on her, willing her to grasp his conviction. "When I get into position, you're going to have to let go the second I tell you. Do you understand?"

The actress offered the slightest nod, the leaves encasing her face following suit.

Mace flattened the soles of his boots against Mother Nature's wall, getting into position. He craned his neck to peek at Ava once more. "I just need you to trust me, okay?"

"I do," she whispered, her tremulous bottom lip betraying her words.

Mace bent his knees, then rendered an explosive kick against the limestone surface. He misgauged his trajectory and peaked a half-meter shy and to the right of where he needed to be. The sound of a branch splitting behind him propelled him into action once again as Ava's makeshift ledge vanished in the vegetation below—its path marked by a wave of echoing *pops*. He took a deep breath as he delivered a second violent kick against the rock wall.

This time, his trajectory proved perfect. All that was left was his timing. A few seconds shy of his target, he yelled, "Now!"

Mace held his breath as Ava closed her eyes and released her grip. A second later, she adhered to his chest—his left arm wrapped tightly around her—and the two of them sailed back toward the limestone surface. His boots found purchase on another generous maple branch, absorbing most of their weight.

Burying her head in the crook of his arm, Ava cleaved to his chest. Feeling her body tremble, he pulled her tighter. He kissed her forehead, which felt clammy; her natural pink hue had vanished. "I've got you," he whispered.

She raised her head, her damp sapphire eyes—shimmering with tears—gazed into his. "That tops any trust fall exercise I've ever done," she cried.

Mace flashed a grin as he stroked her tear-streaked cheek. "Are you hurt?"

"Well, I think I had a heart attack on the way down… and"—she winced—"my ankle is killing me."

"It's a miracle you're even alive." Mace squeezed her tighter, averting his gaze as his eyes welled with tears.

Ava planted a tender kiss on his cheek, luring his stare back to her. "Only because of you," she whispered. With a beautiful, fleeting smile, she added, "I feel like you're my guardian angel."

"You're the angel." Mace pressed his lips to hers, treasuring their lush feel. A second kiss almost caused him to lose his balance.

Ava's eyes widened with the close call. "Can we please get outta here?"

As if on cue, a booming Scottish accent penetrated their ears. "Bloody hell, Mace! What's going on down there?!"

Ava locked her arms around Mace's neck, her cheek grazing against his steely chest, and entwined her legs with his. Mace issued three distinct tugs on the cable, signaling to the Scotsman. A moment later, the line went taut, and the two of them ascended as one.

Chapter Thirty-One

Whispers of apprehensive excitement grew louder with each intermittent pull of the rope. Civil twilight's golden hue washed over Mace and Ava as they broke through the canopy of foliage. Ava kept her head buried against his chest, suggesting she wasn't ready for the impending flurry of activity that awaited them. Mace kept his eyes fastened on the ledge as they elevated in one-meter increments. The crew had gathered around the edge, their peers glued to Mace and Ava. Some wore shocked expressions, most looked stunned, and others pointed with their phones. Mace was glad to see that Reed had the sense to help Scotch with the cable.

"Is her face messed up?!" Pierre called down to them, his tone wracked with worry.

Mace felt an anger brewing within him. The civilian response to distressing events was a hell of a lot different than in the military—and he wasn't sure he liked it.

Mace continued to shuffle his boots against the vertical limestone wall as they approached the edge of the plateau, careful not to let their bodies scrape against it. Reed greeted them first; his body weight distributed across the ground, as he extended his hand to help Ava disembark. Scotch and Redge worked in tandem, biceps bulging with each heave, until Mace climbed over the edge. Collapsing onto his back, he drew in a gulp of fresh air to replenish his lungs. He just needed a moment.

Pierre made a beeline for Ava as the crew closed in around her. "Put your phones away, or you're fired!" the director ordered. "All of you!" His tone boiled with anger. "And find me Hartley! She'll never work a day in her life again!"

Redge and Scotch proffered a helping hand to Mace. They lifted him to his feet, then pulled him into a brotherly hug.

"Mate, I thought you two were cooked!" Scotch's arms sliced the air; his glimmering jade eyes loaded with relief.

Mace unwound himself from the cable and brushed off the fragments of foliage that hitched a ride on his clothing. "We would've been—if it wasn't for you two."

"Remind me…" Redge gave him a big pat on the back. "How many times has the U.S. Navy bailed out the Royal Marines?" he asked with an impish grin.

Mace's chest heaved with warmth. With a gentle shake of his head, he added, "Thanks, mates. I owe you."

Scotch waved a dismissive hand. "Buy me a beer, and we'll call it even."

Mace pushed his way through the human shield surrounding Ava and discovered her ensnared in Reed's arms. "I was so worried about you," he whispered. "We need to get you checked out to make sure you're okay."

Pierre's head moved up and down and side to side as it scouted her body, pausing long enough to slide his black glasses higher on the bridge of his nose. "It's a miracle you are not more cut up!"

Ava tucked her hair behind her ears, revealing blotchy cheeks. "I'm fine." She shifted her weight to one leg while the other bent at the knee, the tip of her hiking boot grazing the stony surface. Specks of blood stained the shins of her leggings.

Mace squeezed in closer. His movement must have caught Pierre's attention, because the director turned to him, extended his arms wide, and said, "Thank you for saving my star!" His lips brushed against both of Mace's cheeks with a pronounced *muah*, as the crew broke out in applause.

Mace swallowed his annoyance; he didn't want their praise. He reached for Ava as she limped toward him, her body leaning against his steady form. Although far from her typical pinkish tint, her coloration had improved. He cupped her jaw in his hand. "We need to get you to a doctor."

"I'm okay," she whispered. "I just need to sit down for a moment." She slid the leaf-covered harness over her hip and let it drop to the rocky soil below.

Mace swiped the gear and launched it to Redge before turning back toward Ava. "I'm taking you to the medical center," he said, his forehead puckering. "There's no point in arguing." The hint of a smile appeared as the actress nibbled her plump bottom lip.

"*Non, non*, I called Dr. Levasque," Pierre waved his hands. "He's on his way up here." The director wore a proud smile—as if his phone call had saved the day.

Mace didn't like the thought of Ava being examined in front of the entire crew. He didn't trust them not to sneak some pictures and leak them online. He could see the social media headlines now. Mace draped an arm around Ava's waist. "No—she needs to rest," he ordered. "Send Dr. Levasque to her cabin." Then, he scooped Ava up in his strong arms and weaved his way through the gawking crew members toward his mates.

"But I need to know if she can continue!" Pierre called out.

Mace's boots pivoted over the rocky soil, sending fine granules of sediment spraying. He locked his steely gaze onto the director. "We're done here," he said, before spinning back around. He marched toward their luxury SUV, Ava stroking his chest as he carried her in his arms, Redge and Scotch on his flank.

Chapter Thirty-Two

The remaining traces of daylight faded as the dark sky swallowed them, and the sleek black Range Rover bounced along the deteriorating pavement, jarring its passengers. Mace caressed Ava's hand as he rested beside her on the leather bench seat. The four of them sat in silence, synergistically sensing each other's need to process the events of the afternoon. Now that they were removed from peril and the chaos that ensued, Mace reflected on the incident. He was forced to confront a harsh truth: someone was trying to seriously hurt Ava—or worse.

"I can walk," Ava said when Redge whipped into the cabin's gravel driveway and threw the vehicle in park.

Mace's brows furrowed. "You don't have to prove how tough you are."

She glanced at him with damp eyes. "I just—"

"You'll only make it worse," Redge said, his stare visible in the rearview mirror.

"Yeah, Ava." Scotch propped his elbow on the console between him and Redge. "So, you're gonna have to let Mace help you." The Scotsman craned his neck to peek at the two of them. "Unless, of course, you want me to carry you," he added with a waggle of his bushy red brows.

Mace rolled his eyes. He shifted his gaze back to Ava. Smoothing a stray lock of hair from her cheek, he leaned close and whispered, "I thought you liked being in my arms."

A beautiful smile emerged. "All right, have it your way."

The trio of titans jumped from the SUV with impressive synchronicity. A moment later, Mace gathered Ava into his strong arms before nudging the door closed with his knee. Then, following Redge's all clear, he marched inside the beautiful cabin.

After setting her on the king-size bed centered in the master suite, he crouched down before her. Despite his delicate touch, she flinched when he removed her hiking boots. The cuff of her boot, tied tightly around her joint, had served her well, but her ankle instantly swelled with its removal.

"That looks like quite the sprain, mate," Scotch said from the doorway as Mace's finger traced the swollen joint, causing Ava to draw in a sharp breath.

"What do you need?" Redge asked.

"See if you can't find a wrap and some sort of ice pack, will ya?" Mace asked. With a nod, his fellow titans scurried off toward the stairs.

"Let's get you out of these clothes." Mace reached for the zipper on her fleece jacket and pulled it down over her chest. "This is normally the part where you say something witty." He rendered a quick grin. "Like, *Oh, Mason, this is hardly the time*," he jested in a melodramatic attempt at mimicking her silvery voice.

Her misty eyes filled with a sadness that pulled on his heartstrings. She pulled her arms from the fleece and examined the through-and-through hole that altered its design. "Sorry—guess I'm not feeling very witty," she muttered.

Mace kissed her hand. "Now, Ms. Ellis, lean back so I can remove your pants." He intended to be a gentleman, but curbing the naughty notions that entered his mind proved futile. Finally, a smile arrived, coupled with a gentle shake of her head. He pulled her glossy leggings over the curve of her hips, exposing a silky black thong panty that made him forget what he was doing.

But the sound of heavy footsteps bolting up the steps reminded him. "Give us a sec!" Mace shouted before Redge and Scotch entered the suite.

"Really, mate? This is *hardly* the time!" the Scotsman's booming voice echoed.

Ava burst into a hysterical fit of laughter, prompting Mace to follow suit. With an affectionate gaze, he unsheathed the remainder of her legs, noting the myriad scrapes and cuts that now adorned her smooth, toned skin.

She scooted up to the head of the bed, and Mace propped two feather pillows behind her back, then draped the sheet over her bare legs.

He kissed her forehead. "I'll be right back," he said, then strode over to the doorway to greet Redge and Scotch.

"This is all I found, mate." Scotch handed him a small first aid kit.

"Here," Redge said, tossing him a bag of frozen peas.

"Thanks," Mace said, stroking his jaw. "Listen…"

Redge fixed his sable eyes on him. "Whatever you need, boss."

"This afternoon… changes things." Mace raked his hand through his spiky hair. "No more speculation. We now know the threat is very real, and whoever is responsible is going to up their game until they succeed or *we* catch them."

"Any idea who might want to hurt Ava?" Redge asked.

"Oh, I have a few ideas." Mace bobbed his head.

Scotch grabbed a fistful of his shaggy red beard. "Yeah, well, so do I."

"Yeah—I get it—but we'll have to brainstorm later." Mace flashed a steely gaze at his friend. "I'd like you two to comb over every inch of Ava's harness. Look for any signs of tampering. First thing tomorrow, see if you can track down Hartley. We need to find out what the hell happened up there."

Redge and Scotch nodded in unison.

"In the meantime, call Brody. Ask him to have his guy run background checks on Homepoint's cast and crew. I want him to comb through their social media accounts, everything."

"Got it, chief," Scotch said.

"I also want to make sure Ava's with at least one of us at every moment." More nods from his mates. "I hate that I don't even have my piece."

Scotch frowned. "Me, too."

A wide smile escaped Redge's big lips. "I've got mine."

Mace and Scotch scoffed. "How'd you arrange that?" Mace asked.

"I have my ways." A roguish glint tinted Redge's sable eyes.

"Well, keep it bloody handy," Mace directed, before walking back into the bedroom.

Chapter Thirty-Three

Mace finished securing the wrap around Ava's ankle, then placed the one-pound bag of frozen peas on top of it.

"I prefer green beans," Ava said with a hint of a smile.

Mace sat on the edge of the bed beside her. He combed her disheveled hair with his fingers and tugged at the neckline of her white tank top to minimize the amount of cleavage peeking out. He didn't need Dr. Levasque getting distracted. "You doin' okay?" his husky voice whispered.

Ava offered a non-committal one-shoulder shrug. Her captivating eyes welled with tears.

With a squeeze of her hand, Mace leaned closer, his gaze fastened to hers. "I won't let anything happen to you."

The welling tears overflowed down her cheeks. "If you weren't there…" her voice choked with emotion.

Mace enveloped her in his arms, swallowing his own anguish. After the incident, he'd packaged that up for delivery at some other time.

A bright light oscillated through the window; the telltale sign of a vehicle pulling in. *It's about time.* The sound of Redge's heavy boots trekking toward the front door reached his ears. Then the door hinge creaked, followed by the sound of three new voices. *Three?*

Several pairs of footsteps pounded over the staircase. Mace craned his neck to see Redge in the doorway, everyone else concealed by his massive form.

"The doc's here," the SEAL announced as he sidestepped to allow a path for the others. The others being Scotch, Pierre, and Reed.

Mace stood and marched over to the man with olive-colored skin and lustrous black hair, combed into a thick pompadour. He carried a bulky bag in one hand, proffered the other as Mace approached. "I'm Dr. Levasque."

"I'm Mace," he said as he gave it a hearty shake. "Appreciate your coming by."

"My pleasure." He wasted no time hurrying to Ava's side. He positioned himself on the edge of the bed, near the outline of her hip. "Ms. Ellis, my dear. I'm sorry to see you under these circumstances."

Ava cast a warm, momentary smile. "Likewise," she murmured.

"We'll wait outside, mate," Scotch announced with a jerk of his head directed at the group.

Mace offered a nod. *Good. Why the hell are Reed and Pierre here anyway?*

Either the doctor sensed Mace's inner thoughts, or his frustration betrayed his face. "I am sorry about the additional guests." The doctor spoke with a soft authority that radiated integrity.

"It's okay," Mace fibbed. He watched as the doctor unzipped his bag and removed a small otoscope.

"As I jumped in my truck to head over, I noticed a flat tire." His voice remained monotone as he shone the instrument into Ava's eyes. "So, I called Pierre for a ride."

Mace massaged the back of his neck as he stood off to the side of the bed. "Seems a bit odd," he mumbled.

"Yes, I thought so, too." The doctor glanced at Mace as he swapped his otoscope for his stethoscope. "They're brand-new tires." He shrugged. "Oh well, I probably just picked up a nail somewhere along the way."

Mace couldn't escape the odd feeling brewing in his gut. He packaged that away, too, for the time being. He'd have to deal with the amassing collection at some point, but not now. He focused on Dr. Levasque as he instructed Ava to take a few deep breaths, repositioning the stethoscope across her chest and back as she complied.

A wide, reassuring smile debuted across the doctor's lips. "Well, my dear, your lungs and heart sound great, and I see no evidence of a head injury—which is nothing short of a miracle." The doctor cocked his head toward Mace. "Is this the gentleman who saved you?"

With an affectionate gleam, Ava peered up at him. "In more ways than one, yes."

Mace's lips burst into a wide grin before he could rein them in.

"Well, you two make a beautiful couple." The doctor said as he placed the stethoscope back into his large, black bag, which rested on the floor.

I'm beginning to like this guy. He appreciated how gentle he was with Ava.

"May I pull the sheet back and examine your legs?"

Ava offered a nod, resting her manicured hands in her lap as he rolled the sheet back, exposing her legs up to her thighs. His eyes inspected the numerous scratches and scrapes. "These abrasions are minor… I'll leave you with an ointment that will facilitate healing and minimize the likelihood of scarring."

"Thank you," Ava said.

He studied her ankle. "This is what concerns me the most, however." With a graceful hand, he unwrapped Mace's handiwork, revealing her purple, distended joint. "Whoever wrapped this did a nice job."

Okay, I'm really liking this guy.

"I'll be as gentle as possible, my dear," Dr. Levasque said before gliding his finger over her injury. He stopped when Ava winced. "The good news is that it's not broken." He smiled at the two of them. "Definitely a sprain, most likely mild." He wound the stretchy compress around her ankle once again and topped it off with the thawing bag of peas.

"You can tell it's not broken just by looking at it?" Mace tried to keep the skepticism out of his tone.

"When you've seen as many skiing injuries as I have, yes." He curled his hand around Ava's as he rose from the bed. "My dear—someone was looking out for you."

Ava swiped a tissue from the nightstand and dabbed it over her cheeks.

"I'd like you to stay off of it for at least twenty-four hours, then see how you're feeling." He turned toward Mace. "Feel free to give her over-the-counter pain relievers should she require them. And keep it wrapped and iced, just like you've been."

Mace nodded.

"I want to see you again before the end of the week." Dr. Levasque reached for his bag. "I want to make sure there are no signs of infection; otherwise, I'll have to prescribe an antibiotic."

Ava opened her mouth to speak, but Mace beat her to it. "She's deathly allergic to penicillin."

"I'm glad you said something." His dark eyes grew wide. "That's primarily what I keep in stock at the medical center. I'll make sure I have some alternatives available."

Mace gave his hand an appreciative shake. "Thanks so much, doctor."

"Please—do not hesitate to call me if she needs anything." Dr. Levasque reached into the front pocket of his bag and removed a card. "This has my personal cell number on it."

Mace escorted him to the door. He swung it open to discover his mates and their guests waiting in the loft. Perched on the russet brown leather sofa were the forms of Reed and Pierre—Scotch squeezed in between them—their shoulders mashed together. Redge raised himself from the wooden rocker, the chair releasing a happy groan as the giant stood, when Mace appeared in the doorway.

"How is she?" Reed asked as the three couch cuddlers stood in harmony.

"Considering she fell over ten meters into a ravine of thick woods—she's fantastic." Expressions of relief fell upon the group. The doctor turned toward Pierre. "I'm putting her on bedrest tomorrow. Then—provided *she's* feeling up to it—she can be back on set the next day. But only if you can figure out a way to film her scenes without her having to put too much pressure on it."

Pierre nodded enthusiastically. "*Oui, oui*, I can do that," he said with a rushed, relieved tone.

The doctor stepped closer to the director and pointed an authoritative finger at his chest. "*She* decides if she's feeling up to it—not *you*."

"Of course," Pierre stated, an injured expression on his face. "May we see her?"

Dr. Levasque bowed his head and gestured to Mace. With a reluctant nod, Mace stepped aside to grant them access.

"I'll wait downstairs," the doctor called out as the others poured into the master suite.

Pierre hurried over to the edge of the bed and clutched Ava's hand. He removed his glasses and placed them on the nightstand. He pinched the bridge of his nose, squeezing his eyes closed. "You gave me quite the scare," he whispered, hanging his head.

"Imagine how I felt." Ava ran her tongue over her lips, then followed up with a nibble.

Pierre exhaled with a loud huff. "This boyfriend of yours is quite the hero," he inclined his head toward Mace.

Ava emitted a gorgeous smile. "You have no idea."

"Perhaps we should write him into the script, eh?"

"No, thanks, mate." Mace shook his head, crossing his arms over his chest.

Ava let out a light laugh. "He functions better *behind* the camera." She offered a playful wink at Mace.

His heart pounded with love for this woman. He was grateful to see her mood improving.

While Pierre chatted with Ava, Reed closed the gap between him and Mace. "I can't thank you enough for saving Ava," he said with a hushed, bassy tone.

Lowering his chin, Mace studied the actor's sincere, silvery eyes as he stood before him. "Well, I sure as hell wasn't going to stand by and do nothing." He struggled to keep his frustration out of his tone.

"I- I don't know how you do it." Reed stammered, his head shaking back and forth. "I mean, you sprang into action *as it happened*." He blew out his cheeks. "I froze like a statue." He ran a hand through his thick, perfect black hair. "I completely panicked."

Consoling some self-pitying, overpaid actor wasn't exactly on Mace's vision board for the year. "Try not to beat yourself up too much," he said through tight lips. Catching a glimpse of Reed's welling tears, he softened his tone. "Most people panic in stressful situations."

"Yeah, but *you* didn't." Reed cupped the nape of his neck. "You were there for Ava when it *really* mattered, and you saved her *life*."

"Just comes down to training, mate." Mace relaxed his shoulders.

"I *pretend* to have your courage on screen." Reed hugged himself. "Really, I'm just a *sham*."

Mace searched his mind for something to say; found nothing. Every one of his mates would've done the exact same thing he did, sans hesitation. He'd built his life amidst the bravest men in the world and had little patience for cowards. He patted the actor on the back. "You just do you, mate."

Before he knew what was happening, Reed flung his arms around him. "Thank you for saving my favorite counterpart!" he sobbed.

Mace caught sight of Redge and Scotch as they smothered their grins. He tapped the bawling actor on the back again. "Okay." He tried to put some distance between himself and Reed—the feel of the man's chest pressing against his made him uncomfortable—but Reed clung tighter. "Okay!" Mace said again.

Reed finally withdrew his arms from Mace and wiped them across his eyes. "Whew!" He patted his sternum. "Sorry, just needed to get that off my chest."

Mace squelched the urge to deliver his biggest eyeroll to date. He stepped outside of Reed's reach and relocated to safer ground—alongside Redge and Scotch.

Ava must've observed the awkward encounter, because she sat in bed with an amused expression plastered to her face as she peered at Mace.

"Focus on healing tomorrow," the director was saying. "But please let me know first thing the next day if you can continue." He smoothed his fingers over his remaining tufts of silver hair. "It would break my heart to have to replace you." His bottom lip jutted out.

"I'm sure I'll be in a position to continue, Pierre." Ava offered a reassuring smile.

"Besides,"—Reed crouched beside the bed—"she's irreplaceable."

"Wouldn't you have to refilm the whole thing?" Scotch asked the question that popped into Mace's head.

"*Non, non.*" Pierre slid his glasses back on. "We simply use another actress for the movements, then utilize AI to generate Ava's face onto hers." The director shrugged. "It's not ideal, but we could make it work if absolutely necessary."

"Of course,"—Reed's eyes darted to Ava—"we'd be hard pressed to find an actress with your, ah, measurements."

Mace's nostrils flared, and he opened his mouth to speak, but Redge beat him to it. "I think it's time we let Ava get some rest," the SEAL interjected as he jammed his thumbs inside his belt loops.

*****

Scotch had to pee. He slipped out of the master suite as Reed and Pierre were wrapping up and dashed down the stairs. He discovered Dr. Levasque sitting on a stool at the kitchen island, scrolling through his phone. The guy was so quiet, he'd almost forgotten he was here.

Scotch delivered a nod as he marched on by.

"You are the Scotsman who visited my sister the other day, correct?" The doctor's frigid tone called out to him.

Scotch stopped in his tracks beside the fridge. He pivoted to find himself the victim of the doctor's scrutinizing glare. "That's right," Scotch confirmed as he propped himself against the hickory cabinet directly opposite the doctor.

Dr. Levasque bobbed his head. His eyes dropped to his phone screen. "How much do you know about my sister?"

"Enough to know that I'd like to *get to know her better.*" Scotch folded his arms over his chest.

The head bobbing continued, with the addition of his tongue poking around the inside of his mouth. "Is that what you were doing by the poolside?" Golden-brown eyes darkened, but not from the ambient lighting. "Getting to *know* her?"

Scotch wasn't in the mood for games. "So, what, mate? I'm not good enough for her,"—Scotch thrust his finger into his chest—"but her butler is?" He tossed his arms out wide.

The doctor's head jerked back, his eyes bulging. "Butler?!"

"Yeah, Geoffrey." Scotch released a loud scoff. *Guess he didn't know his sister was screwing the help.*

The doctor glared at him. "*Tu es un idiot!*"

Scotch scrunched up his face. *What the hell did that mean?*

"Geoffrey is not her butler!" Dr. Levasque shoved his phone into his pocket. "He is her husband!"

Chapter Thirty-Four

The moon's spotlight hovered over Mace as he held his sleeping beauty in his arms. Her body skimmed against him as he lay naked on his side, his engorged bicep serving as her pillow, leaving a trail of golden hair to tickle his stubbled chin. He felt the soft touch of her petite foot across his shin. With gentle strokes, he brushed his hand over her smooth, toned stomach, the undulating motion comforting him. Normally, the feel of her barely shrouded derriere pressing against his hip would be the catalyst for his sleepless night. But tonight, another package was to blame—the amassing bundles he'd wrapped tight and buried within him.

His mind couldn't erase the sight of her falling from the zipline. The horrified sensation that traveled up his spine... the feel of his heart shutting down. Despite the cumulative trauma of the battlefield and the first-hand witnessing of precious lives lost, he'd never been so petrified as the moment he watched helplessly as her hand slipped from that tether. His body trembled, and tears, unstoppable, fled from his eyes.

Filled with a foreboding regret, he reached an important decision. There was something he needed to address back in London. Something that had been weighing heavily on his mind before travelling back here to see Ava. And he finally had the courage to do it. He peeked at his titanium diver: zero six hundred in the U.K. He toyed with the idea of sneaking out of bed to call her. He knew she'd be awake.

With measured movements, he started to slide his arm out from under Ava. A few inches in, a moan escaped her lips, and she rotated in his arms; her tank-covered breasts threshing against him. She peered up at him through half-shuttered eyes. Her fingers danced across the definitions of his chest, resulting in the instant swelling of his mast. Darkness failed to conceal the hunger in her gaze as she pulled him to her mouth, the tip of her tongue tasting his thin lips. Lifting her tank over her buxom chest—her nipples hardening with the unveiling—his rugged hands caressed her luscious peaks of flesh.

Soft, euphonious moans filled his ears as he transferred his mouth to her breasts, his tongue tracing their beautiful, bountiful form. She slid her panties from her hips, granting his desire free will. With the tip of her breast gingerly positioned between his lips, he—careful to avoid her injured ankle—rolled on top of her, his rock-solid forearms supporting his weight with ease. A moment later, his engorged mast had found its home, easing into her beckoning body. She tilted her head back, pleasure-filled sighs echoing throughout the suite with every loving penetration.

Mace latched his gaze onto her sapphire eyes, sparkling under the moon's limelight, as her healing arms draped around him. His beloved beneath him, his soul became weightless, unencumbered by the burdens that boggled his mind. His passion mounted inside his shaft, crescendoing with an untempered fervor of rhythmic thrusts, until his love—serendipitously timed—flowed into her.

His lips again found hers as she snuggled up to his chest. "I love you," she whispered, in between tender kisses.

He caressed her smooth jawline. "I love you, sweet angel." Then he wrapped her in his arms and pulled her tighter against him. He buried his head in her hair. "I thought I'd lost you." He squeezed his eyes shut, attempting to hold back his tears.

Ava pressed her lips to his cheeks, kissing the teary streaks, before whispering, "The thought of losing you is what gave me the strength to hold on."

This woman gave his life a new horizon. The phone call he needed to make could wait.

Chapter Thirty-Five

Long, sparse blades of grass disappeared beneath the hood of the Range Rover as the aggressive vehicle traversed the narrow two-track's steep, rising grade. Redge gripped the leather-wrapped steering wheel and navigated the difficult terrain with ease. With a faint, low humming sound, the passenger seat drifted back, and Scotch stretched his maniacally bouncing legs as far as the dashboard would allow, emitting a loud sigh. He shoved his hand into the side pocket of his black cargo pants and retrieved a protein-packed granola bar—his third of the morning. He tore open the silvery plastic and then shoved half of it in his mouth.

Redge swallowed his annoyance. "What's wrong?"

"Nothing, mate," Scotch responded, sending half-chewed traces of oats down his beefy chest.

Redge's eyes drew to a slant with his sideways glance. "Didn't your mom ever teach you to chew with your mouth closed?"

"Aye." He nodded, sending more crumbs tumbling before shoving the remaining half between his lips.

Redge eased off the accelerator for a sharp curve, then let his heavy boot fall back upon it as the grade increased. *They had to be near the summit.*

Scotch discharged a second, louder sigh as he turned his head to look out the window.

Redge eyeballed the perpetual adolescent beside him. "What's *wrong?*" he asked again.

"I'm fine, mate." Scotch shot him the eyes.

Redge shook his head, slowed for a brief dip in the track, then said, "Whatever." Another steep climb before the dreary morning sky opened into view, and their path leveled out. They had reached the plateau's peak. He spotted the zipline adventure's wooden platform in the northwest quadrant. A minute later, he pulled up beside a dark blue Jeep Compass and switched off the ignition with the touch of a button.

Redge and Scotch exited the vehicle, the simultaneous sound of car doors slamming announcing their presence, prompting an about-face from the lone figure standing atop the platform. The two titans made their way up the two-story structure, two steps at a time, where a short but robust woman greeted them with a glower.

"You must be Hartley," the retired SEAL said. At six-foot-seven, Redge towered above the compact form of the zip line operator. He estimated her to be in her mid-to-late twenties, but something told him those round, worried eyes held a lifetime of experience.

A hesitant nod.

"I'm Redge and,"—he gestured to the Scotsman beside him—"this is Scotch."

Hartley didn't seem interested in a customary introduction, so Redge refrained from offering his hand. She flung her short, ebony hair, shaved to a stubble on one side, and glared at them with cappuccino eyes.

"Thanks for agreeing to meet with us," Redge said, hoping to break the ice.

"Yep," Hartley said through tight lips, her fingers toying with the zipper holding her oversized, gray hoodie together.

"How long have you been doing this?" Scotch asked. The titans stood side by side, leaving plenty of space between them and the zipline operator.

Her expression remained stoic. "For more than five years."

"Have you ever had an incident like this before?" Redge asked. He defied the urge to cross his arms over his chest; instead, he kept his hands clasped in front of him.

"I've never had an incident, *period*," Hartley said, her fists clenching.

Redge observed the pile of equipment lying beside her. "May we see the tether?"

Hartley corkscrewed down and snatched the requested gear. "Here," she tossed Redge the piece of red nylon that had attached to Ava's harness.

The retired SEAL lifted it with his palm to allow for a thorough inspection. He ran his finger over the threaded edge that had connected to the carabiner—now frayed—as he studied the strap.

Scotch inched closer to examine the tether as Redge held it in his hands; the two of them exchanged a knowing glance. "Has anyone else seen this yet?"

"Nope." Back to seesawing the zipper.

"Look," Scotch's hands found his waist. "We're not accusing *you* of tampering with this, but someone bloody did."

Hartley's shoulders relaxed, her cappuccino eyes glazed with sadness. "I would *never* have let Ms. Ellis do this if I'd suspected there was the *slightest* chance something could go wrong."

"I believe you," Redge stated.

The young woman discharged a hefty breath. Her hands moved from her zipper to the nape of her neck.

"When did you check the gear?" Scotch asked.

"When I got word that the camera crew was setting up… maybe an hour before." She scrunched up her face, her eyes darting to the left. "Two tops."

"So, this," Redge held up the tether, "sat up here for up to two hours unsupervised?"

The glare was back in full force.

"Look, we're just trying to figure out how much time someone might've had to tamper with it," Scotch soothed.

Hartley shrugged. "I've never had this happen before."

"Did you notice anyone up here yesterday?" Redge asked. "Anyone who shouldn't have been?"

She bit down on the fingernail stemming from her thumb. "No, but—"

"But what?" Scotch asked.

"I-," Hartley's gaze fell to the ground. "I… wasn't here the whole time. I took a call from my boyfriend," she mumbled.

Redge ran his large hand over his smooth ebony head. "Can you think of any crew members who might want to hurt Ms. Ellis?"

Hartley offered an emphatic shake of her head. "I work with a lot of celebrities, and most of them, honestly, I want to screw with their harness myself. But I *actually* like Ms. Ellis. She treated me with respect, ya know?" Redge and Scotch nodded. "I can't imagine anyone wanting to hurt her… though—" her eyes shifted to the eastern horizon.

"Though?" Scotch prompted.

"I dunno … I mean it's *showbiz*… everyone is an actor, right?"

Redge caught Scotch bob his head in understanding. Seems his bartender role allowed him to relate.

"Plus,"—Hartley tossed the hair on the right side of her head—"anytime a gorgeous woman has the spotlight, people are gonna be jealous… no matter how nice they *act*."

Chapter Thirty-Six

Tranquilized by the gentle morning breeze, Ava tilted her head back against the varnished Adirondack chair. She propped her ankle on the seat opposite her. It was already starting to feel better, and she was tempted to limp downstairs to help Mace make breakfast. But a promise is a promise.

Yesterday, as she clung to the tether with all her might, gripped with terror, she had been convinced the day would be her last on this precious earth. The sensation of the nylon slipping from her grasp, the sickening lurch in her stomach as she plummeted into the woods below, would never escape her memory. The chance of a new day made her heart swell; the evil of the world erased from her mind, at once replaced with Mother Nature's comforting beauty.

That zipline had been operating for years, incident-free. Of course, it would be my luck that something would go awry just when I happened to be using the equipment. What were the odds? Unless… it wasn't an accident and someone…

Ava kneaded her forehead. She untied her plush cream robe, wrapped it tighter over her torso, then secured it around her waist. She just couldn't imagine anyone in the crew tampering with the equipment; they were all on wonderful terms, or so she thought. It's often difficult to trust anyone in this industry. A wave of dread rolled over her. *What if Osian Thomas was responsible?* The threat that her titans had saved her from last fall had been eliminated, to her knowledge anyway. *But what if—from prison—he was able to orchestrate another attack?*

Ava felt herself grow weak; the thought of him targeting her again made her stomach churn. After all, she was the reason he remained behind bars. He could've been sitting in prison for months, obsessing over how to exact his revenge. She took a deep, calming breath. *That's ridiculous.* Why would he organize the ransacking of her room? Then a fall from a zipline? *No, he'd probably just arrange for a hitman to snipe me one morning when I happened to be relaxing on the deck.* The sudden urge to roam back inside swept over her.

A shadowy movement materialized in her peripheral vision. With a jerk of her head, her eyes zeroed in on the dark-clad figure that emerged from the side of the cabin below, the open slats of the railing providing a peek-a-boo view of the imposing form. Her shoulders fell with recognition. Mace appeared to be pacing, one hand on his hip, the other holding his phone up to his ear. *Thought he was making breakfast? Must be important. Maybe it was Redge or Scotch with an update; I know they were planning on meeting with Hartley this morning. Or maybe it was Annie. Ugh. Maybe Mace needed to unload after yesterday's incident. I can hear Annie's chirpy voice now… Your poor thing! How scared you must have been! It's a good thing I came here! Let's meet so we can discuss this in person!* A sick feeling again plagued her stomach. Mace's mental well-being was of the utmost importance to her, but there was something about Annie she simply did not trust. *Honestly, the woman flew here from London to check on him? As a friend? Gimme a break.* She loathed that Mace was so nonchalant about it. *He'd blow a gasket if my therapist did that—not that I have one—but I might NEED one by the time this film wraps up.*

An obsessed therapist treks halfway across the globe in pursuit of a former patient, convinced they're a match made in heaven. Ooh, that has great cinematic potential. The reality of it was far less appealing, especially considering it involved Mace. Incredible didn't even begin to describe him, and Ava thanked her lucky stars for his presence in her life. But—as with any marvel of design—he captured the attention of admiring eyes, despite his presumably pure intentions.

Her ears strained to pick up the exchange, but she heard nothing beyond the buzzing of nature. Mace continued to pace alongside the eastern side of the cabin—his back to her and expression hidden—intermittently disappearing from her viewing angle. She reached up to fix her windswept hair and then leaned back against the wooden chair, resigning to respect his privacy.

****

Mace pocketed his phone and bolted up the front steps in one leap. He strode across the living room and into the kitchen, where he flipped on the coffee maker. He inventoried the fridge, found the eggs and a variety of fresh vegetables, then selected a ceramic skillet from the cabinet beside the gas range. He cracked two eggs into a bowl, spent twice as long removing the eggshell shards, then whisked and added the vegetables and a sprinkle of cheese. He'd grown proud of his breakfast abilities over the past few years and enjoyed having the chance to show them off to Ava. He wondered if Kent ever made her breakfast, before the image of the two of them enjoying the first meal of the day in bed together sent a surge of irritation through him. He slid the omelet onto a plate, then repeated the process, sans half the fixings. Two cups of steaming hot coffee later, he loaded the porcelain platter and trotted up the wooden stairs.

He was greeted by a vacant bedroom. The sheer curtain, billowing with the breeze from the open glass slider, directed him to the balcony. He discovered Ava leaning over the wooden railing, arms folded, her wrapped foot skimming the top of the cedar deck board.

"Ava Rosemary Ellis!"

With a flinch and a gasp, she turned to face the sound of Mace's deep, booming voice. A beautiful smile crept across her pink lips. "It's just Rose, thank you very much."

"No, it's *Rosemary.*" Mace set the platter on the bistro table's glass top, then marched over to the actress. "According to your mum, anyway." He cupped her smooth jaw in his hand and got lost in her fetching eyes. He ran his thumb over her soft, full lips. After planting a tender kiss upon them, he whispered, "You're supposed to be resting your ankle."

"I know…" Her eyes fell to his chest. "But it's already feeling so much better," she murmured as she slid the zipper on his fleece jacket downward. She smoothed her slender hands over his snug black shirt, then rested her cheek against it. His eyes drew to a close as her intoxicating scent wafted up to him. He pulled her tighter against his hard chest and kissed the golden crest of her head.

A split second later, he scooped her into his arms, carried her across the balcony, and through the open slider into the bedroom. He draped her curvaceous form across the blue and green plaid that covered the king-size bed. He stepped away just long enough to retrieve the porcelain platter.

Ava's eyes lit up when he placed the tray across her lap. "Impressive," she whispered with an incline of her head. He placed a mug of coffee in her hands, prompting a radiant smile, before sliding the oversized armchair from the corner and positioning it beside the bed. Pierced with admiration, her peer locked onto him. "Thank you," she whispered.

Mace grinned. "My pleasure." He kissed her forehead before plopping down in the chair. He took a bite of his omelet and washed it down with a sip of burning hot coffee. A soft vibration drummed his left pec, and he reached into his chest pocket to extract his phone. Following a quick swipe and a pause, he announced, "Redge and Scotch are on their way back," before setting his phone down on the nightstand.

Ava nodded, placing her mug aside. "Is that who you were talking to earlier?"

Mace's brows snapped together before he could recover from her surprise question. He didn't realize she'd spotted him on the phone. He had stepped outside to eliminate the risk of being overheard but hadn't anticipated her moseying out onto the balcony. His eyes searched hers, trying to discern whether she'd gleaned any details of the conversation. "No," he whispered.

Expectant eyes remained fastened to his. He took another sip of the scorching morning brew. "I wanted to check in with your family at the Embassy... see how Maximus is doing," he said after his esophagus recovered.

Her semi-convinced eyes would have to suffice. She ran her fingers across the gold chain attached to her neck. "I trust you didn't mention this incident? I don't want them worrying for no reason."

"No, of course not." Mace shook his head. "Ava—can you think of anyone in the crew who might want to see you…" He struggled to say the word out loud.

A wounded expression overtook her face. "So, Redge and Scotch don't think it was an accident?"

Mace cupped his chin between his thumb and forefinger. "I won't know till we debrief, but if I had to guess…"

"Well, I can certainly think of someone *outside* of the crew who might want me out of the way." Her arms locked together over her chest.

Mace bobbed his head. He knew who she referred to and didn't want to belittle her concern. "I can see why you'd think that."

Sapphire eyes glared at him. "I wish you weren't so naïve about her intentions."

"Ava, look," he reached for her hand—fought to free it as it clung to her chest—then planted a tender kiss. "Annie and I go way back." Ava's eyes spiked with displeasure. She withdrew her hand from his and tucked it under her chin. *Probably not the best way to start my rebuttal.* "I just mean," Mace cleared his throat, "that she knows my history. She helped me through some really difficult times." Mace searched her softening eyes as he massaged the back of his neck. "The deaths of my parents, my divorce, trying to work through the trauma of my life's work…" his voice trailed off as his gaze dropped to the floor.

He felt the medicinal touch of her fingers over his forearm. His eyes ascended to meet hers, their warmth restored. "I wish I could've been there for you," she whispered.

Mace rendered a gentle shake of his head. "Ava, those were some dark days." He fought to keep the pain from surfacing. "You get a far better version of me now."

"I'd love any version of you."

Mace felt his heart pulsate with affection. "I admit it's odd that she came here, but I really think she views my well-being as directly tied to her professional success." He laced his fingers with hers. "If I regress, she'll see that as a failure on her part, career-wise." He stood from the chair and lowered his mouth to hers. Her coffee-flavored lips tasted delicious.

Ava returned his kiss, then parted from him. "Mason,"— she stroked his cheek—"I'm not a fool, I can see in her eyes that she wants *more* from you."

Mace didn't know how to help her move past this. Her opinion of Annie was clouding her ability to view the crew through an objective lens. The distant hum of a V8 engine debuted, followed by the sound of gravel spraying. He combed his hand through her long locks. "Let's see what Redge and Scotch have to say." He kissed her forehead again before lumbering toward the door.

****

Normally, she treasured his intuition, but it bothered her that he was so blind when it came to this issue. Ava watched his gorgeous rear end as it escaped her view, followed by the sound of his heavy boots on the staircase. She finished the chef-grade omelet that rested on the plate beside her. Breakfast was *definitely* in his wheelhouse… dinner, not so much, but she loved that he tried. She longed to finish filming and fly back to northern Michigan. Time seemed to move more sluggishly there, and she relished every comforting, protracted moment with her wondrous warrior.

She laid her fork across the ivory plate, then rested it on the nightstand. She caught sight of Mace's phone; he must have forgotten to grab the large, charcoal-gray device before he marched from the room. Temptation soared within her as she stared at the lifeless screen. She wanted to believe that he'd called the Embassy, but her gut suggested otherwise. Trepidation brewed in her stomach, fueled by the thought that he may have lied to her. Her eyes remained glued to his phone as it sat there, taunting her. She knew his password— and he knew hers—they had agreed long ago to forge a foundation of trust and never keep secrets from each other. *If either of us is doing something we don't want the other to know, then we shouldn't be doing it,* he'd said, and she agreed wholeheartedly. She'd never felt the urge to actually *employ* the knowledge of his password, though… until now.

She snatched his phone from the nightstand. It weighed twice as much as hers due to its military-grade shell. She tapped a long, glossy pink nail against the summoning screen, her finger trembling. *Why am I so nervous? Mason had given me his password and his permission to look through it anytime—there's no reason to feel guilty.* She closed her eyes, releasing a slow breath. It wasn't guilt she feared—it was the truth.

Chapter Thirty-Seven

Mace glanced at the nylon tether Scotch tossed to him. It took him all of three seconds to discern that the fabric had been scored. He laid it across the pine dresser opposite the master bed.

"How can you tell?" Ava asked, her expression souring. Her robe still clung to her frame as she rested in bed, her injured right ankle stretched out in front of her while the other leg bent at the knee.

"Half of the thread's edges are neatly severed," Scotch stated from his position in the doorway.

"Exactly," Mace nodded. He swiped the strap from the dresser and strode beside her as she propped herself higher against the stack of pillows. "See how this first half has an even, well-defined edge?" Ava's eyes followed his gesturing finger. "This other half is frayed and stretched thin, indicating that's the only section that supported your weight."

Ava emitted a sharp sigh before hanging her head in her hands. "Guess there's no denying someone's trying to hurt me."

Mace tossed the tether to Scotch, then wrapped his arms around her. He hated that he couldn't guarantee her safety. Last fall, in Michigan, he'd felt confident about his ability to protect her. Here, there were too many elements outside of his control—starting with too many damn people.

"Ava," Redge clasped his large hands over the log-shaped footboard. "Did you notice anyone besides Hartley when you were up on the summit?

Ava lifted her head to meet the retired SEAL's eyes, then rendered a vigorous shake of her head, sending her long locks swinging across her back. "No—no one."

"And Hartley seemed like her usual self?" Mace asked, taking a seat on the edge of the bed next to her. He laced his fingers with hers and offered a gentle squeeze.

Ava craned her neck to peer into his eyes. "Yes." Her gaze shifted to Redge, then Scotch. "I mean, she's never been super friendly, but always professional." They nodded in sync. "And I've never gotten any strange vibes," Ava added, tucking her hair behind her ears.

"I think it's time we consider someone besides the crew, mate," Scotch said as he rooted himself beside Redge.

"Agreed." Redge shoved his thumbs inside the belt loops of his cargo pants.

Scotch smoothed the tip of his beard. "Any thoughts?"

Mace nodded. "Kent—"

"Annie—" Ava blurted at the same time. She flashed an annoyed look at Mace. "Kent wasn't even in Canada when my room was ransacked!"

"Or so he *says*…" Mace watched as Ava's beautiful eyes rounded their lids. He glimpsed the gold pendant that hung from her neck, peeking out from her posh ivory robe, hovering over the crease of her cleavage. He ran a finger over the warm, smooth, precious metal, then flipped it right side out. Leaning back against her pillow, he stretched an arm under her head, which resulted in Ava snuggling closer to his chest.

"Is it possible,"—Ava paused to nibble her bottom lip— "that Mr. Thomas is behind this?"

Mace cupped her chin in his hand and fixed his steel-blue eyes onto hers. "No." Though a part of him had wondered that same thing at first, which is why he asked Scotch to reach out to Brody. He locked eyes with the retired sniper and gave the slightest nod; the silent gesture granted permission to proceed.

"According to Brody's *guy*,"—Scotch's long, milky-white fingers quoted the air—"Thomas hasn't had any visitors or any mail in the past few months."

"It would be next to impossible for him to orchestrate something like this from prison," Redge assured.

"Besides, why go to all this trouble?" Scotch shook his head, sending ginger-red hair askew. "Nah, it'd be far easier for a sharpshooter to take you out while you were lying around in bed."

Mace watched as Ava's eyes—growing wider with each passing second—rolled down her body and across the bed, then darted to the massive, radius window at the front of the room. Mace shot Scotch a glower. "You have great timing, mate."

The Scotsman shrugged. "Just sayin."

Mace decided to move on. "How long have you known Pierre?" he whispered to Ava as he held her in his arms.

"Long enough to know he wouldn't hurt a fly. I admit Pierre can be… eccentric—but all the good directors are."

"That's fair." Mace nodded. "Can you think of any crew members who've seemed a bit off?"

A pensive expression appeared on her face as she ran her finger across her pouty bottom lip.

Redge seated himself on the opposite edge of the bed. "Anyone arriving at the set early, or leaving late, that sort of thing?"

"No… I haven't noticed any odd behavior on behalf of anyone." With downcast lips, Ava added, "Though, in all honesty, I haven't been paying close attention." She glanced up at Mace, her eyes moist. "I've just been focused on filming so we can wrap up and get home."

His fingers stroked her soft, rosy cheek. "You have no idea."

Scotch slid his fingers back and forth over the frayed tether. "Maybe it's time we get the police involved."

Mace blew out his cheeks. A silence settled over the room as three sets of eyes stared at him. "My gut tells me that's not the right play."

"Agreed," Redge added. "That'll only complicate things."

"And cause a further delay," Ava said as she smoothed her plush robe over her legs.

"So, what?" Scotch reached into his scraggly beard to address an itch. "We just keep up the premise that we believe this was an accident?"

"Exactly," Mace directed. "No sense alerting the perp. Let's see what Brody's guy turns up and proceed from there."

Redge and Scotch nodded in unison. The retired SEAL rose from the bed and jerked his head toward the door. "We'll let you get some rest," he announced as he strode toward the loft, Scotch on his heel.

Mace wasted no time. He nuzzled Ava's neck, savoring her smooth, creamy porcelain skin. "It's time for your bath, Ms. Ellis," he whispered in her ear.

Ava arched a skeptical brow, prompting Mace to flash a wide, crooked grin. "Doctor's orders."

As he rolled from the bed, he spied his phone on the nightstand—lying in a different position than he'd placed it. His eyes froze open as he stared at the resting device. *Did she look through my phone?* He glanced at Ava, her eyes shifting away under his gaze. He felt a knot tighten inside his stomach. *If she did, then she now knows I lied about calling the Embassy.*

Chapter Thirty-Eight

Scotch propped his feet on the wooden table centered in front of the maroon leather couch, while his fingers enjoyed the coarse texture of his beard. He glanced at his cell, which rested on the cushion beside him: twelve-thirty hours. He swiped to reread the text that came through a few minutes ago: "Cannot wait for my massage!" followed by a series of kiss emojis.

Scotch slid his feet off the table and dropped them to the polished oak floor. He jerked forward, resting his elbows upon his bouncing knees. Another sideways glance at his phone told him three minutes had passed. The wringing of his hands did little to aid his dissonance. He bolted up from the couch, called to Redge that he'd be back in a bit as he snatched the keys to the Range Rover, then hurried out the front door.

He guided the high-end SUV around the multitude of potholes that plagued his path. A few miles later, he slowed to a stop. His eyes hovered over the blue sign posted at the junction. A large, white arrow pointed to the right—the word *Hôtel* above it.

Heart thumping with discord, Scotch hesitated. His fingers drummed the leather-wrapped steering wheel at the twelve o'clock position. He tugged the wheel to the right before a split-second change of heart made him spin to the left, tires squealing with the abrupt movement.

His route led him onto a familiar cobblestone. Midway through the circular drive, he guided the Range Rover to a gradual halt, then threw the vehicle in park and cut the engine. A moment later, he found himself staring at a pair of elegant glass doors accented with intricate wrought iron scrolling. He drew in a measured breath, slowly exhaled, then pressed the illuminated round button.

One minute felt like ten before Scotch heard the muffled sound of footsteps approaching. One-half of the massive door swiveled open to reveal the imposing form of Julietta's husband. His clothes, a vermilion button-front shirt, the cuffs rolled back over his forearms, deftly tucked into black dress pants, appeared custom-tailored to his athletic frame.

Geoffrey's arms crossed over his chest, his eyes slanting with the movement. "Julietta isn't here," his smooth, commanding voice—laced with frustration—announced.

"I didn't come here to see *her*."

Geoffrey's dark eyes narrowed to slits as a truculent expression overtook his face.

Scotch stroked his jaw while he studied the presence before him: the man wed to the woman he'd pleasured poolside a few short days ago. "Look, mate," Scotch began, his stare falling to the cobblestone at his feet. "If"—he forced himself to look her husband in the eye—"I'd known Julietta was married, I never would've let what happened… happen."

With a heavy sigh, Geoffrey's arms fell to his sides. "I appreciate that," he muttered.

"Why didn't you stop us?" Scotch blurted, tossing his hands out.

Geoffrey ran a hand through his spiky espresso hair as his chin lowered to his chest. "Julietta is… a complicated woman."

"Yeah, that's an understatement." Scotch's brows furrowed.

Her husband shifted sideways in the half-open door. "Bourbon?" he asked, gesturing for Scotch to step inside.

Scotch offered a shrug of resignation and then followed Geoffrey into the palatial home. He passed by the grand cherry staircase and into the sumptuous kitchen before his eyes swept over the opulent pool that butted up to the terrace. The memory of Julietta tugging on his zipper stormed his mind… wrapping her mouth over his… Scotch shook his head and palmed the cold quartz to steady himself.

Geoffrey reached into a polished white cabinet and removed a large crystal decanter. After splashing the honey-colored bourbon into two lowball vessels, he slid a glass in front of Scotch with a faint grating sound. Following a nod, Geoffrey tossed his back before Scotch could even raise his to his lips.

With a resounding *thunk*, Geoffrey dropped the glass to the glistening quartz. "You must understand," he met Scotch's stare. "Julietta and I love each other very much. But—since her parents passed—she's been struggling with her own mortality. She's been seeking… new *experiences*, shall we say."

Scotch bobbed his head. "I'm guessing I wasn't her first *new* experience?" He took a swig of the expensive liquid.

The creases around Geoffrey's eyes crinkled into gorges as he released a deep, belly laugh. "Not by a long shot, Scotsman."

Scotch felt foolish for allowing himself to be one of her—apparently many—pawns. "That explains why she doesn't wear a wedding ring," he mumbled.

"I gave that fight up long ago."

Scotch swirled his glass over the counter. "Doesn't that bother you?" he asked, struggling to keep his tone even. He was all for fun and games in a relationship, but even he had his limits.

Geoffrey tipped the decanter into his glass for the second time, then gestured to Scotch, who shook his head. "Of course it bothers me." He took a long, slow pull from his replenished glass. "But restraints have never worked with Julietta. She needs to run free for her spirit to thrive."

Perhaps it was the harsh kitchen lighting or the heavy topic of conversation, but the man standing opposite him seemed to age before Scotch's very eyes; his wife's lifestyle choices had surely taken their toll on him. Scotch swallowed the remaining golden liquid his glass offered, its sweet heat warming his throat. "Why do you stay?"

A series of muffled chimes from a grandfather clock hiding nearby broke the silence. Geoffrey turned his head to peer out the window. "My promise to love and honor her till death do us part isn't null and void just because she cheats on me."

Chapter Thirty-Nine

Ava stretched her long leg out straight, then rested her bruised ankle on the acrylic rim of the whirlpool tub. She had been nervous to see how bad it might look when Mace unwrapped it, but found herself pleasantly surprised. As long as she babied it on set tomorrow, they should be able to proceed with filming. *Fingers crossed.* She didn't want any more delays. She just wanted to get home. She missed Carolyn. She missed the gorgeous, tranquilizing view. She missed having Mace to herself.

Closing her eyes, she leaned her head back and found refuge in the warm blanket of shimmering suds that covered her body. Her mind wandered back to a short time ago, when she held Mace's phone in her hands. *Perhaps I should have checked his call log.* No, she reassured herself. *I trust him. If he says he called the Embassy, then I'm sure he called the Embassy.* She had her mind convinced, but her gut seemed to be putting up a fight.

"A hot towel for my favorite patient!" The sound of Mace's voice traveled to her sodden ears. Ava lifted her head out of the water, her long, wet hair gliding against her bare skin, to discover Mace standing beside the tub holding a fluffy white towel.

She flashed a beautiful smile. "And you're certainly my favorite nurse."

"Really? I don't get to be a doctor in this scenario?" He draped the towel over a hook, then knelt before the tub, an embellished frown attached to his mouth.

"Well," Ava lifted a bare shoulder to her cheek. "You're already my *hero*, but I can promote you to…"—a long nail tapped her pursed lips, her eyes ascending to the ceiling—"perhaps, physician's assistant, if you prefer," she added with a coy smile.

He pulled back the long sleeves of his form-fitting shirt, then immersed a hand in the heated water to scavenge for hers. He lifted her wet, delicate fingers to his lips, then mumbled, "I'll take hero any day."

As she peered into his spirited eyes, her heart swelled with adoration. Desperate to feel his body against her, she resisted the urge to tear off his clothes and pull his shredded frame into the bath—worried their combined weight might send the tub crashing through the floor.

Ava savored the feel of his tender, repeated kisses spanning the length of her forearm. The embodiment of strength and all things masculine, he seemed to shelter a secret layer of compassion revealed only to her. The frequency of his kisses slowed, as his gorgeous steel-blue eyes clouded with concern. "What's bothering you?" she whispered.

He raised his eyes to hers, his chest expanding as he drew in a long breath. "I've just been wondering whether you've thought any more about Kent's offer," he mumbled in his made-her-heart-flutter British accent.

"I have…" She surveyed his expression as she paused. "Quite a bit, actually."

Mace scooped some bath water into his hand and let it funnel through his fingers, warming her exposed shoulder. "Seems like a great opportunity." His tone held a disquiet.

"It does… but I find myself conflicted."

"Why?"

A raspberry-red painted toenail rose from beneath the sudsy surface and found purchase along the satin-nickel faucet that jutted over the tub. "After what happened a few years ago, I swore I'd never have anything to do with that production company again."

"But you always said that was your favorite role…"

"That's true. And a sequel would be amazing." Her toe tapped the neck of the faucet in cadence. "But I just don't know if I want that energy in my life anymore. Plus…"—Ava glimpsed the concern that saturated his soul-baring eyes— "I worry it would be difficult on you…"

"I can handle it," his words reassured. "Besides, I would never want to be the reason you turn down an opportunity."

"I love you for saying that." She brushed her lips over his hand. "But, if we're being honest, I know certain scenes can be difficult to watch. And there would be a *lot* of those scenes in this film…"

Mace's eyes grew wide but recovered quickly. "I can handle it," he reiterated with a shrug. "I worry more about what happens after the film."

Ava canted her head. "What do you mean?"

"Well… once you're involved with that studio again, it might be hard to walk away." He kneaded her exposed shoulder. "There'll be more opportunities, both in terms of films, and…"

Ava flashed a quizzical look. "And?"

The turmoil brewing in his eyes strengthened. "Other people in your life."

"I'm not sure I follow?"

"Ava, you'll be schmoozing with all the A-listers again." The kneading stopped, but his rugged hand remained cupped over her bare shoulder. "It'd be easy to get sucked up in that lifestyle."

Ava's brows knitted together. "I think I deserve a bit more credit than that… I'm pretty grounded."

"I know *you* are—but hanging out with all those celebrities"—the creases on his forehead puckered—"it can be intoxicating."

"Intoxicating?" Ava arched her brow. "Are those *your* words or Annie's?"

"It doesn't matter."

"Yeah, it kind of does." She lifted her head. "Seems to me like she's planting the seeds of discord."

Mace stroked her forearm again, his tender touch pacifying. "I just worry that being around all of those *stars*… those handsome *male* stars…"

"Mason…"

His insecurity appeared in the form of a one-shouldered shrug. "You'll want to trade me in."

Ava lifted herself upright, water cascading down her frame. She leaned over the edge of the tub, her plump, wet breasts pressing against his powerful chest. "You're the only *star* I'm interested in." She kissed the stubble of his cheek, prompting a beaming smile to spread across his lips. "You're my Polaris,"—she delivered another tender kiss to his cheek—"the star by which I orient my life."

Chapter Forty

*S*he's *absolutely stunning. It's just not fair.* From the shadows, she peered through the crude slit as Ava reached around her back to unzip her teal maxi dress; the garment slinked off her curvy frame and fell to the floor. With a graceful bow, she retrieved it and draped it across the tufted pebble accent chair positioned in the corner. The actress's private makeshift dressing room, cordoned off with heavy, blackout curtains in the southwest corner of the resort's filming section, provided the perfect clandestine location. She smiled at the thought of her cloaked presence. *If Ava only knew!* The actress would be horrified to discover she'd been observed on several occasions as she meandered about the space—often in the nude—oblivious to her watchful eyes.

Ava stood, one leg bent at the knee, before a clothing rack overflowing with carefully curated outfits, all custom-designed for her frame. Her blush-colored lace bra stretched to cover her breasts, showcasing her protruding nipples. She wore matching bikini panties, cut high over her toned thighs. Ava sifted through numerous options, appearing to struggle with finding the right choice for whatever scene they would be filming next.

A forbidden fascination continued to lure her to the actress's dressing room; her original intentions hadn't been to spy on her. But the way in which Ava's graceful, denuded form sashayed about enchanted her. Men had always made her weak in the knees—especially the tall, athletic ones. She'd never opened herself up to the possibility of enjoying another woman's company. But this one seemed to stir a dormant desire. Her entire body tingled with... envy? Excitement? *A combination of both.*

But my world would be so much better without her in it.

After several minutes, Ava removed a hanger from the rack and limped—her purple-stained ankle must still be hurting—over to the floor-length mirror and held it up to her frame. The actress pursed her lips and tilted her head from side to side, apparently giving considerable thought to the ensemble. At last, she cast a satisfied smile at herself in the mirror, then tossed the outfit over the same accent chair that held her original outfit. Ava slipped into a black silk robe that barely covered her thighs, tossed her hair, and then limped her way through the heavy curtain that served as a door.

She backed away from the slit she'd cut in the fabric. The actress would be heading toward her makeup chair at this very moment, and she knew she'd better hurry.

****

Ava plopped down in her stylist's chair. It felt good to give her ankle a rest. Although it had improved significantly since the incident, she feared complete healing was a way off. But she didn't want Pierre to know that. She committed to suffering through the remaining scenes in silence.

She glanced at her diamond-encrusted watch. *Where was Nikki? Normally, I'm the one who runs late.* Her long nails drummed against the metal arm of the chair in a soft tapping cadence. As she peered at her reflection in the mirror—partially concealed due to Nikki's penchant for Post-it notes—her mind led her to a contemplative state. *Most actors would kill for an opportunity like this... Why am I not jumping at the chance? Because it's a big deal, that's why. Filming would take at least three months. Then, of course, there'd be all of the post-production-related events. Could Mace really support that kind of commitment? He said he could, but his virtuous eyes contradict his words. Let alone the fact that it would require a temporary move to California... Granted, I could simply fly back and forth from Michigan, but it would be less tedious to stay in California till the sequel's premiere.* Her mind drifted to memories of lavish parties and mingling with Hollywood elites. They had once made her feel like a goddess, and it pained her to admit—but Mace was right—it could be intoxicating.

"Ava!" The sound of Nikki's animated voice jolted her back to reality. She watched her trusted stylist appear in the mirror as she rushed into the room, then took her customary spot beside her.

"I'm *so* sorry I'm late!" Nikki cried, struggling to catch her breath.

"It's all right." Ava flashed a warm smile. "I trust everything is okay?"

Nikki tilted her head back and gathered her long, chocolate curls into a ponytail and secured it with a band. "Oh, my goodness!" Her usual almond complexion appeared pale. "That seafood pasta I had for lunch did not sit well with me!" she said, patting her stomach.

"Oh." Ava frowned. "I'm sorry to hear that."

Nikki tossed her hands out wide. "Like, do not go in the bathroom!"

"Don't worry, I won't," Ava murmured through tight lips; she watched her own eyes grow wide in the mirror. "If you're not feeling well, Nikki, I can certainly do my own hair and makeup." She started to lift herself from the chair.

"Oh, my gosh, no!" Nikki palmed her shoulders and, with a gentle touch, pushed her back down in the chair. "Pierre would flip out if I didn't do my job!"

"Yes, but if you're not feeling well…" Ava slid forward in the seat, freeing herself from Nikki's grasp.

"Oh, I'm feeling much better now." Nikki marched around the chair and began digging through her daisy-print satchel next to the makeup counter. "Lemme just grab a piece of gum, then we'll get started."

Thankful she opted for the kale salad instead, Ava nodded.

"There, all better." Nikki proclaimed as she tossed the silver wrapper into a small, rectangular garbage can. She combed her fingers through Ava's long locks. "Your hair is so beautiful, Ava. I just love styling it."

"Thank you." Ava smiled. "Given that you've been styling it for almost two years, I'd think you'd be getting bored by now."

"Heavens, no!" Nikki's reflected expression grew serious. "Plus, between you and me—it drives Jasmine crazy that I get you and she gets stuck with Reed!" Nikki released a sudden high-pitched laugh.

"Really?" Ava watched her face scrunch up. "I had no idea."

"Oh, yeah!" Nikki sized up three different ceramic curling rods, settled on the medium-sized one, and plugged it in. "She keeps begging me to swap, even for one day, but"—she gave an emphatic shake of her head—"there's no way I'm agreeing to that!"

"Reed has a beautiful head of hair."

Nikki finger-combed her tresses again. "Oh, absolutely! But it takes all of ten minutes to do it. There's virtually no room for creative expression—unlike with you!" She pulled a yellow Post-it from the corner of the mirror, one of several adhered to the reflective surface. "Let's see… Pierre said he wants your hair down for this scene with relaxed curls."

"Doesn't leave much room for creative expression, I'm afraid," Ava said with a smile.

"No worries. There's always tomorrow," Nikki said with a shrug. "That is—unless you plan on abandoning us for California."

Ava drew in a sharp breath. She craned her neck to face her stylist. "Excuse me?"

"Oh, everyone's talking about it," Nikki whispered, leaning in close.

"Talking about what, exactly?" Ava's inquiry came out harsher than she intended, and a startled expression overtook Nikki's face.

"Well, just that," a sheepish tone crept into her response, "Mr. Kincaid desperately wants you back in California to film the *Studio Nine Eleven* sequel…"

Ava swiveled in her seat to face the mirror. "Just so we're clear—I have no intention of abandoning my role."

"I'm glad to hear that!" Her stylist reached for the curling iron. She laced it with a small section of Ava's hair, then rolled upward.

Following their working dinner the other night, which Kent and Annie so gleefully crashed, she had asked Pierre, Reed, and Stephanie to refrain from sharing the opportunity

Kent presented. The fewer people who knew, the better—at least until she'd reached a decision—and the three of them assured her they would keep it in confidence. *So, one or more of them lied to me. Unless, of course, it was Kent who spread the word in hopes of putting more pressure on me, which definitely fit his modus operandi.* Her mind retraced the timeline of that evening. It couldn't have been Annie, because she had joined them *after* Kent mentioned the sequel. *The only way Annie would know… is if Mace told her.*

Lost in thought, Ava's eyes had traveled to her clasped hands resting in her lap. The *screech* of the curtain door sliding open drew her back into the moment. Behind her, in the mirror, Jasmine's image competed with Nikki's.

"Hey," Reed's stylist said as she entered the well-lit, cozy space. Her black mane swept to the right in a shaggy pixie cut that obstructed one dark eye.

"Hey, back at ya," Nikki replied as she freed another section of Ava's hair from the hot iron.

Jasmine wandered over to the makeup counter, her eyes poring over the multitude of colorful bottles in varying sizes and shapes. "I'm outta shine spritz."

"Oh, crap, so am I." Nikki's free hand flung to her hip. "Better add it to the list." She motioned toward the mirror, lined with yellow three-inch-square reminders. Nikki patted the pockets of her apron with her free hand. "I don't have my pen…"

"No worries." Reed's stylist stepped beside Ava as she sat in the chair, held captive by the burning hot rod that clinched her hair. "I've got it," Jasmine said as she proceeded to pull a red dry-erase marker from her smock's front pocket. Below the supplies needed Post-it, she scribbled "shine spritz" on the mirror.

Ava watched the color drain from her face as she stared at her reflection. The image of her ransacked room, mirror message and all, overpowered her senses, and—despite the bright LED lighting—the room went dark.

Chapter Forty-One

I t's the seafood pasta!" Ava heard Nikki's booming voice echo from behind. She faltered out of her stylist's cordoned-off section of Basecamp, her vision fading with each clumsy step. She lunged against a glass door that opened onto a secluded courtyard, bright sunlight at once coating her, as the warm, late-April air breathed life back into her lungs.

The camphoraceous scent of cedar filled her nostrils as her bare feet gingerly trekked across the golden-hued woodchip-lined terrace. A green-coated steel bench rested among a colorful array of tulips, and Ava planted herself upon it, the metal cold against her bare thighs. She controlled her breathing, restoring her heart to its resting rate. A gentle gust washed over her, the black silk of her robe billowed in response, and Ava felt a flash of foolishness for bolting out of the resort in her bare feet and dressing gown.

But she was sure she would have passed out otherwise. Watching Jasmine write on the mirror had triggered a surge of unexpected panic. *What were the odds that Reed's stylist just happened to have a red dry-erase marker? She looked perfectly comfortable writing on the mirror, as if she'd done it thousands of times. Not like the practice is that uncommon. And lots of people have red dry-erase markers… that they carry in their pockets… Could Jasmine have been taunting me? I barely know the woman—we've hardly spoken over the last two years. Why would Jasmine want me out of the way? It didn't make any sense.*

Yielding to the intrusive thoughts, Ava leaned forward and massaged her forehead, her eyelids drawing to a close. Her senses synergized with the environment, bringing an awareness of every flutter, whir, and rustle around her—and allowing her to recognize the distant shuffle of approaching footsteps much sooner than would typically be the case.

"Ava, my dahling," a chirpy voice called out. "You do not look well."

Ava straightened her spine, her eyes fluttering open. She forced a smile. "Well, I assure you, Annie—I am."

"Well, that's a relief," Mace's former therapist replied. She appeared as if she'd just concluded an afternoon run, wearing blue spandex swarming with white swirls, and a coordinating high-neck tee. Her short, dirty-blonde curls were pulled back, resulting in a caramel-colored pom centered behind her head.

As Annie's scrutinizing eyes swept over her, she fought against the searing heat creeping up her cheeks. She tugged at the hem of her flimsy silk gown. *Why did they make these things so short?* She wrapped the fabric tighter over her chest and buried her bare, petite feet in the loose woodchips. "What are you doing here?" Ava asked, struggling to keep her tone even.

"I just finished my afternoon jog." She emitted a proud smile. "Thought I'd hang around the set in case Mace needed me today."

"How thoughtful of you." An anger thrummed through Ava's veins. *He doesn't need you—period.*

Annie pursed her lips and tilted her head toward her shoulder. "How's your ankle, by the way?"

"All better," Ava lied.

Annie tugged on her caramel pom, sending her tight curls bouncing free. "You sure gave everyone quite the scare."

"Well, that certainly wasn't my intention." Ava folded her arms over her chest.

Doubt seemed to speckle Annie's mossy-green eyes; her nonchalant shrug suggested a silent, *Perhaps.*

Ava studied Annie's expression as the corners of the therapist's mouth curled with the slightest of smirks. This woman made her blood boil, but she was used to dealing with Annie's type. After all, she'd encountered more than her fair share of pretentious, supercilious types in this industry—just never in a tiny silk robe and bare feet. Mace's former therapist had discovered her in vulnerable form and—by the looks of it—was enjoying the perceived susceptibility. "I presume you question my sincerity." Ava fought to project her usual, confident tone.

The smirk arrived in full force. "Well," she shrugged. "The timing seemed rather *convenient*."

"Let me get this straight—the timing of *my* fall was convenient?" Ava cast an icy glare. "To whom, exactly?"

"Oh, dear,"—Annie waved a dismissive hand—"I just mean in the sense that Mace, Redge, and Scotch were all on site. Naturally, if an accident were to happen—whether accidental or *self-inflicted*—their presence would all but ensure a favorable outcome."

Ava sprang from the cold metal bench. Her fingernails dug into her palms as she clenched her fists at her side. "Self-inflicted?" A suffocating fury coursed through her as she analyzed Annie's spurious eyes. "I certainly hope you're not suggesting I somehow altered my own zipline equipment?"

Annie shrugged. "Oh, what is it you Americans say… *if the shoe fits?*"

Yeah, cause no one in England has ever said that. "Annie—that is the most unconscionable thing I've ever heard."

"Is it?" Her face contorted as she continued, "The accident did take place after Mace arrived…"

"It also took place after YOU arrived."

Annie gasped. "Oh, goodness, that's preposterous! I wouldn't hurt a fly!"

The throbbing in her ankle teetered on unbearable, but she wouldn't dare let Annie know that. "Why are you *really* here?"

"As I've mentioned *several* times,"—Annie tucked her chin to her chest—"I'm here in case Mace needs help getting through this difficult time."

"Difficult time?" Ava scoffed. "You make it sound like he's back in Afghanistan."

Annie's mossy-green eyes cast daggers her way. "Ava—how *dare* you belittle what Mace is going through?"

The afternoon breeze picked up, delivering a gust that threatened the tie around Ava's waist. "That's not what I meant. I would never—" *This damn robe!*

"Mace is a very loyal man, Ava. He deserves to be with a woman who isn't going to toy with his emotions… in real life or under the guise of *acting*." Traces of spit sprang from Annie's bottom lip.

Ava inched forward, their faces on the brink of colliding. The blood pounding through her body turned ice cold. "The only *actor* here is you." Ava took her index finger and pushed it against Annie's sternum. "I see right through your pathetic attempt at triangulation—and so will Mace." Annie scoffed and took a step backwards, freeing herself from Ava's reach. "You're playing a dangerous game," Ava scolded. Desperate to maximize every fiber of silky thread as it billowed with the breeze, she yanked at her robe.

Annie's eyes narrowed to slits. "What rubbish! How dare you suggest I would employ such a tactic!"

"Well, *if the shoe fits*, doc," Ava sassed with an arch of her brow.

"Listen." Annie inched closer. "I've known Mace a lot longer than you have."

"Perhaps." Ava's lips pursed. "But I know him in ways that you will never."

"You can't keep playing the victim forever, Ava." Annie's hands flew to her hips. "Mace will grow bored of feeling like he's got to protect you all the time."

Ava had never actually hit anyone before. Except for that one time during a Taekwondo lesson when she missed the target and clocked her training partner. Even her fight scenes on set were perfectly coordinated to minimize any *actual* contact. She'd never even *wanted* to hit anyone before… but this woman elicited a wrath completely foreign to her. The desire to tackle Annie to the ground swelled within her, but the thought of disappointing Mace kept her from acting on it. "I may be a lot of things, Annie, but a victim is not one of them."

"I can attest to that." A smooth, baritone voice sounded from behind. Ava whirled around to see Kent approach, his gait strong and steady over the uneven cedar woodchips that lined the terrace. He flashed a charming smile as he approached. "Ava's far too resilient to adopt a victim mentality."

She never imagined she'd be so happy to see her ex-fiancé.

Annie scoffed at Kent's remark. She flashed a haughty smile at Ava. "Saved by the bell, it would seem."

"Thought only Americans used that phrase?" Ava touched her finger to his chin.

Kent stroked the corners of his lips, as if his well-kept fingers might mask the developing grin. He appeared to be enjoying their not-so-friendly banter.

Following a sharp intake of breath, Annie said, "Well, I best be getting back to my run." She began to jog in place. "I find it to be such a great way to process my thoughts." She whirled around and called out, "Cheerio!" as she darted over the splintered cedar and disappeared around the side of the resort.

"Good riddance…" Ava uttered before swiveling toward Kent and allowing her eyes to drink in the sight before her. He wore khaki pants tailored to his athletic frame and a blue button-front dress shirt—the man didn't subscribe to the concept of casual—that offered the slightest glimpse of his amber chest hair. Then his smile showed up. His swoon-worthy, charismatic smile that once lured her into his arms—and his bed—time after time.

"Did the therapy session not go well?" Kent asked with a waggle of his brows.

Ava shot him a look. "I'm not sure I've ever disliked another human being as much as I do her…"

Kent laughed. "I suspect the feeling is mutual."

Ava again tugged at the robe tied to her waist. "I mean, it's pathetically obvious why she's here."

"Agreed." Kent smiled. "Even I can see that."

Ava studied his expression for traces of sincerity. "Right? I'm not crazy—she's trying to steal Mace."

"I know you're not crazy, Ava." With a gentle touch, Kent rested his hand over her forearm.

The wind began to pick up again, and Ava had to smooth her hands over her thighs to keep the slinky fabric from revealing too much. "Thanks."

Kent lowered his gaze. "How's your ankle, by the way?"

"It's feeling a lot better."

"Really?" Kent crouched down on one knee for a closer look. "It's pretty bruised. I'm not sure you should be working today."

"I'm fine. Truly," Ava reassured.

Kent shook his head. "Okay." He lifted himself upright. "Your dedication is admirable, that's for sure." Hazel eyes glimmered with hope as they fixed onto hers. "Have you given any more thought to my proposition?"

Ava's gaze shifted to the colorful tulips at her feet. The answer should have come easily for her, yet she remained riddled with conflict. She gathered her blowing, half-curled hair in front of her chest. "I'm—" the rest of her words refused to materialize.

"It's okay." Kent's hand found its way back to her forearm. "Take all the time you need," his voice soothed. Lifting her chin, she discovered his eyes brimming with affection. This was the Kent she remembered. The Kent she fell in love with. "I just don't want you to have any regrets," he whispered, as his fingers glided over the silky fabric.

A strong gust of wind swept through the terrace, teasing the tie at Ava's waist free. She clutched the hem of her robe—a second too late. Kent's eyes lit up as he glimpsed her barely sheathed breasts, and his charming smile was back in full force. "It would seem today's my lucky day."

A scorching heat jolted up her cheeks as her fingers worked feverishly and clumsily to knot the silk tie around her waist. "Okay, let's just pretend that didn't happen, please." Ava held her arms, palms wide, over her chest.

"Yeah, no dice." Kent delivered a roguish grin. "They're even more incredible than I remember."

Ava scoffed. "I'm going to head back inside."

"Better make sure that thing's tied nice and tight." With a glint of mischief in his eyes, he reached for the knot over her navel and gave it a gentle tug.

Ava opened her mouth to protest just as a loud *clack* then *squeal* sounded as the exterior door burst open. She craned her neck to see Mace emerge, his stoic expression replaced by shock as his eyes registered the sight of Kent standing before her with his hand locked onto her waist.

"What the *fuh*—" the sound of the door slamming behind him drowned out the remainder of his question.

Chapter Forty-Two

Mace crossed his brawny arms over his broad chest as he watched her clutch the nape of her neck, her sapphire eyes wet with tears. The sparkle disappeared from her bottom lip as it vanished inside her mouth. "I promise—it's not what it might have looked like," Ava whispered.

They huddled in a quiet alcove just outside Basecamp, away from the inspecting stares of the cast and crew. Mace studied her contrite expression as she stood inches from his chest. Despite her formidable acting ability, he believed she was telling him the truth. But his gut also suggested she left something out.

Mace threaded a hand through his tousled hair. "Why the bloody hell were you outside anyway?" His hands shifted to his hips. "I left you safe and sound in your dressing area."

Ava filled him in on what happened with Jasmine. "I felt like I was going to faint if I didn't get out of there."

Mace grew thoughtful for a moment as he processed the information, noting the need to investigate Reed's stylist.

"You could have called for me." His tone proved harsher than he intended, and he softened his voice as he continued, "I'd been looking all over for you."

Tears dangled from her thick, bottom lashes. "I'm sorry."

"Ava! There you are!" Pierre's voice echoed, spotlighting their secluded corner. The director stomped over, his wingtip shoes silent over the soft carpet. "We're behind schedule, my dear!" His eyes dropped to the floor, then ascended the length of Ava's form. With a grimace, he flung his arms out wide and said, "*Quoi*? You are not ready!"

Ava wiped her eyes on the silky fabric that covered her arms. "Sorry, Pierre."

"Nikki? *Nikki*!" The director shouted. Ava's stylist scurried over from another corner of the room, a sheepish expression rooted on her face. "Last looks! You have ten minutes. *Ten minutes*!" Pierre flashed a look of contempt at Mace, then stalked off toward the camera equipment.

"If we can just finish this scene,"—a glimmer of hope penetrated her teary eyes as she lifted herself on bare tiptoes—"then hopefully we can wrap up early and spend the evening together." Her glitter-free lips brushed his stubbled cheek before she limped off toward Nikki, her barely sheathed frame weaving through the crew.

Mace's chest bloated with a deep breath before deflating through tight lips. As the crew's frenzied activity slowed, he made his way closer to the set. He'd been dreading this scene—but not as much as tomorrow's. His eyes canvassed the crew; everyone appeared to be in full work mode. He shifted to the cast; Reed stood near Pierre, chatting about something Mace couldn't make out, and the extras, wearing eager expressions, were nestled in their designated area. Mace pored over the guests; all of the faces were familiar to him at this point. He spied Redge in the opposite corner, his usual black tactical garb stretched over his ebony skin, but this time, black sunglasses rested on the bridge of his nose. His heavy arms folded over his chest. The guy sure looked the part. Anyone stupid enough to mess with him was… well… just stupid. His eyes continued their path, scouring over the guests. He spotted Stephanie, Reed's girlfriend, standing near a well-dressed man. Although his back was to Mace, his perfectly groomed California-bronzed hair gave him away… *Kent*… *Bloody hell*… he couldn't escape the guy.

Anger had stabbed his chest when he spied Kent's hand on Ava's waist a short while ago. He hadn't been that worked up since Ben Baylor tried to convince Ava to fire her trio of titans last fall. He thrust his large hand into the front pocket of his black utility pants and squeezed his tiny, squishy Newfoundland companion. The odd-shaped stress ball collapsed, then expanded at a snail's pace. Two more squeezes and his pulse had returned to its resting rate.

A vibration against his rock-hard arse cheek lured his hand from his front pocket to his back. With a swipe, he brought his phone to life to discover a video selfie of Scotch as he rounded the corner of their vacation rental, evidently conducting another perimeter check, captioned *Just wanted ye to know I'm doin' my job*! Mace glanced over at his SEAL friend, who eyed his own phone, no doubt watching the very same footage. Seems the Scotsman still didn't trust Redge's doorbell camera. *How the guy became one of the Royal Marines' most decorated snipers is beyond me.* Mace groaned and shoved his phone back into his pocket.

A loud *clacking* sound from the eastern corner of Basecamp drew his attention. Mace spied a two-man crew rolling a queen-size bed into position as the set was prepped for tomorrow's scene. The crew parked the large bed in the designated spot, its sky-blue upholstered headboard resting against the paneled façade. The two heavy lifters scurried off while another crew member methodically arranged several fluffed pillows. *Squeeze.*

Two white nightstands were carried in and placed on either side of the prop bed. The pillow fluffer placed small, identical bedside lamps on each, followed by a simple flower arrangement on the right. *Squeeze.* The bed crew reemerged, carrying a small table in a natural wood finish, which they placed off to the side. The pillow fluffer, hands on hips and lips pursed, stared at the piece of furniture. After a long moment, her index finger gestured to another area of the set, and the bed crew responded with haste. With the table in its new location, the pillow fluffer's head bounced up and down. Seconds later, a crisp white linen covered the four-legged piece of furniture, and she arranged a variety of realistic-looking fruit over it. In the center, she placed a malachite, cone-shaped champagne bottle. The finishing touch: two long-stem silver-coated flute glasses, each engraved with an inscription.

As Mace zigzagged closer, the black etching became clear enough for him to read: *Soon-to-be Bride* and *Soon-to-be Groom*. He froze as he stared at the prepped scene—the one which he'd been dreading most of all. His heavy lids fell closed, and he took a slow, deep breath. Then he squeezed.

"Action!" Pierre's voice echoed throughout Basecamp, and silence ensued.

With muted steps, Mace stalked back over to the western corner, which had been rigged for today's scene. Darkness shrouded the set, and all was still. A disquiet hung in the air, ready to greet the clandestine actors. Following the cue, a dim, shadowy light revealed a barren set and a lone figure sitting in a wooden chair, hands bound. A burlap sack veiled the actor's head, but several inches of golden curls escaped its breadth.

Mace watched as Reed, his tall, athletic frame covered in black from head to toe, approached with simulated caution—his prop gun oscillating with each step. The seasoned actor knelt before the figure in the chair and set his weapon aside. Camera one's operator extended the boom for a close-up as Reed gingerly removed the brown cloth that covered Ava's head. Wrists restrained behind her back, Ava sat with disheveled hair, an off-white rag stuffed between sparkly lips. Feigned fear forced her eyes wide, and tears streamed down her cheeks.

Mace averted his gaze. Acting aside, he loathed watching these scenes. He'd seen too many in real life, and the sight of Ava in this position—albeit for cinematic purposes—triggered him. The mini-Newfoundland in his pocket felt his wrath.

Reed removed the rag from her mouth. "You're safe now," his husky voice proclaimed.

"Oh, Luke!" Ava cried. "You're my hero!" *Squeeze.*

Mace watched as Reed cupped her face in his hands. Camera two panned in. "I'd never let anything happen to you." He freed her hands, then camera one zoomed in on the huge diamond attached to her left ring finger. Reed pulled her hand to his lips and planted a kiss. *Squeeeeeze.*

"Luke," Ava whispered as she stared into her co-star's eyes. "I don't know how I'll ever repay you."

Reed remained crouched before her. "Just love me, Ava—like I love you." The mini-Newfoundland, now pea-sized, might never regain its form.

"Cut!" Pierre yelled before the actors burst into laughter.

Ava gave Reed a playful shove. "Maybe you'll remember my character's name by the time we wrap."

"Sorry 'bout that!" Reed stood and laced his fingers behind his head. "Freudian slip, I guess," he said with a chuckle.

He felt Redge's presence approaching before visual confirmation. The retired SEAL stood beside him as he watched the crew members rush to reset the scene. A few minutes later, Ava was again bound to the chair, her pouty lips touched up, and the same rag stuffed back into her mouth.

"From the top!" Pierre yelled as the burlap sack lowered over her head and the set went dark. "Do try to get her name right this time, *si'l vous plaît!*"

Redge cocked his head toward the exit. "Why don't you get some air? I've got this."

Chapter Forty-Three

He let the heavy door slam behind him. Crisp, cool, spring air filled his lungs, providing an instant shred of relief. He locked the zipper of his charcoal-gray jacket and slid it upward, the soft fleece warm against his neck.

His heavy boots soundless, Mace made his way across the brushed sidewalk toward the woods that outlined the resort and dialed into Mother Nature's theatre. A variety of winged insects danced across the emerging blooms of the life-bearing season, coupled with the cautious tread of a hooved animal in the surrounding forest of trees.

The tread of another animal debuted behind him, and Mace pivoted to spy Annie approaching.

"'Ello!" she called out, her voice cheerful.

"Hey." He paused in place to allow her time to close the distance.

"I was just coming to check on you when I saw you exit the set." She stopped beside him. "You seem upset." Worry clouded her green eyes. "Is everything okay?"

Mace shrugged his shoulders. He came out here in hopes of some time alone and wasn't sure he felt like talking.

Annie rested a hand on his forearm. "It's okay. We can simply walk, if you'd prefer." She tilted her head and cast a wide smile. "Like we used to when I first started treating you all those years ago."

Mace's focus shifted to the adjacent dirt path as he recalled their history. They'd spent his first three sessions hiking around the outskirts of London in silence. She'd been a trooper; of course, she was getting paid to be. Mace nodded.

"Great!" Annie tugged at her ponytail, sending her shoulder-length curls bouncing free as they embarked on their journey.

The most desirable time to visit the northern country excluded late April, and Mace was thankful for the pre-tourist-season solitude. They trudged along the well-worn dirt trail as it wound through the dense foliage of the forest. Their path, often narrow, zigzagged around massive Sugar Maples and Northern Red Oaks native to the beautiful Canadian landscape. A familiar sound traveled up to Mace's ears, summoning him deeper into the peaceful biome—the hushed percussion of running water. He picked up his pace, Annie complementing his aggressive stride behind him.

The muted thunder grew louder with each inclined step. Several meters later, his keen eyes spotted a curtain of white amongst the green backdrop. The trail curved right, then back to the left, before revealing a worn wooden overlook obscured by the branches of a large Norway Spruce. Mace rested one hesitant foot on the structure to test its integrity. Satisfied, he ventured across the weathered cedar boards and cupped his palms over the railing. A moment later, his former therapist stood beside him.

One of nature's most powerful elements, water had always been a calming force in his life—eliciting both fear and awe, often simultaneously, within him. Even as a child, he could sense its majestic precariousness. His fondest memories with his mum and dad involved the water, and he cherished the memories of many summer holidays spent at Lake Windermere in England.

Soothed by the resonating symphony of echoes produced by the plunging water, Mace's breathing slowed. As his eyes bathed in the beauty before him, his intrusive thoughts faded with each drop of water as they fell to the basin ten meters below. All of a sudden, he felt like talking.

"This schedule has me bloody knackered," he muttered.

Annie turned to him; her eyes filled with softness. "I can imagine."

"I mean, this is her third film in four months." Mace tossed up his hands. "We've hardly spent any time together since the start of the year."

"I fear it may only get worse," Annie whispered. Mace cast a sideways glance at his former therapist. The corners of her mouth fell downward. "Especially when she moves to California for the *Studio Nine Eleven* sequel.

Mace blew out his cheeks, then rested his forearms over the railing, redirecting his focus to the plunging water.

"I worry that the sudden change in status… might really lure Ava back into that lifestyle. After all, was it not what she once craved?" Mace was silent as Annie continued. "Let alone the fact that Kent will be right by her side. It's certainly hard to deny his charm."

Mace craned his neck to face Annie. "Thought your role was to help me feel *better*?"

"Oh, Mace." Annie nudged closer, her shoulder brushing against his bicep. "My role isn't to make you feel better—it's to help you anchor to your reality."

Mace offered a slight nod as he stroked his chin. He fought against the unsettling feeling in his gut. "I'm not worried about Kent. I'd be right by her side, too."

Annie reached for his forearm, her eyes glistening. "Mace—that's a horrible idea." Her emphatic head shake reinforced her statement and sent her short curls into a frenzy.

Mace's eyes narrowed to slits. "Why?"

"Because!" With a gentle squeeze of his wrist, she continued, "Ava's fame will skyrocket with this production. She'll be welcomed back into Hollywood's inner circle with open arms, and"—Annie fixed her concerned eyes upon him—"it pains me to say this—but she'll grow tired of you."

"Well, that's some reality check, doc." Mace let his head fall into his hands.

"I'm so very sorry to say all of this." She reached into the pocket of the hoodie tied around her waist and produced a red tube of lip balm. "I know how much she means to you."

Mace let her words sink in. *Would Ava really grow tired of me? I can't compete with that lifestyle.*

"I've seen it happen too many times," Annie continued. "Couples whose relationship forms from a transitory need—in your case, serving as her bodyguard—often struggle when that need is no longer necessary." She smoothed the cherry-red lip balm over her lips, then stuffed it back into her pocket. "I'm quite sure that Kent would insist on his own team in California should Ava require protection. Leaving you to serve as just the *jealous boyfriend*."

Any calming effect the water once had on him vanished. He felt his blood pressure rise. He wanted to argue every word she spoke, but—deep down in his gut—he worried she might be right. "Ava hasn't even decided whether she's going to take the role," he muttered through clenched teeth.

"Oh, Mace." Annie brushed her hair from her shoulder. "I've seen the longing in her eyes when she's on set. Being an actress is her dream! She wouldn't give that up for anyone! And—mark my words,"—she shook her index finger—"this opportunity will prove too good for her to pass up. Even if it means…"

"Even if it means what?"

"Mace, I don't… I don't want to upset you," she continued, her head bowing. "Perhaps we should keep walking."

"Even if it means *what*, doc?"

Annie let out a pronounced sigh. "Even if it means *losing you*."

Mace's heart sank. He didn't want to be an obstacle for Ava as she pursued her dreams. A pink spear of light, courtesy of dusk's setting sun, pierced the earthbound water, creating a miniature, misty rainbow which drew his gaze. The sight before him imparted trickles of tranquility, which were short-lived.

"I may have a solution." He heard Annie whisper.

Mace cast a quizzical look her way.

"You could come back to England with me. Oversee some of the veteran support groups I'm starting." Mace's peripheral vision glimpsed her inch closer as she continued. "Give Ava the space she needs to pursue her dreams." A warm smile spread across her lips. "That way, you're not burdened with having to watch her in any compromising positions with her co-star, nor will your presence hinder her… shall we say… *ambitions*? Once that is behind you, the two of you can figure out the best way to move forward." Annie rested her hand on top of Mace's as it gripped the rail. "Assuming you'll even *want* to move forward."

His gaze shifted from the cascading water to Annie's mossy-green eyes. They beheld a new, different gleam: a sparkle of affection either never before portrayed, or he simply hadn't noticed. For a moment, he canvassed the passion-filled eyes of the woman he'd known for over ten years. The woman who'd made herself available—day and night—as he traversed some of the most difficult paths of his journey. *I can't believe I didn't notice it before.*

"Annie, look—" Mace slid his hand out from under hers and pocketed it in fleece.

Her hand trailed his, parting at his waist before coming to a rest on his bicep. "Mace, you mustn't confuse this perceived need-based infatuation with genuine love." Her tone softened to a whisper as she stepped closer, her form pressing against him.

Mace took a step in reverse, then another before realizing he had backed himself against the adjacent railing, the cedar pressing into his spine. Before he knew what was happening, Annie raised herself on her tiptoes, her glittery red lips, slightly parted, rushed toward his.

Chapter Forty-Four

Ava nibbled on a long, raspberry-red nail, entranced by the too-hot-to-yet-consume golden liquid before her. *Where was Mace? Why wasn't he answering his phone?* A loud slam severed her thoughts.

"Take that, dawg!" Redge called out, his smooth ebony lips spread wide as his wrist pinned Scotch's against the black granite for the second consecutive time.

Scotch disentangled his grip from the retired SEAL's. "Damn you, bruv," he mumbled while smoothing his unruly ginger beard to a point.

"What'd you expect?" Redge asked. "The only thing you've lifted lately is that bottle of beer."

"Hey, mate, I work hard to keep this incredible physique." He jerked up his snug shirt, revealing his creamy-white washboard abs. Ava couldn't resist stealing a glance, though it only made her miss Mace more.

Redge responded accordingly: he slid his painted-on shirt up over his chest, exposing chiseled abs, each muscle group carved to perfection. "Those bones have more meat on 'em than these."

Scotch scoffed. "Left-handed this time," he ordered, propping his elbow back up on the counter.

Ava's gaze fell back to the teacup. *He's supposed to be looking out for me, yet he's nowhere to be found.* Unease plagued her stomach with the myriad possibilities that might explain his disappearance. *He knew we were hoping to wrap early tonight... where could he have gone?* Wherever it was, Ava had the sinking suspicion that he wasn't alone. She couldn't banish the thought of her earlier encounter with Annie from her mind. From the second that woman appeared at the restaurant last week, Ava knew she'd set her sights on Mace, and this afternoon's chance meeting only served to confirm it. The woman would stop at nothing to get her hands on him.

A gruff Scottish accent stole her musings.

"Hmm?" She glanced up from her captivating cup of tea to discover Scotch's emerald gaze.

"Ava, my bonnie lass, what's wrong?" Scotch plopped down on the stool next to her.

Her eyes darted between sniper and SEAL, channeling their inner strength. She wanted to respond with *Nothing*, but her mouth didn't cooperate. Their beautiful, soulful eyes, serving as her safety net, summoned her vulnerability, and warm tears drifted down her cheeks.

Scotch wrapped his strong arms around her.

"You're worried about Mace," Redge whispered.

"I just don't understand where he could be," Ava murmured, wiping stray tears on her cotton sleeve.

"I'll try calling him again." Scotch jumped up from the stool, reached into his back pocket, and retrieved his phone.

"It's pointless." Ava gave a gentle shake of her head. "Just goes straight to voicemail."

"I'm sure he'll be back before dark," Redge reassured as he tugged his sleeves up to his elbows. His smooth, baritone voice sounded less confident than it had thirty minutes prior.

Scotch trudged over to the large window beside the stacked-stone fireplace and peered out of it. "Yeah, well, he's got about twenty more minutes before that happens."

Ava fought against the second round of tears trying to escape.

"Look,"—Redge's hands locked onto his hips—"no one is better at navigating in the dark than Mace, and that's coming from a SEAL."

Scotch, pacing the expanse of the cabin, halted. "Yeah, maybe ten years ago, mate," he said, scrunching up his face.

Ava rolled her eyes. "Well, that's reassuring."

Scotch shrugged. "Just sayin'."

Hoping the hot beverage might magically calm her nerves, Ava chanced a sip of the steeping tea. *No such luck.* She watched as Redge vanished into his bedroom only to emerge a moment later wearing a camouflage field jacket and carrying a large tactical flashlight.

"Hey, mate," Scotch held up his palms. "We don't need to be sending out two search parties."

Ava swiveled on her stool to face Redge. She could make out the faint outline of a handgun in his chest pocket. "Scotch is right. I don't want to chance you getting lost."

Redge narrowed his eyes. "Thanks for the vote of confidence."

Ava sauntered over to the bald behemoth and wrapped her arms around him. "I'm sorry, Redge. I just don't want to be worrying about you, too."

He cupped her chin between his thumb and forefinger and lifted it to meet his gaze. "Look, I've run five miles on these trails every day since I arrived. I know them better than the park rangers."

The soft tapping of raindrops colliding with the window stole Ava's focus. Scant traces of light clung to the darkening sky. "Maybe the three of us should go."

"No way." Redge waved a dismissive hand. "Mace'll kill me if anything happens to you. You two stay here," the retired SEAL directed as he zipped his jacket and made a beeline for the front door.

✳✳✳✳

Bright LED light pierced the darkness, forming a tunnel of visibility in front of him. Redge pulled his hood over his head, sheltering it from the delicate drizzle. "Mace!"

he called out for the third time. No response other than a soft, intermittent rapping against the leaves.

He started with the path closest to the cabin, knowing it connected to the main trail network. When Mace had stalked off set earlier this afternoon—no doubt distraught by the scene they were filming—he most likely ventured onto one of the trails that led from the resort. *I'll start here and backtrack towards the hotel.*

Mace was one of the finest navigators he'd met during his time as a commando. *There's no way he'd get lost in a simple trail system like this.* The guy was either being a big baby and pouting, ignoring their calls, or, more likely, his phone didn't have service. Unless he encountered something on his hike. Something or *someone.*

About ten meters into the first trail, Redge's light picked up a glint of silver. He bent down for a closer look. Another gum wrapper. Since his discovery a few days prior, he'd scoured these trails every day in search of signs of activity. Nothing—till now. He picked up the wrapper— littering pissed him off—and slowed his pace, his eyes studying the dirt and nearby brush line for disruption.

A thunderous crash shook the surrounding trees. Redge knew he needed to find Mace soon. He broke into a slow jog, about to call out to his friend again, when he noticed another track. Bathed in bright LED light, he could make out the footprint clear as day. An aggressive tread, similar but different than the one from the other day. He positioned his foot beside it. Gauging by the size of his boot, the print came from a man's size eleven or twelve hiking shoe. He inspected the nearby path and found another—two prints side by side this time. Redge stood beside the prints, then turned and faced the rear of the cabin. Just as before, even at this distance, the side of the cabin—Ava's suite and balcony— was exposed. Redge followed the tracks with his flashlight for a few feet before they disappeared into the thick of the woods. He'd have to inspect later. Right now, his mission was to find Mace.

Chapter Forty-Five

Mace jerked his head to the side just as Annie's moist red lips made contact, brushing against the corner of his mouth. "Stop," he said, his steel-blue eyes bulging. "Just stop." He clasped his large hands over her shoulders and gave a gentle push, creating enough space for him to free himself from the railing. "I think it's time you head back to London, doc."

Shaded by more than the evening sky, the softness faded from Annie's eyes. "Mace," she called out, again stepping close. "We could be so incredible together."

The loud crash of distant thunder momentarily drowned out the calming swoosh of the plunging water. Mace threaded a hand through his hair; a cool, wet droplet of rain danced across his skin. "My heart—and *every inch of me*—belongs to Ava."

"Can't you see how unhealthy your relationship has become?" Desperation sounded in her voice. "You're not suited to her lifestyle!"

Fine droplets began to fall at irregular intervals, resulting in a faint haze. "I know," Mace muttered. He retreated across the slippery cedar, which led to the narrow trail, and proceeded in the same direction from which they came.

"So what? You're just going to accompany her to California?" Annie's voice called out from behind him.

"Yep."

"Even if it wreaks havoc on you?"

"Even if it kills me."

"That's masochistic!"

Mace didn't feel like acknowledging the obvious.

****

Multiple knots now plagued her stomach. With a heavy sigh, she stood from the raised stone hearth. Ava locked her arms over her chest and cupped her neck. She proceeded to pace the southern half of the living room while Scotch shoved a powdered sugar-laced lemon bar into his mouth, his coarse beard collecting the crumbs.

"Hey," he said, still chewing. "It's gonna be okay."

Stopping in place, her eyes met Scotch's from across the room. Her voice broke out in a whisper, "I can't help but feel like Annie is somehow behind this."

Scotch's eyes filled with a rare sincerity. "Ava—Mace is the most loyal man I know."

She massaged her forehead. *I want to believe that.* But between this evening and the peculiar phone conversation from the other morning, she now found herself questioning whether she'd too easily extended her trust. Mace was the most incredible man she'd ever met; if she couldn't trust him, there was no sense in even trying with anyone else.

"He'd never disrespect you like that," Scotch continued as he carved another lemon bar from the glass baking dish. "For my first stag party,"—the powdery treat disappeared with one bite—"he organized a party bus to take us to—get this—race bloody remote-controlled airplanes!" Scotch shook his head in disbelief. "No strippers, nothing!" Scotch threw his hands out wide. "If it weren't for the beer, I would've abandoned his arse right there." He dusted the evidence from his chest, then stretched his colossal arms behind his head. "And don't even get me *started* on what he planned for my second stag party."

Ava let out another sigh. "I appreciate that you're trying to help Scotch, but—"

Just then, the outside motion light kicked on, casting a bright, orange-tinged glow across the covered porch. Ava darted across the room in awkward hobbling fashion, flung open the door, and limped through it. She braced herself against the wooden rail and peered out into the vast darkness. An outline began to take shape, dark against the evening sky, its intimidating form growing more distinct with each step. Redge marched toward the stone path that led to the porch. On his flank, another formidable shape emerged: *Mace!*

Heart swelling, Ava—ignoring the piercing pain radiating from her ankle—sprang from the porch and dashed toward her titan. Within the motion light's radius, her peripheral vision picked up yet another form approaching. This one slight—with shoulder-length curls.

Mace pulled her into his arms, and soothing swept over her as he held her tight against his powerful chest; his musky scent filled her nostrils. After a long moment, she propped her chin on his chest and gazed into his shaded-with-the-evening-sky eyes. "I was so worried about you," she whispered.

"I'm sorry," Mace mumbled, stroking her rain-drizzled hair. Ava's eyes adjusted to the dim reach of the porch light, and she took in the details of his natural, impassive expression. The day-old stubble that defined his cheeks, the fine creases that lined his forehead and stemmed from the corners of his eyes. He was breathtakingly handsome… Aside from the splash of red sparkle that stained the left corner of his lips.

Ava's heart sank with the discovery. She recoiled from his clutch, inducing a puzzled expression across his face. Mace's steel-blue eyes glazed with angst as she took her middle finger and sluggishly wiped the uninvited stain from his mouth. "This color is *all* kinds of wrong for you," she said, her velvety tone ice cold. Then, she spun on her heel and—her anger fueled by the throbbing pain in her right ankle—made a beeline for Annie.

She'd never been the jealous type. Years in and out of the spotlight, mingling with top models and actors, the swoons of other, younger women—ulterior motives notwithstanding—who tried to charm Kent right in front of her... None of it ever fazed her. She knew who she was. Although not inflated, her sense of self-worth was strong, keeping her grounded. Until this moment, she'd never felt threatened—irritated and insulted, yes—but never *truly* threatened by another woman. But then, she'd never been with someone she was so terrified of losing.

"Ava, look—" Annie toyed with the sleeves dangling from the hoodie tied to her waist as Ava approached, the therapist's words competing with the pounding in her head.

"Tell me, doc." Ava laced her arms over her chest, her dagger-filled eyes piercing the wannabe seductress. "How might the British licensing board respond when they learn of your antics?"

Annie stumbled backwards, fading from the motion light's range, as if the exposure would reveal her true nature. "I admit,"—her voice sounded strained, feeble—"it's *possible* I may have misread the situation—"

"Go home, Annie. Not back to the resort—back to London!" Ava pivoted and limped back towards the porch. She stormed past Scotch as he rested a hip against the railing and through the open front door.

Chapter Forty-Six

Mace felt crestfallen. *How could I be so stupid?* His naivety—exactly what Ava warned him about—got the best of him, and he had failed her. His feet found their pace as Ava vanished through the front door. He climbed onto the porch, the wide, wooden steps creaking under his weight, and aimed for the entry, till a retired sniper blocked his route.

"Listen, mate." Scoth threw his palms out toward Mace. "Maybe you should give Ava a little space."

Mace shot him the eyes. "Get outta my way."

Scotch shrugged. "Just sayin'," he said, stepping aside. "What are we supposed to do with her?" He cocked his head towards his soaking-wet ex-therapist.

"The resort's shuttle will be here any minute," Mace replied as he crossed the threshold into the living room. He kicked off his wet boots, then bound up the log stairs, his sock-covered feet silent over the lacquered surface. In the loft above, he paused outside the closed bedroom door, fully anticipating it to be locked. Following a deep, calming breath—because the mini-Newfoundland now resided in one of the several dumpsters behind the resort—his fist imparted a light rap against the pine door.

No response. He palmed the round black knob and gave it a twist, surprised to discover it jiggled freely with the movement. He nudged the door open, only to have it halt a few centimeters in. *She moved the bloody dresser in front of it.* Simultaneously frustrated and impressed—she was a lot stronger than he realized—he gave the door another nudge. This time it gave, and he realized—with the dresser still in its resting place—that the plaid rug had gotten caught under the door, hindering its mobility.

After a moment's hesitation, he plodded into the room, his eyes browsing the dim space. The only source of light stemmed from the bear perched on the bedside table, its bottom resting on the lamp's base. "Ava?" he whispered, spying her faint outline on the bed.

He closed the distance and plopped down on the bed beside her. She lay on her side; her porcelain skin blotchy and her eyes mired with tears. Her long, blonde hair trailed past her shoulders, ceasing at the pronounced curve of her hip. She looked ravishing, and his arms craved her… along with his already swelling mast. But instinct told him to be a gentleman, because he had *a lot* of explaining to do.

"What the hell happened tonight?" Ava's velvety whisper held a fiery inflection.

Mace's large hand plowed through his damp hair as he blew out his cheeks. "You were right," he murmured, reaching for her soft hand.

Ava retracted her appendage and shoved it under the pillow, out of his reach. "I typically am, but what *specifically* are you referring to?"

Mace felt a flush creep up his cheeks. "About Annie."

The actress nibbled on her bottom lip; her eyes locked onto his. "I hate that you didn't believe me."

"I hate that I was so foolish."

Welling tears began to spill over. "I also hate the thought of her lips on yours."

That's how I feel when you're with Reed. "They weren't *exactly* on me," he soothed. "It was more of a split-second graze."

The actress arched a skeptical eyebrow.

"Scout's honor. I turned my head as soon as I realized what was happening." Back to nibbling on her pouty bottom lip. Mace chanced lying on his side next to her. Thankfully, she didn't push him off the bed.

"But you must've been tempted, given that you were standing so close to begin with." An ethereal glow, courtesy of the bear-wielding lamp, projected across her snowy skin. Her breath, warm and sweet, drifted across his face as he inched closer, her plump lips within reach.

Mace tucked a strand of golden hair behind her ear. "Not at all," he whispered.

Another skeptical brow arch, coupled with narrowed eyes.

"Ava,"—Mace stroked the soft skin of her cheek—"my devotion to you trumps any earthly temptation."

The tear dangling from her bottom lash at last lost its hold. "Oh sure, you say that *now*…"

"I'll *say* it now,"—he wrapped his arm around her taut waist and pressed his body against her luscious form—"but I'll *prove* it every day of my life."

A beautiful smile emerged. Ava tugged his shirt free and caressed his chest, allowing him to bask in her healing, angelic touch.

Chapter Forty-Seven

He preferred his gin chilled as opposed to on the rocks, but the substandard beverage would have to suffice. Quite frankly, he expected more from a resort of this caliber. At least they had the decency to serve a well-respected brand.

Kent searched the deserted lounge. Drenched in rich walnut, the soft lighting reflecting its sheen, the space, unlike his gin, did not disappoint. The bar's mirrored backdrop was tasteful, not overdone, which seemed so often the case. He felt certain he'd seen this place in a movie or two, but the names evaded him.

A high-pitched giggle followed by the familiar *click-clack* of stilettos prompted him to crane his neck toward the entrance. A buxom thirty-something with smooth, long hair the color of honey traipsed in, her arm locked onto a well-built, well-dressed man several decades her senior. The man escorted her up to the bar, leaving a series of empty stools between them and Kent. After helping her onto a cognac leather stool, he took his time sliding his athletic arms out of his sports coat before draping it across the vacant stool to his left. The man stole a glance at Kent as he made a spectacle of rolling his sleeves back to his elbows and adjusting his diamond-trimmed gold watch. Then, he nuzzled his companion's bare shoulder, inducing another high-pitched giggle.

The woman wrapped an arm around the nape of his neck and planted a lingering kiss on the man's lips. She was nothing short of striking. Her well-crafted figure demanded attention, which Kent gleaned to be her objective. He spied the massive diamond attached to her ring finger; instinctively searched for the telling piece of jewelry on the man. Found it. *So, they are married.* Whether to each other remained unknown.

The professional presence behind the bar approached the couple. "*Bonsoir*, Mr. and Mrs. Martinus." *Well, that answers that.* "What may I get you?"

"Two glasses of your chardonnay ice-wine." The man glanced in Kent's direction. "Actually, just bring the entire bottle." A fetching smile appeared on his wife's plump lips before her hand fell into his lap, disappearing from Kent's view.

The man had good taste… In wine, watches, and women. Kent tossed his gin back and then rested it on the bar with the slightest of *thunks*. Mrs. Martinus made a display of whispering something into her husband's ear, while her mahogany eyes locked onto Kent. The smile spreading across her husband's lips took its time. Kent glanced at his own inappropriately priced Swiss timepiece. *Three minutes before she strikes up a conversation with me.*

The woman didn't even make it past the two-minute mark. "What is it you do, *Monsieur…?*" Her light, flirty voice held a thick French inflection.

Kent studied the two of them for a moment before responding. "Kincaid." He stroked his chiseled jaw as their pairs of eyes remained fixed on him in anticipation. "I'm a producer."

The woman's eyes beamed. *They always do.* "Ohhh! How exciting!" As her hand rested on her husband's chest, her fingers splayed as she emphasized the word *exciting.*

The husband's expression appeared skeptical. "Where are you from?"

Kent took the opportunity to roll back his sleeves. A man of his taste would certainly recognize the million-dollar accessory attached to his own wrist. "California," Kent added, with the slightest of smiles. *Thirty minutes before your wife invites me to your suite.* He was no stranger to the game. Nor was he a stranger to hot wives who'd grown bored with their husbands, or young women desperate to break into the industry. He considered himself an attractive man, but through limelight-seeking eyes, his attractiveness became unparalleled. He'd behaved, though, for many years when he had the privilege of being with the most extraordinary woman he'd ever met. Even after Ava left him, he'd shied away from temptation, in hopes he might one day win her back. He hated himself for being so foolish—for letting his ego flourish. She was the only woman he'd ever trusted, and losing her was his biggest regret. A regret that haunted him every day.

The bartender delivered the bottle of ice wine along with two stemmed glasses. He popped the cork, then poured a trace amount in one glass, and, with a gentle slide over the lustrous walnut, presented it to Mr. Martinus. The man gave it a slow swirl, then brought it to his lips before inclining his head at the bartender. "What brings you to our northern neck of the woods?" he asked while tipping the chilled liquid into his wife's glass.

Kent sighed. "Let's just say I'm pursuing my favorite actress." He'd hoped, after enough time had passed, that Ava might warm up to the idea of giving him a second chance. Then he heard about her new bodyguard slash boyfriend, and he felt his odds slipping away. The guy didn't fit into their world. Then again, he wasn't so sure Ava did either.

The age-gap couple continued their sizing-him-up chitchat, careful to weave in statements that hinted at their excessive wealth. Kent suppressed the urge to roll his eyes around his lids. *If they only knew of the fortune I'd amassed, they'd fall flat on their French asses.* He glanced at his watch. *Eighteen minutes into his thirty-minute projection.* He wouldn't take them up on their offer, of course, but he *so* enjoyed the pursuit.

While the man went on and on about having his yacht prepped for the season—*I bet mine's bigger*—Kent allowed his eyes to hover over his wife. Her tight black, corset-style dress shoved her large breasts skyward at an unnatural angle. Speaking of unnatural… by the looks of her, the only thing she'd retained from childhood was her eye color. He didn't necessarily mind surgeon-crafted enhancements; his industry was chock-full of them, and he'd grown accustomed to the standard. Which made it all the more incredible when he encountered genuine beauty. He released an indistinct sigh. Man, he missed Ava.

Another whisper in her husband's ear, followed by a coquettish giggle, her stare fixed on him. *Here we go.*

"Would you care to join us for a nightcap?" the husband asked.

A lascivious smile appeared on his wife's lips. "Our suite is incredible… especially the bed."

Chapter Forty-Eight

Kent couldn't wait to see their shocked expressions when he turned them down flat. A shrill squeak sounded in the lobby behind him, repeating itself in cadence. Kent swiveled on his stool to discover Annie trekking across the marble floor, every inch of her dripping wet. Kent spied her running shoes, the source of the annoying sound.

He jumped up, reached into his wallet, and tossed a crisp one-hundred-dollar bill onto the bar, then bolted to catch up with the therapist. Just as the elevator began to close, he reached her, turning sideways to squeeze in between the encroaching doors. His eyes fell upon a pathetic sight. Water began to pool on the carpet at her feet as she stood in place before him. Her teal spandex leggings looked dry, but her white tank, now see-through, revealed the outline of her bra, failing to shroud the stiff tips of her breasts. The water weighted her dirty-blonde curls, like a hard-worked mop turned upside down. "You look awful," Kent managed to say without thinking.

Annie simply glared at him as she untied the hoodie that clung to her waist. She tried to slip her arms into it, but the soaking-wet cotton impeded the action.

"What happened?" The elevator slowed to a stop, and the doors yawned open. Kent followed behind as Annie trudged down the hall, leaving tiny puddles with each step. She reached into the hidden pocket of her waistband and pulled out her keycard. Following a quick beep, the door swung inward. Kent stared at her with expectant eyes.

"I need to take a shower. Then we'll talk."

"Fine," Kent said, stepping into the suite as she vanished into the bathroom, closing the door behind her. Kent ventured into the well-appointed standard room. It felt cramped compared to his spacious suite. No matter, he'd only be here for a little while. He meandered over to the window and browsed the glowing lights of the resort's courtyard below. He preferred his lake view. He took a seat in the wingback chair beside the window to wait for Annie. *Whatever happened with Mace this evening, it didn't appear to go as expected.* During their chance encounter in the elevator a few nights ago, she had accompanied him back to his suite. Just as he suspected, Annie admitted her feelings for Mace. She'd surprised him by not making a pass as they polished off the bottle of champagne. Not that he would've taken her up on it; she was a far cry from his usual temptress. However, he had hoped she'd serve as a temptation for the commando, leaving a sliver of opportunity for him to swoop Ava into his arms. *What a great story that would make! A retired commando's therapist tracks him halfway across the globe and steals him away from his celebrity girlfriend by confessing her love. It had Homepoint written all over it. They'd no doubt offer the lead role to Ava.*

With a prolonged creak, the bathroom door retracted, and Annie stepped out, wearing a white plush robe that landed at her knees. She dropped her wet clothes on the floor near the bed, then plopped down with a weighted sigh in the chair opposite him.

Resting an ankle over his knee, Kent said, "I'm guessing your evening didn't go as planned." He smoothed the pronounced crease of his pants over his shin.

"This has been a fool's errand, I'm afraid." Annie thrust her hand in her hair and gave it a shake. "Mace doesn't seem to care that the odds are stacked against him. He's planning to stand by Ava's side, *even if,* and I quote,"—Annie's fingers quoted the air—"it kills him!"

"Sounds rather senseless." Kent stroked his chin between his thumb and forefinger.

"Exactly!" Annie scoffed. "After all I've helped him through over the years." She hung her head and rendered a slow shake. "He wouldn't be half the man he is today without my guidance."

Kent steepled his long fingers in front of his chest. "You'd think he'd be grateful."

"Precisely!" Annie flung her hand to the side. "And don't go getting your hopes up about your precious *Ava*." Annie's brow furrowed as she wagged her finger. "She's not giving him up without a fight."

Kent's heart sank. *She gave me up without so much as a word*. For the past few years, he'd clung to the dream that she'd eventually want him back. That their time together pre-scandal would prove strong enough to warrant a second chance. "Did he say anything about her deciding to go back to California?"

Annie pursed her lips. "Just that she hadn't *officially* decided." She issued a dramatic eye roll. "But, even if she does, he's planning on joining her."

"What?" Kent leaned forward in his chair. "You were supposed to tell him that I'd hire my own security team to look after Ava."

"Oh, I did!" Annie's eyes bulged. "But he just loves spending every minute with her. Plus, she fancies having him on set." Annie tossed her wet curls, sending droplets splaying. "It's pathetic, actually."

"She said that?" Kent grimaced. "She really said *she likes having him on set*?"

"Uh-huh."

"She hated when I'd visit her on set..." he mumbled, half to himself. "Said she felt *scrutinized*." Kent lowered his chin to his steepled fingertips. After a long, contemplative moment, a resigned smile escaped his lips. *How could I be so foolish? I had loved her with all of my heart—my selfish, greedy heart. Clearly, the neanderthal commando was a better man than I.*

A soft knock at the door whisked him from his self-defeating thoughts. He glanced at Annie, then the two of them eyed the door in sync. He stood and soundlessly made his way toward the entrance. With a peek through the peephole—*but how? The puddles must have given away their location*—a suppressed thirst began to stir.

He glanced back at Annie—a quizzical expression slapped over her face as she stared at him. "Doc, I say it's time we cut our losses." A salacious smile crept across his lips. "Tonight—let's focus on our own self-care."

He swung open the door. With an incline of his head, he proffered a silent greeting to Mr. and Mrs. Martinus as they waited outside the suite.

"We just wanted you to know that the offer still stands," the woman, her husband's arms wrapped around her cinched waist, declared with a come-hither expression.

Annie took a hesitant step forward, exposing her presence, her hands clutching the fabric of her robe. The man's eyes lit up with the reveal, feasting upon the recently showered therapist—no doubt a pleasant surprise. Kent translated Annie's expression: her hunger rivaled his own.

With the slightest of nods, Annie extended her permission, and Kent gestured for the married couple to join them.

A bottle of champagne materialized, its juniper glass condensating. Laced between the man's long fingers were the stems of three crystal flutes. "I'm afraid I only brought three," Mr. Martinus announced as he held out his palm.

"I'm happy to share," his wife announced as she wandered beside Annie. With a tender touch, she brushed the therapist's damp hair from her shoulder. Her husband peeled the foil off the neck of the champagne bottle, then popped the cork, unleashing a resounding *pop*.

But that wasn't all he unleashed. Years of bottled-up desire raced to the surface, filling Kent with an acute, primitive urge. *If I can't have Ava, then I'd might as well have… whomever I want.*

The four of them clinked glasses as a formality. Kent downed his in one sip—noticed his counterpart did the same—while Annie and whatever her name was giggled between sips of their shared glass. Her husband wasted no time—*respect*—and yanked at the tie around Annie's waist. Her robe fell open, revealing her thin frame and petite, pink-tipped mounds. He lowered his mouth to hers, his hands cupping her breasts. The therapist responded by reaching for the zipper at his waist.

Kent fixed his sights on the missus. She set the stemmed glass on the bedside table, then whirled around to meet his ravenous gaze with a naughty gleam in her eye. She peeled off her little black dress, revealing bare, delicious curves. Kent freed the hem of his shirt from his pants and unbuttoned it, exposing his bronze, defined chest—her eyes sparkling with the visual. Poised on the generously-sized bed, she reached her long, shapely legs out toward him; her slender ankles latching onto Kent at the waist, beckoning him toward her.

He appraised the voluptuous form before him. For three years, he'd shunned the advances of glamorous women, saving himself in hopes of reuniting with Ava. *Three years!* No matter, he'd make up for it tonight. Starting with this guy's trophy wife.

Chapter Forty-Nine

Just get through today. Mace stared at his reflection in the bathroom mirror. They were scheduled to film the one scene he'd been dreading since Ava read the script for *Mystery and Mayhem: More Mayhem* to him. The remaining scenes consisted of filler footage and retakes, and Pierre anticipated wrapping by the middle of next week. *Just get through today.*

Mace felt the remnants of this morning's breakfast churning in his stomach as he raked his hand through his mussed chestnut hair. His mates, as if sensing his anguish, had offered to chauffeur Ava to the set this morning, and he was grateful for the reprieve. *Maybe I should sit this one out. Ava would understand.* She had suggested multiple times that he "Take the morning off." *And, bloody hell, did I want to.* He took a deep breath, watched his lips in the mirror as they parted slightly, and exhaled, a small circle of fog forming. He didn't want to be the reason Ava felt like she couldn't pursue her dreams. He didn't want to risk her harboring any resentment toward him down the road. He had to show her that he could handle her intimate scenes—that he wasn't just the *jealous boyfriend.*

He decided to try a light dose of imaginal exposure therapy. Clearing his mind, he closed his eyes, then channeled the memory of when Ava first explained the scene to him. He pictured Ava in Reed's arms, snuggled close to his chest. They begin to kiss. A bed appears behind them. Reed slips her sweater over her head and runs his hand over her swollen breast… *It's just a quick bra shot,* she'd reassured. Reed collects her into his arms and carries her to the bed. He lies on top of her, planting a series of kisses along her neckline before drifting down to her heaving chest. The camera fades, then reawakens to find the two of them in bed, the bright morning sun filtering through the window. A sleeping Ava is curled up next to Reed, the sheet tucked under her arms, covering her bare body… *Wait—you'll be naked?* He'd asked. *Of course not! My body will be shielded by the sheet, so I won't be naked onscreen… But the two of you will be naked UNDER the sheet?… Well, we'll wear modesty garments… What the bloody hell is a modesty garment?… Reed will wear something to cover his, you know, and I'll wear little shorts and pasties to cover my… So, BASICALLY, you'll be naked and kissing in bed!… Well, only for a few minutes,* she'd explained *with a wounded expression that clenched his heart.* He pictured Ava and Reed in bed, his strong arms enveloping her. With a whispered good morning, she kisses him, her warm, plump flesh pressing against his bare chest. *Modesty garments, my ass.*

Mace's eyes shot open. He dashed to the toilet just as his morning breakfast reappeared. With his stomach still in knots, he stepped into the shower to rinse off. *Why the bloody hell can't I handle this? For cryin' out loud, this should be easy for me. I'm one of the finest marksmen the Royal Marines has ever produced, with the medal to prove it. I've jumped from planes at high altitude—low and high open. I've spent years kicking down doors in close-quarter combat, ready for whatever was on the other side. I've taken out targets at long and close range—in and out of the water. I've rescued hostages in the dead of night. I've mastered the art of explosives… I can do this! I have to prove to Ava that I can handle this.*

Exiting the shower, he drew the plush towel across his torso, then secured it around his waist. He shook his head and regained focus, then found himself again staring into his reflected eyes. *Yes, the Royal Marines had prepared me well for everything in life—except for matters of the heart.*

Chapter Fifty

Crew members dashed about in frenzied excitement as they finished preparing the set for the forthcoming scene. Mace stood between his mates, the trio in their customary coordinated garb: black tactical pants and busting-at-the-seams shirts. His keen eyes inspected the crew and guests, alert for anything out of the ordinary. Earlier, he'd remained outside Ava's dressing room while she dressed for today's scene; afterward, he waited while she sat in Nikki's styling room while the stylist "worked her magic," as Ava put it—but Mace never saw the results of anything magical. There wasn't a moment in the day, every day, that she didn't take his breath away.

While he'd kept watch over Ava, he'd enlisted his mates' help with scoping out Reed's stylist. Things hadn't sat well with him since Ava shared Jasmine's proclivity for writing on mirrors.

With Ava back on set, running through the scene alongside Reed and Pierre, Mace intended to debrief.

Continuing to survey the crew, he whispered, "Status update?"

"Nothing to report, chief," Scotch replied, keeping his tone on par.

"Reed's stylist is squeaky clean," Redge added.

Mace's head vacillated to the Scotsman on his right, then to the SEAL on his left. "Seriously?"

"A red dry-erase marker isn't exactly a smoking gun, mate." Scotch thumbed his belt loops. "We found three more throughout the set in the first fifteen minutes of our search."

Mace stroked his jawline. He'd hoped for a lucky break.

Redge smoothed his hand over his clean-shaven head. "Let alone the mirror thing."

"Yeah, mate, Pierre's assistant did the same thing on the mirror in the hall when he barked an order to her." Scotch ran his hand through his scraggly beard. "Seems like that's the go-to method of jotting down impromptu notes 'round here."

Mace expelled the air from his lungs. He couldn't shake the feeling that Kent somehow played a role in all of this. *What better way to get Ava to abandon this project and jump at his?* After Annie's pass at him last night, he'd wondered if he'd been blind to the possibility that she could have orchestrated the ransacking of Ava's room and the scoring of her zipline tether. But instinct suggested he look elsewhere. Annie may have developed feelings for him over the years, but she wasn't *entirely* off her rocker. Ava's mere threat to notify the British licensing board resulted in an expression of pure panic. He just couldn't see her jeopardizing her entire life's work. Plus, he awoke to find a lengthy text message from her, which included a seemingly sincere apology and details of her plans to fly home to London this morning. He glanced at his watch. She's probably somewhere over the Atlantic at this very moment. Ava wouldn't have to worry about her interfering anymore.

A beautiful giggle rang out from the center of the set, redirecting his attention. He glanced up to see Reed haul Ava in his arms and deliver her to their first position. "No sense putting unnecessary strain on that ankle," he said with a laugh. The actors stood beside the small, linen-draped rectangular table that had been set the day prior. A beautiful assortment of authentic-looking fruit, arranged on glazed turquoise platters, rested on one side, while a crystal vase filled with colorful flowers rested on the other. In the middle sat the slender, curved shape of a champagne bottle, accompanied by two stemmed pewter flutes.

Mace was beginning to miss his Newfoundland-shaped therapy ball. He felt the tickle of hair against his bicep and turned to see Stephanie squeeze in between him and Redge, her long ponytail sashaying from her swift movement.

"You feeling okay about today's scene?" she asked, her voice one notch above a whisper.

Hell no. Mace shrugged. "I guess."

"This is the scene I've been dreading the most, to be honest with you." She tugged at the diamond attached to her earlobe.

"Yeah, that's an understatement," Mace mumbled.

She peeked up at him with a sideways glance, then rendered a sly smile. "I'll let you in on a little secret for getting through these scenes…"

Mace whipped his head to look at her, desperate to absorb every ounce of her forthcoming wisdom.

"I always reenact them later with Reed," she whispered with a waggle of her brow. "That way, it removes the image of *them*,"—she pointed her index finger at the co-stars—"from my mind and makes me feel connected to the scene in a more positive way."

Mace pinched his breath as he let her words sink in. "That's… utterly brilliant."

"Thanks—I think so, too." She nudged his shoulder, then traipsed off, disappearing amongst the crew.

I can't believe I hadn't thought of that. An invisible weight lifted from his broad shoulders.

"Quiet on the set!" A woman's voice bellowed. Silence, as requested, followed.

"Action!" Pierre's voice called out. Mace spied the senior director as he sat perched in his custom chair behind his viewfinder.

Camera one closed in on Reed and Ava. With a sonorous pop, Reed uncorked the champagne, Ava's eyes sparkling with anticipation. With a joyful smile, his eyes roaming over Ava, he tipped the green bottle into both glasses, then passed the *Soon-to-be-Bride* vessel to Ava before reaching for the one etched with *Soon-to-be-Groom*.

"Here's to another job well done," Reed whispered with a charming smile. A *ting* sounded as they clinked the heavy glasses.

Ava emitted a gorgeous smile, then poured the contents of her glass down her throat. Both actors returned their flutes to the table. "Luke,"—she captured his hand and stared into his silvery eyes—"I almost don't want this mission to end," she whispered.

Reed wrapped his arms around her, locking his wrists at the small of her back. "It doesn't have to, Leslie." He gazed into her eyes.

So far, so good. I could totally do this with Ava. Mace pictured himself pouring their champagne, then enveloping her in his arms.

"I liked pretending we were married," Ava stated.

"Oh, Leslie!" Reed lifted Ava's chin and brushed his lips over hers. "I don't want to pretend anymore."

Mace watched as Reed and Ava began to kiss fervently, their lips locked onto each other, his hands roaming freely over her back. Mace pictured himself in Reed's place. The imagery was spotty at best.

Impassioned kisses raged on as Reed fumbled with the top button of her form-fitting cardigan sweater. Success. He moved onto the second button, the crease of Ava's cleavage on full display. Barely a touch and the third button popped free, revealing a plump mound of bra-covered flesh.

Mace's vision blurred. Despite his best concentrated efforts, his mind struggled to erase the image of Reed as he ran his hands over her chest. Mace shook his head.

"You okay, mate?" Scotch whispered.

Mace glared at his Scottish friend. "You could at least have the decency to look away," he mumbled.

"Sorry, geez…" Scotch scrunched up his face.

Mace noted that the Scotsman failed to avert his eyes. His peripheral vision glimpsed Redge, his chin lowered to the floor. *Good man.*

Mace forced himself to focus. *I have to prove to Ava that I can handle this.* Reed had removed Ava's sweater, his broad arms semi-cloaking her from the camera's view as they engulfed her. Clinging to each other, they side-stepped toward the bed.

Mace felt the bile rise in his stomach, and a sweat broke out across his forehead. His knees grew weak, and he felt as if he might pass out. *I guess I can't handle this.*

He needed to find a bathroom—a garbage can, anything. About to turn away, he caught sight of Ava jerking free from her co-star's arms. Reed's shocked expression mirrored Mace's sentiment. Ava clutched her stomach before doubling over. Then, with projectile trajectory, she vomited all over the set.

Chapter Fifty-One

Mace sprang into action, hurdling the waist-high rope that separated the set from the crew, bolting toward Ava. He reached the actress's side just as she fell to her knees, sliding in place beside her. One arm braced her back while the other held her head—her face ashen. Her skin felt clammy and cold, and her eyes lolled upward. A split second later, both Scotch and Redge appeared at his side.

Mace ordered, "Grab my phone and call Dr. Levasque!" Quick to oblige, Scotch reached into Mace's chest pocket and extracted his phone. A few taps later, the unit was sandwiched between his shoulder and ear as he scooped Ava's sweater, along with a throw blanket that rested beside the bed, into his large hands and tossed the items to Mace.

"Back up!" Redge's baritone voice could be heard. "Everyone, stay back!" A stunned and pallid Reed cupped his hand over his mouth, giving the impression he might be next. Redge pointed to the bed in the scene and instructed the actor to "Go sit down." Pierre clutched his chest as if his heart might burst through it at any moment, and Redge motioned for him to join Reed on the bed, followed by a noticeably worried Stephanie.

"Something's wrong," Ava murmured as Mace held her in his arms.

His herculean body shivered with a pervading sense of fear. "I've got you. You're gonna be okay." Mace tried to convince himself, in addition to Ava, as he uttered the words. He eyeballed the spray of vomit across the floor. *My God*. In his experience, only two things could cause such a sudden, violent reaction. His eyes darted to Scotch—the phone still rested against his ear; then Redge—the SEAL's eyes met his and, without so much as a word, he nodded, then swiped the pewter flute marked *Soon-to-be-Bride* from the table.

In the distance, the muffled wailing of a siren sounded, growing louder with each passing second. Ava's life now depended on Dr. Levasque. So did his.

Mace gathered Ava into his arms. The piercing squeal of rubber on pavement traveled to Mace's ears as he—Scotch and Redge on his flank—raced toward the exit. Whispers of disbelief echoed amongst the stupefied crew; their expressions stained by shock as the titans passed by.

The glass doors parted sideways, and Dr. Levasque dashed through them, wearing a look of concern that transitioned to alarm when he caught sight of Ava's lifeless form in Mace's arms. "I need to get her to my emergency room this instant."

Despite his innate desire to keep her wrapped in his heavy arms, Mace allowed Dr. Levasque's paramedic team to strap her to their gurney and load her into the resort's ambulance.

"Come with me," Dr. Levasque directed the titans, jerking his thumb toward his full-size pick-up truck. Mace studied the ambulance as the team loaded into it, his feet planted in place. "There's no room for you in there," Dr. Levasque stated as Scotch and Redge jumped into the cab.

Worry pricked every nerve of his body. He climbed into the passenger seat and covered his eyes with his hands.

Dr. Levasque didn't wait for him to get buckled. He threw his truck into reverse, the aggressive eight-cylinder engine responding with a roar. The doctor maneuvered the vehicle around the ambulance and torpedoed toward the medical center on the other side of the resort.

"What precipitated this?" The doctor asked.

Mace blew out his cheeks. "She seemed perfectly fine one minute, then—"

"Mace," the retired SEAL called out from the rear of the truck. "You'd better have a whiff of this."

Mace craned his neck to peer at his mate as Redge passed off the empty champagne flute. Mace swirled the tall, narrow glass below his nostrils and caught the faint scent of mold. "Son of a bitch," he murmured.

Dr. Levasque shifted his eyes from the road to Mace, and the retired commando thrust the glass into his palm. With one hand on the leather-wrapped steering wheel, the doctor raised the glass to his aquiline nose. "Penicillin," the doctor whispered. The realization seemed to register a split second later. "She's in full anaphylactic shock." He gunned the engine. "I have to prep my ER before they arrive."

"How can you be sure?" Scotch asked from the back.

"Penicillin has a distinct, mold-like odor due to its penicillium compound," the doctor explained. "The liquid formulation in particular has a stronger, more distinct odor than the powder."

"Which would explain why there's no residue in the glass," Mace added.

"Exactly," the doctor confirmed.

"Whoever put that in Ava's glass clearly wanted there to be no trace," Redge chimed in.

Following a sharp right turn at a reckless speed, the heavy truck heaved to the left in response but held firm to the pavement. A single-story brick building appeared, with a sign reading *Centre Médical*. A moment later, the trio jumped from the truck and followed the doctor into the building, matching his hurried pace. The familiar sound of the ambulance's siren amplified behind them.

The doctor led them into a cozy exam room outfitted with a hospital bed and standard medical equipment. "The three of you will have to wait in the lobby," he ordered as he gathered a scalpel, syringe, and what looked to be some kind of gel.

"No chance, doc," Mace said.

Dr. Levasque eyed the retired commando as he slipped into a white polyester coat. "Look, my staff and I need to have room to work. I know you're worried about Ava, but getting in the way will cost precious time."

"Fair enough," Mace nodded. "They'll"— he cocked his head toward Scotch and Redge—"wait outside, but I'm not going anywhere."

Dr. Levasque paused to meet his steely stare. "Fine," he conceded. Then added, "But stay in that corner," with a modulated tone as he pointed to the angled space opposite the bed.

Just then, a rhythmic clatter sounded as the paramedic team wheeled Ava into the room. Within seconds, they had her transferred to the bed, then went straight to work hooking her up to a multiparameter monitor—the device coming to life with a series of lights and beeps. Mace scanned the digital readings. He didn't need a medical doctorate or even a nursing certificate to know that Ava was in critical condition: her blood pressure registered fifty over thirty, and her pallid, feeble form appeared to be unconscious.

Dr. Levasque turned her sallow head to one side while his assistant sterilized her neck. Mace felt like his heart might erupt through his chest at any second, his entire future on the brink of slipping away. Placing a blue, plastic cover over her neck—the center transparent and adhesive-backed—the doctor unfolded it in sections down her blanket-covered torso. Mace took a deep breath and exhaled through narrowed lips.

Scalpel in hand, Dr. Levasque, a determined look in his eye, turned toward Mace as he pressed himself into the designated corner of the room. "Given that Ava can't offer her consent—I'll ask you." Mace clenched his jaw. "This procedure could collapse a lung or cause a blood clot, but it's the only thing that might save her life. Do I have your permission to pro—"

"Yes." Mace pinched his breath as Dr. Levasque lowered the scalpel to Ava's carotid artery. Then, as gravity took control of his heavy eyelids, he prayed. The room grew impossibly still and remained so for what seemed like an eternity.

Chapter Fifty-Two

"M s. Ellis, my dear, we simply cannot keep meeting this way," Dr. Levasque's smooth voice whispered.

Mace opened his eyes to discover Ava's lids fluttering open. A relief unlike any he'd ever known surged through him with the sight of those precious sapphire gems. Disregarding the doctor's command to confine himself to the corner, Mace leapt beside her bed and whisked her hand in his.

Golden hair piled under her cheek as her head remained tilted to its side, the catheter still attached to her neck. "Thank you," she murmured.

The doctor squeezed her free hand. "I'm just glad I got it right." He emitted a warm, broad smile. "I haven't had to do this procedure since my residency."

Mace crouched beside the bed for a better view: her eyes again flickered with life, and a pinkish hue crawled over her cheeks. The faintest of smiles broke out across her lips as he admired her.

"I'd like to continue to monitor you for a few hours before I remove the central venous line, but I'll give you two a few minutes." Dr. Levasque swiveled away from her bed and strode from the room.

A thousand statements populated his mind: *I'm so grateful you're alive! I'll kill whoever did this to you! I was so terrified! I can't bear to live without you! Will you have my children?!...* But his salivary glands decided to quit working, and he couldn't seem to form any words. Instead, he planted a tender kiss on her forehead. Then, he pinched the bridge of his nose, hoping to ward off the deluge of tears welling in his eyes.

"There she is!" Redge cried out as he and Scotch burst through the door wearing wide grins.

Ava tilted her head to greet them. "I'm sorry, I must look awful."

Tears streamed down Mace's cheeks. *You're more beautiful than ever.*

"Nah, you're gorgeous—even when covered in plastic." Scotch imparted a playful wink.

Ava's eyes grew misty. "Once again, I find myself forever indebted to the three of you."

"I don't know, Ava... you give us a much-needed purpose." Redge laced his fingers behind his neck. "So, I think we're the ones who should be indebted to you."

"Dude, are you crying?" Scotch asked, scrunching up his face as he stared at Mace.

Redge glared at the Scotsman. "I'm guessing the Royal Marines didn't offer sensitivity training?"

Scotch stroked his beard to a point. "Sorry—I've just never seen him cry before."

Mace's eyes rounded his lids, prompting Ava to release a hushed giggle. Fleece-covered sleeves wiped his cheeks. "Let's just move on."

Scotch had always struggled with that directive. "I mean, I didn't even see you cry at your parents' memorial," he continued, resulting in a slow head shake on behalf of the retired SEAL. "I'm just sayin."

Following a soft knock against the door frame, Dr. Levasque reappeared. Redge and Scotch repositioned themselves to huddle in the corner, allowing him room beside her bed. The four of them waited in silence as he reviewed Ava's stats on the multiparameter unit. Then, he smiled. "I'm most pleased with how quickly you're bouncing back, Ms. Ellis." He slid his stethoscope from his neck and stuffed it into a big square pocket. "Assuming this continues, I don't see a reason to keep you overnight."

"Thank you, doctor," Ava whispered, her rich, velvety tone reinstated.

"That being said,"—his eyes ascended to Mace—"I'm required to report this to the authorities. Clearly, this was attempted homicide."

With an unyielding gaze, Mace raised himself into an upright position and homed in on the doctor. "It's imperative we maintain the façade that this was an unfortunate accident."

"Yeah, mate." Scotch ventured out from the corner and took up position beside Mace. "Or else we'll just scare away the perp."

Mace crossed his arms over his massive chest. "We need to catch this guy—or girl—without rousing their suspicion." He paused to gauge the doctor's expression. "Otherwise, these attempts will continue to plague Ava until one proves successful."

"Well, this attempt was pretty damn close," the doctor scolded as he stepped closer to Ava. The three men wreathing her hospital bed now stood with shoulders back and arms crossed over their chests: their stares resolute.

Redge stepped out from the corner. "Look, Ava's an American citizen, under our protection." He gestured to himself, Mace, and Scotch. "Legally, she's our responsibility."

"I'm not sure the law sees it that way." The doctor shook his head. "I'm obligated to report this."

"Report it as an accident," Ava whispered as she reached for Dr. Levasque's hand and gave it a gentle squeeze. "That glass was an old stage prop. It wasn't cleaned before use, which, unfortunately, happens all the time."

"I don't know." The doctor ran his hand through his thick, dark hair. "This makes me really uncomfortable."

"Just give us twenty-four hours," Mace pleaded.

Dr. Levasque released a loud breath. "Fine," he said. "Twenty-four hours—I'll offer you no more."

Chapter Fifty-Three

I t's the most incredible footage we've ever filmed!" Pierre exclaimed, clasping his hands over his heart. "Homepoint loves it!"

"I'm so glad… I think…" Ava massaged the back of her neck, careful to avoid the bandage over her carotid, as she lay curled up next to Mace on the supple leather sofa. She feigned a smile in an effort to combat her uncertainty; she wasn't sure if she should be pleased or offended.

"Considering she practically died in the process," Mace mumbled as his thick, powerful arm pulled her closer.

"Of course, of course," Pierre slid his black-rimmed glasses higher over the bridge of his nose. "Naturally, I'm so relieved you are okay." With a paternal touch, he patted her shin. "After all, you are my favorite actress," he said with a smile. "Though,"—he stroked his chin—"I can't say I've ever met a more accident-prone one…"

Ava planted her cheek against Mace's firm chest, his musky scent tranquilizing. "How does this alter your vision for the closing scene?"

Pierre stood and addressed the group. "Picture this!" His excitement teetered on child-like while he drew his splayed hands apart, as if parting a stage curtain. "Instead of you and Reed in bed—which is so overdone these days—Luke proclaims his love as you're being lifted into the back of an ambulance!"

Ava couldn't curb her amused smile, inspired by the ear-to-ear grin that Mace wore. "I couldn't agree more, Pierre," he said, issuing a firm nod. "Bedroom scenes are bloody overrated."

"My thoughts exactly!" The director inclined his head toward Mace. "This will give it a fun, unexpected turn of events. Though again, I am sorry you had to endure that, my dear."

Ava slid the gold pendant hanging from her neck back and forth across its chain, then tucked it into her ivory cable-knit cardigan sweater. "*I'm* sorry to have caused yet another production delay."

Pierre waved a dismissive hand. "Nonsense. I want to retake the coffee shop scene with the extras anyway, and we could use more footage of the resort. Now,"—he bent forward and kissed her forehead—"I'll let you get some rest."

"Good night, Pierre." Ava watched as the senior director moseyed out the door, then vanished into the darkness. A moment later, the sound of his four-cylinder rental and a stabbing light sweeping across the living room affirmed his departure.

"Clock's a-ticking, mate," Scotch announced.

Mace blew out his cheeks, then raked a large hand through his tousled hair, the traces of silver disappearing with the action. "I know."

"What's the plan, chief?" Redge asked.

"Brody's guy came back empty-handed. There's nothing that links any crew member to anything even remotely concerning." Mace rested his chin against the top of Ava's head, smoothing her long hair. "No social media evidence that would suggest someone holds an unusual interest in you. Honestly, everyone seems to love you."

"And that's a bad thing?" Ava lifted her head from its favorite position—against Mace's chest—to peer up at him, eyebrow raised. His piercing eyes rendered an impish glint. She stifled a yawn before resuming her preferred post.

"Of course not," he whispered, squeezing her tight. "But it definitely makes our job harder."

"What I don't get," Scotch chimed in, "is how no one caught the fact that the liquid penicillin was in your glass *before* Reed poured the champagne?"

"I wondered that, too, but pewter flutes aren't exactly see-through." Mace propped his strong calves on the coffee table. "Reed would've had to look directly in the glass before he poured it, which we know he didn't, because his eyes were fixed on *Leslie*."

"As far as we know, that liquid coulda been sitting in there all day." Redge strode over to the fireplace and flipped the switch hidden under the mantel. A moment later, the blue-tipped flame vanished.

"Seems to me," the retired sniper drummed his fingers over the arm of his chair, "that all this circles back to one of two people."

"Unless those two people joined forces," Redge added as he plopped back down on the adjacent sofa.

Mace massaged his jaw. "Interesting," he mumbled, with a far-off look in his eye.

Ugh. The thought of Annie made her feel ill again. Ava's gut had never led her astray, and she knew that woman was up to no good the second she'd arrived. She abhorred that Mace had fallen victim to her conniving. "My money is *still* on Annie." With her head pressed tight to Mace's chest, she detected the faintest increase in the tempo of his beating heart.

He gave a gentle shake of his head. "She's already back in London. Left first thing this morning."

Ava's eyes nearly drew to a close. "Really?"

"Yes." Mace removed his phone from the zippered pocket attached to his thigh. "I received a nice apology this morning." He handed her his phone. "See for yourself."

Pleasant, albeit begrudging, surprise set in as Ava skimmed the message. It, in fact, received a passing mark in terms of an apology, assuming the words were sincere, which was a big assumption. Regardless, a sliver of peace coursed through Ava with the thought of not having to worry about this woman interfering in their lives. With a tap of her long nail, the message vanished, only to reveal Mace's call log. She glimpsed a few exchanges with Brody, then her eyes drifted to another London number—an early morning call three days prior. And it wasn't made to the Embassy. *Why would he lie to me?*

Mace plucked his phone from her fingers and pocketed it. "Feel better?" he asked, wrapping his arms tighter.

I'm not sure... "A little... It was a nice message... I suppose." *I just hope it's true.*

"So that leaves one primary suspect?" Redge asked.

Mace nodded. "First thing tomorrow, I'll track him down for a little chat."

Ava's attempt to suppress a second yawn failed, and the melodic sound soon had her three titans *aaahnning* in response. She was too tired to argue about Kent. She was also growing tired of defending him. Perhaps Mace and the others saw something in him she didn't. After all, Mace was right—he did ruin her Hollywood career—even if it hadn't been intentional.

Brushing a long lock of hair from her shoulder, Mace leaned close and nuzzled her ear. "Let's get you to bed." His warm breath, simultaneously soothing and arousing, erased the phone call from her inquisitive mind.

Taking her hand in his, he stood and led her toward the stairs, his solid gait steadying hers. "Good night," she whispered to the lounging commandos with an incline of her head.

"Glad you're feeling better, Ava."

"'Night, lass," Scotch said as he relocated to Mace's spot on the couch and propped his pasty white feet on the coffee table.

Alongside her warrior, Ava minced up the stairs. Her ankle, although recovering nicely, still hurt under her full weight.

"*Diehard Four* or *Cobra*?" She heard Scotch ask as they reached the top step.

"Definitely *Cobra*," the sound of Redge's response echoed from below.

"I'll get the popcorn!"

After sliding the suite door closed, Mace pulled her to his chest, her head coming to a rest over his heart. His rugged hand cupped her cheek and lifted it to meet his loving gaze. "This marks the second time in less than a week that I thought I'd lost you." He lowered his mouth to hers. She relished the touch of his stubble-trimmed lips and the moist graze of his tongue. "I had no idea loving you would prove so dangerous."

Her hands slipped under his tight shirt. "Why is it that danger feels less threatening when I'm with you?" she asked through a breathy whisper, her lips brushing over his. Her fingers danced across the breadth of his chest, savoring his chiseled-to-her-concept-of-perfection form.

His rugged hands reciprocated. "Guess that means I'm doing my job." He tugged the top button of her cardigan free, then moved on to the second. A moment later, his hands found her lace-covered breasts, caressing them as if just discovered.

"I don't want to be your *job*," she murmured between kisses.

Mace pulled his lips from hers. He locked his steel-blue eyes onto her. "You're not a job, Ava. You're my *entirety*."

Her sweater slipped from her arms and fell to her petite feet before her hands landed at his waist. With well-honed ability, she released his belt and the button of his heavy cargo pants. She glided his zipper downward, the motion proving difficult as she gingerly maneuvered around his massive protrusion. A moan escaped his lips as he unfastened her bra—her breasts spilling against his chest. The world seemed to slow as they continued to shed their clothes, freeing their bodies to marvel in each other's touch. Cupping her derrière, Mace's rugged hands lifted her to hip height, her legs instinctively splaying, before planting her on top of the lacquered pine dresser.

Back braced against the smooth,   cream-colored wall, her eager lips locked onto his as he eased himself inside of her, then traveled to the lobe of his ear, teasing it between her teeth. Her hands roamed the sculpted muscles of his chest, delighting in every inch. Mace's lips journeyed from her mouth south to her décolletage, then back again. While a rugged yet gentle hand latched to her hip, the other fondled the creamy flesh of her bountiful breasts. Bodies entwined, their passion peaking with every rhythmic thud against the drywall, until Mace, breathless, rested his forehead against hers.

Chest heaving, Ava panted, "I love you."

"Sweet angel,"—Mace paused to catch his breath—"you have no idea."

Chapter Fifty-Four

It's like living with a six-foot-three-inch toddler. Mace leaned against the black granite counter, willing the coffee maker to expedite its offering.

"It's not fair!" Scotch stomped the heel of his tactical boot against the hard oak floor.

"Quit being a baby," Redge grumbled before cramming a forkful of scrambled eggs into his mouth.

Mace filled his mug with his favorite morning cocktail, then spiked it with creamer. "Mate, I need you here."

"But I should get to go!" Scotch threw his large arms out wide, then folded them over his shredded chest as he continued, "Redge can handle things on this end!"

Mace shot him the eyes. He knew his mate was chomping at the bit for some excitement, but this teetered on pathetic. "It's too risky. I need to know Redge has *backup* if something happens while I'm out."

"But we,"—Scotch made a grand circular gesture with his hand—"all know I'm the better interrogator!"

"That's because you enjoy it a little *too* much," Redge mumbled as he broke a piece of extra crispy bacon in half.

"Hey, mate, I can't help that I—"

Two consecutive chimes, similar to that of a doorbell, sounded from Redge's back pocket. He withdrew his phone and placed it in the center of the island for all to see. A passcode and swipe later, the trio watched as a small, forest-green SUV slowed to a stop next to Ava's Range Rover. Mace swallowed his frustration. He strode across the polished floor and swung open the front door to reveal an enormous bouquet that spanned the width of the door frame, two waists, and four legs.

"May we come in?" Reed asked.

Mace shuffled to the side, permitting him, his model girlfriend, and the exorbitant bouquet to enter. Stephanie wiped her athletic shoes on the welcome mat while Reed slipped his hiking boots from his feet. He set the purple vase on the coffee table, then tucked his hands into the back pockets of his fitted black jeans. Turning toward Mace, concern speckling his bright eyes, he asked, "How's my leading lady doing?"

"Much better," Mace said.

Reed blew out his cheeks, his shoulders slumping with the action. "Well, that's a relief." Stephanie placed her hand between his shoulder blades and offered an affectionate rub.

"Can we see her?" Reed asked.

"She's still in bed."

"I told you we should have called first," Stephanie whispered. She plucked a long, stray hair from her black leggings, then laced her fingers with Reed's.

The actor's handsome face produced a one-sided frown. "Sorry, I just assumed she'd be up by now."

His tone, both pleading and hopeful, chipped away at Mace's reluctance. "She's actually awake..."

"Oh!" Reed's face brightened.

"I think it'd be best for her to get some rest, though. When she gets out of bed, I'll see if she's feeling up to company."

"We understand completely," Stephanie smiled. "We just wanted her to know we've been worried about her."

Mace marched toward the door. "I'll let her know you two stop—"

"Mind if we hang for a while?" Reed asked, his eyes darting from Mace to Redge, then Scotch.

"Uh..." Mace tried to rein in his flaring nostrils.

Stephanie looked just as surprised by Reed's question. "We wouldn't want to impose."

Reed fixed his eyes—those damn puppy dog eyes—on him.

"I have an errand I need to run," Mace replied. *Bloody hell, can't this guy take a hint?*

"Perfect!" Reed's tone teetered on elation. "Stephanie and I can stay here and help watch over Ava."

Mace raked a hand through his hair. He glimpsed Redge leaning against the counter, his expression stoic. Then his eyes shifted to Scotch—a huge smile stretched across his milky-white face. With a waggle of his brow, the Scotsman mouthed the word, *Backup*!

Chapter Fifty-Five

With a sudden jerk, Mace spun the leather-wrapped steering wheel to the right, narrowly avoiding the pothole. Scotch rode shotgun, one ankle propped on his knee. His long fingers thrummed the side of his powerful thighs to the rhythm of the music drifting through the speakers—a '70s hit from a British band.

Dissonance rattled his brain. He wasn't sure letting Scotch tag along was the right play. He trusted Redge without question, but Reed hadn't *exactly* proved useful during times of distress. He'd frozen in place when Ava fell from the zipline, and damn near lost his chyme yesterday after Ava got sick. The guy could throw a punch, all right—at least a scripted, perfectly-timed one—but how would he respond to a threat while Redge was on duty? His commando sense suggested he make it quick.

"How lucky are we that Stehanie knew Kent's hotel room number?" Scotch asked.

"Yeah." Mace slowed and maneuvered around a family of bicyclists.

Scotch bobbed his head. "Do you buy her story that his room just happens to be right around the corner from theirs?"

Mace scrunched up his face. "Why would she lie about that?"

"Just seems *awfully* convenient," Scotch said with a shrug. "Plus, ye know, Kent's a good-looking guy."

"Yeah, well, so is Reed." *I can't believe I just said that.*

"Just seems to me like maybe she's been keeping tabs on him." Scotch craned his neck to face Mace. "After all, the guy can offer her what she wants careerwise." Scotch stroked his beard. "Maybe she, uh, offered him a private audition…" His far-off tone suggested he enjoyed the imagery.

Oh, good God. "I dunno… she seems pretty into Reed."

"It doesn't take much for a woman to stray, mate."

Mace knew he spoke from experience. Casting a sideways glare at the Scotsman, he opened his mouth to say, *Not ALL women are like your ex-wives, Scotch*—then thought better of it.

With the first of May, which marked the official beginning of the tourist season, drawing near, the resort seemed to blossom overnight. Several long aisles into his parking-spot search, he pulled between two yellow lines near the section marked *Employé*. He didn't mind the long walk; he just felt fortunate to find a spot toward the front of the resort, leaving plenty of distance between them and the studio's designated section. He wasn't in the mood to engage with any crew members and relive what happened to Ava yesterday afternoon.

They strode through the revolving front doors of the main entrance, garnering stares that turned to glares as the ear-piercing, repetitive squeak of their footwear echoed throughout the lobby. Mace tried to match Scotch's stride to minimize the annoying sound, but his timing proved the slightest bit off, resulting in protracted squeaks. At last, they crossed into the elevator lobby.

Scotch punched the arrow pointing up. A moment later, he pressed the round button labeled thirty-two, and the car ascended with a lurch. Mace leaned against the stainless-steel wall of the cab and appraised his mate. The Scotsman rested against the silver panel opposite him, an eager glint in his eye. In his hands, he clutched a medium-sized black fabric case. Mace had seen that case before, though he preferred to forget it.

"What's in the case this time?" he asked, gesturing to the unit.

A roguish smile appeared, and the glint in his sparkling emerald stare grew into a maniacal gleam. "Just a few toys."

Mace rolled his eyes. "You realize we're just going to have a little chat with him, right?"

"Oh, yeah, of course." Scotch shrugged—but the gleam remained.

The elevator slowed to a stop. The shiny doors parted to reveal a gilded paisley carpet and ivory wainscoting that extended the length of the hall. Following a glance at the plaque on the wall, Mace headed to the left. They then hung a right at the end of the hall and proceeded to pass several sets of double-door alcoves before coming to a stop in front of one marked 3227 in elegant gold letters.

Mace took a deep breath before raising his fist to the door. No response. He rapped louder this time, then pressed his ear against the door. No sound traveled through the barrier.

"Maybe he's on set, mate," Scotch said.

Mace shook his head. "Pierre said they'd only be filming the extras today." A third knock elicited the same response. "Why would Kent care about seeing that?"

"Maybe he's scoping out new talent."

Mace shot him the eyes through a sideways glance. He recalled their sauna encounter from the other morning. "Let's go check the pool." A half pivot in, he noticed a small, white triangle poking out from the bottom of the door. Mace crouched down for a closer look.

He ran his forefinger over the edge. "Feels like a business card," he announced for Scotch's benefit. He attempted to slide the card out from under the door, but inadvertently pushed it further inward. "Great," he mumbled.

"Move outta the way." Scotch bent down and unzipped his black bag, exposing several thin steel instruments of varying size and sharpness. He slid a pair of elongated tweezers from its pocket and lowered his head to the floor, his unruly ginger hair scraping the paisley print. He slid the thin metal implement under the doorframe and extracted the glossy white card.

Gold foil letters spelled out the name of the resort's spa. Scotch flipped the card over, and an image of a woman lying on her stomach, her back partially cloaked by a towel, materialized. Below it, the words *'date'* and *'appointment time'* were listed. Bright blue handwritten ink indicated today's date. Mace glanced at his titanium diver watch, then his lips spread into a wide, crooked grin.

Chapter Fifty-Six

Reed, you're making me nervous!" Ava exclaimed as she watched the six-foot form of her on-screen love interest lean precariously over the wooden balcony.

"It's just so beautiful out here," Reed murmured. He retreated to a more stable position, the bulk of his body now behind the railing, and rested his elbows atop the oil-stained cedar.

Ava stared out over the serene Canadian horizon as she sat in one of the Adirondack lounge chairs her balcony bestowed. A cloudless baby-blue morning sky stretched across the wall of thick evergreens that lined the back of the parcel. "Agreed," she whispered. Her eyes drifted to the ground, some thirty-plus feet below. "But I don't need you falling."

"Yeah, otherwise, everyone will think this film is cursed!" Stephanie added as she combed her fingers through her long, caramel hair.

The corner of Ava's lips crept up. *If they only knew.* She peeked at her ankle. Once deep purple, the bruise had begun to fade, forming an unsightly blackish-yellow tint across her joint. Although it still hurt to put her full weight upon it, the swelling had abated, allowing her full range of movement.

Reed swiveled around to face Ava and Stephanie; the small of his back braced against the railing. "You gotta admit—this production has been pretty crazy." He rolled the cuffs of his alabaster button-front shirt up to his elbows, exposing his muscular, dark-haired forearms. "What, with your zipline accident and the moldy flute yesterday…" Reed shook his head. "Honestly, it makes me never want to drink from a prop cup again! I hope Pierre fires whoever was responsible for cleaning that stuff."

Ava offered a repetitive arch of her brows. "Maybe we should incorporate a zipline accident into the script for *Mystery, Mayhem, and Marriage.*"

"That's great!" Reed's head flung back with an exuberant laugh. "See? That's why you'll be such a great screenwriter!"

Ava crossed one satin-covered leg over the other, her injured ankle dangling. When Reed and Stephanie first arrived, she'd grown flush with the thought of them seeing her in her pink and black polka-dot pajama pants. On set, immersed in her character's mind, she could handle anything. Conversely, at home, she was simply Ava, and she didn't like feeling exposed. She toyed with excusing herself to get dressed, but hadn't yet showered, and the realization that both of her guests had seen her in far more compromising attire sank in.

Stephanie rested her head against the high back of the wooden chair positioned next to Ava. "You're sure you two want to venture into the realm of screenwriting?" She swept her thick, long hair over her shoulder and parted it into three sections. "They're always the first ones thrown under the bus if viewers don't like the plot."

Reed fixed his silvery-blue eyes on Ava. "Definitely. After this schedule, I could use a little break from acting." He cast a charming smile. "And there's no one I'd rather work with than you, Ava."

Stephanie began to weave her hair into a loose braid. "You two sure seem to know how to give the audience what they want."

Ava drew in a long breath of the fresh Canadian air, held it for a moment, then exhaled. "I'm looking forward to a break from acting as well, Reed—a permanent one."

Reed's eyebrows snapped together. "What?"

Stephanie whipped her head toward Ava, a shocked expression on her youthful face.

Reed marched across the deck and plopped down in the open chair beside Ava. "Don't let these freak accidents scare you away, Ava!" Panic seemed to plague his penetrating eyes as he reached for her hand. "You're far too incredible an actress to throw in the towel."

"It's not just that, Reed," Ava whispered with a shake of her head. "I just don't love it like I used to."

"But, Ava, your career is really starting to take off again!" Stephanie flung one long leg over the other. "The *Studio Nine Eleven* sequel could be huge!"

Ava pulled her knees to her chest. "None of that matters to me anymore, Stephanie. Besides,"—she turned back toward Reed——"you know I've never really felt comfortable in the limelight."

Reed's hand tightened over hers, his grasp pleading with her to reconsider. "But you're such a natural!"

Ava brought a shoulder to her cheek, her bottom lip finding its way into her mouth. "I'm hoping I might be a natural screenwriter, too."

The silver of his eyes glimmered with affection. After a lengthy moment, he said, "As long as I get to work with you in some capacity."

Stephanie tossed her thick, long braid over her shoulder. "Mace must be ecstatic!"

Her gaze shifted to Reed's model girlfriend. "Actually… I haven't told him yet."

****

The security camera app on his phone chimed intermittently. Redge studied the visuals on his device, switching between recorded footage and live feed. He lifted himself from the barstool, grabbed his empty coffee mug and Scotch's too—the guy was seriously becoming a slob—and rinsed them in the sink. Then, he wandered into the bedroom and grabbed his roof prism binoculars before heading out onto the front porch.

An eerie stillness hung in the dank spring air; a foreboding hush that belied the blossoming season. Redge stood at the base of the wooden steps, alert for any sounds that didn't stem from nature. Nothing. Aside from the premonition churning in his gut. He moseyed toward the back of the cabin, traversing the large swath of level ground that connected to the trails beyond—careful to steer clear of the eroding soil that led to the steep drop-off below the rear balcony.

He raised the compact binoculars to his eyes. Adjusting the focus, he zeroed in on the trail that led from the back of the parcel. The narrow path appeared to be deserted. His head oscillated left to right as he scoured the dense foliage lining the path. The woods appeared vacant. Until a splash of red caught his eye—moving toward the trail.

Chapter Fifty-Seven

Bathed in shadowy light from the gloaming corridor, Mace and Scotch stood outside door number three. He was amazed at how little effort it had taken to convince the receptionist that they needed to deliver an urgent, personal message to the producer on Pierre's behalf. Then again, Scotch could be pretty damn convincing. The commandos' eyes met, and following a brief, synchronized nod, Mace, with the slightest of pressure, nudged the door inward.

Greeted by the soothing sound of water lapping the shore, the earthtone room didn't disappoint, although the lighting proved much brighter than Mace expected. The east-facing room absorbed every ray of early-morning sun, despite the drawn shades. His nostrils registered the faint scent of lavender wafting from a diffusing mist in one corner. Positioned in the center of the cozy room was a massage table—Kent lying face down on top of it. An ivory satin sleep mask shrouded his eyes, his cheek resting against folded arms. His perfectly tanned body lay exposed, save for a crisp white towel draped across his buttocks.

Mace stifled an annoyed sigh. The sight of Kent's body—the very one Ava caressed with loving hands for years—triggered trace amounts of bile in the back of his mouth.

"Finally, Flo," the producer mumbled, his tone cross. "I was beginning to think you forgot about me."

Several stealthy steps later, Mace and Scotch stood on opposite sides of the massage bed. Scotch, with measured movements, unzipped his black case and set it on the small accent table that held the miniature fog machine.

"I've been really tense—so much has happened since I was here last." The unexpected sound of Kent's irked voice caused the Scotsman to flinch. "I need you to *really* work my rhomboids," the producer ordered.

Mace wrung his hands in front of his powerful chest. He pictured himself pounding his fist between the pompous producer's shoulder blades. *How's that? Still tense? Let me dole out another, mate.*

He severed the vision when he realized Scotch's eyes were locked onto him. The retired sniper held a high-carbon steel knife out in front of him, his jade eyes glimmering. He'd seen that look in Scotch's eye before.

Mace glanced at Kent as he lay across the massage bed. "What's taking so long, Flo? You're teetering on a two-star review, *at best*, and don't expect a tip!" Mace met Scotch's excited stare. Then, with a slow, diminutive motion, he slanted his head.

Scotch, his furtive footsteps dodging sound, positioned himself at the head of the massage bed. He raised the blade to waist level, held it out for a split second, his hand rock steady. Then, quick as a flash—he slid it across the producer's head—parting his sun-kissed hair in two halves and slicing the elastic band of his satin sleep mask.

The sliced ivory band spilled onto Kent's forearms as the mask angled forward, unveiling his wide eyes. "What the—" Kent propped himself up on his arms, sending the crisp, white towel plummeting to the floor, and exposing the front half of his body.

"Ugh!" Mace jerked his head to the side, his rugged hand protecting his eyes. "Why are you always bloody naked?" The sound of Kent's bare skin skidding across the leather bed traveled to his ears.

"You two are lunatics!" Kent yelled.

Mace chanced a quick peek between his fingers. He breathed a sigh of relief when he discovered the towel resting across Kent's lap as he sat upright on the massage bed. With his hand no longer needed for visual protection, Mace folded his arms across his chest.

"I suggest you keep your voice down, mate," Scotch whispered. The six-inch blade seemed to take on a life of its own, tracing an invisible pattern over the fabric covering Scotch's thigh.

"Or what?" Kent asked. "One scream for help and this place will be crawling with people." His tone suggested exasperation, but his hazel eyes clouded with fear.

"Aye." Scotch bobbed his head. "Women carrying warm towels and body oil are my worst fear, mate."

Mace stroked his chiseled chin. "We just want to ask you a few questions."

"This isn't how you go about asking someone a few questions!" The fear ebbed from Kent's eyes, and his tone had grown bold. Mace reminded himself that the producer was used to high-pressure situations in his industry.

Mace stepped closer, fixing his steely gaze on Kent. "Just cooperate and—"

"Hel—" Kent opened his mouth to scream, but Mace's powerful hand cut him off, gripping tight over his jaw. Fear again plagued his eyes. *Good*.

The feel of Kent's beard stubble tickling his palm repulsed him. "I was hoping we might have a productive conversation," Mace said, loosening his grip on Kent's jaw.

Kent nodded, his eyes wide.

"Brilliant," Mace mumbled. He slid his hand from Kent's face and stepped back, anxious to put more distance between himself and the naked producer.

"Why weren't you on set yesterday?" Scotch asked.

A smug smile appeared. "I had a threesome." Mace clenched his fists. "Golf,"—Kent's eyes jutted out of his head—"ever heard of it?"

The guy's ability to bounce back was nothing short of incredible. Mace glanced at Scotch as he tossed the knife between his hands. The Scotsman's eyes conveyed a desperate plea: *Can I have a turn? Can I? Can I???* Mace crushed his hopes with the slightest shake of his head, then fixed his stare back on the producer. "I find it hard to believe you'd want to miss Ava's bedroom scene."

Another closed-lip smile. "Why would I care to see her *posing* in bed when I possess the memories of *actually* being naked next to her?" His tight smile grew wide, his impossibly white teeth on full display. "The many, many memories."

Mace combated the rage thrumming through his blood. The guy had no idea what he was capable of. Before Mace could respond, Scotch's combat knife whipped past him, end over end, narrowly missing his chest. Mace's eyes followed its path—until it came to a rest—its tip buried between the narrow gap of Kent's thighs.

Kent's entire body shuddered. His strong jaw fell open as he lowered his head to assess the damage. "You could have cut off my penis," he mumbled.

Mace stepped into the open space between Kent's legs. "From what I saw in the sauna the other day, there was plenty of room." He grabbed the handle of Scotch's knife and pried it from the massage table. A fraction of a second later, the tip of the blade pressed into Kent's chin and lifted it at an angle until his panicked eyes met Mace's glare. The color drained from Kent's face, and a trickle of bright-red liquid glided down the blade. Mace dropped his wrist to the slightest degree, relieving the pressure, but allowed the weapon to hover beneath the producer's chin.

Why does it matter where I was anyway?" Kent's voice trembled. Another droplet of blood fell onto the towel that covered Kent's thighs. "Oh my God—something happened to Ava." He stared at Mace with pleading eyes. "Please tell me she's okay!"

After a long moment, Mace handed the knife off to Scotch.

"What happened?" Kent's shoulders fell forward, the sweat beading across his forehead becoming more pronounced. "Please—I must know," he whispered.

Mace's thumb traced the path of his thin lips as he studied Kent's worry-filled eyes, gauging their sincerity. "Someone put penicillin in her cup on set." His peripheral vision caught Scotch flashing him an annoyed look. *Yeah, I know—I'm losing my touch.*

Kent ran his hand through his perfectly styled hair, then squeezed his eyes shut. "I always knew someone would try to hurt her."

"What makes you say that?" Scotch asked.

"She's phenomenal... a once-in-a-generation actress. Despite her career setback, most people in this industry adore her and would do anything just to be a tiny part of her success." Kent rolled his bare shoulders back. "Conversely, there are those who perceive her as a threat... to their career, their self-esteem, their relationship… the list goes on and on. Some people would love nothing more than to see her disappear."

Mace stared at him through narrowed eyes. "You seem to be well-versed on the matter."

"This is nothing new, if that's what you're insinuating," Kent said with a shrug before smoothing the towel draped across his legs. "Actors receive empty threats all the time, and Ava received more than her fair share while she lived in California. Threatening messages on set, at home, dead flowers—you name it."

"Then why didn't she have a security team?" Mace asked.

"She did, off and on. I got her the best crew money could buy,"—Kent thrust out his chin—"but none of the threats ever materialized. Plus, she hated having a team. Said she felt *confined*." His right eyebrow arched. "Imagine my surprise when I heard her new man was a bodyguard."

Mace stroked his chin, his mind processing.

Scotch combed his beard with the combat knife. "Funny how you spent a lot of money trying to protect her, when you were the one who destroyed her reputation."

Kent glowered at the Scotsman. "Look, man, that haunts me every day. Losing Ava just about killed me."

A wave of gratitude washed over Mace. For a fleeting moment, he thought about thanking Kent for screwing up so royally. Had he not, Mace would still be holed up in his condo trying to stave off Scotch's sister, instead of beside the woman he loved more than life itself. Mace locked his hulking arms over his chest. "You were one of only a handful of people who knew she was deathly allergic to penicillin."

Kent scoffed. "Are you kidding? *Everybody* on the set knew!"

Mace's brows snapped together. "What do you mean?" A puff of mist appeared from the accent table, sending a fresh dose of lavender into the room.

"I *always* made a point of telling the crew of *every* project she worked on. Guess some habits die hard." Kent rendered a heavy sigh. "Anyway, I informed Pierre that first day I was on set, and he made a big announcement over the lunch hour. He adores her. I swear, the man would drop dead of a heart attack if something happened to her."

A flush crept across Mace's cheeks—a result of chastising himself for not thinking to do the same—followed by the realization that his suspect list just grew exponentially.

"That means…" Scotch said with a concerned look.

"Yeah. *Anyone* could've done it." The retired commando blew out his cheeks and began to pace the length of the cozy space.

"This threat…" Kent started. "Why do you suppose they want Ava out of the way?"

"Still trying to figure that one out," Mace mumbled as he wrung his hands in front of his chest.

"Determine whether they want Ava out of the picture because of her life *onscreen* or *offscreen*." He paused to roll his neck from side to side. "Figure that out, and you'll narrow down your suspects."

Mace squelched the impending eye roll. "No offense—but we got this," he said, tossing out his hands.

"Yeah, this ain't our first rodeo," Scotch scolded.

Kent shrugged. "Have it your way." A loud *thrrrp* sounded as Kent slid down from the massage bed, exposing his pale backside.

"Ugh!" Mace pivoted a second too late.

"Anyway," Kent said as he fastened the towel around his waist. "If I were you, I'd start with your little therapist friend."

Mace was taken aback. "She's in London, mate. Left yesterday morning. I don't see how—"

Kent's lips spread wide with a knowing smile. "No, she's not."

"What the bloody hell are you talking 'bout?" Scotch asked.

"Her plane had some kind of mechanical issue, and her flight was cancelled. She spent all day here at the resort."

Mace's entire body tensed. "How do you know that?"

A naughty gleam appeared in Kent's hazel eyes.

Mace flashed a look of disgust. "You're pathetic."

Kent shrugged. "Look, I went almost three years clinging to the desperate hope that Ava might take me back."

"So, what, you've finally decided to move on"—Scotch jerked a thumb toward Mace—"with his therapist?"

"Oh, please!" Kent's hands landed on his hips. "Annie was just…"—his eyes drifted upward and angled right—"an outlet."

"Why now? After all that time?"

Kent stepped closer to Mace. He tilted his chin north—his pinprick injury already clotted—and fixed his gaze on the retired commando towering above him. "Despite my hope… coming here and seeing Ava again after all this time… made me realize something." Kent swiveled, his back to them, as he continued, "What she and I had was real, that I'm sure of. At least as real as it could be, given my self-absorbed ways." Kent pivoted back around to face Mace. His hazel eyes projected a sadness, a regret that Mace hadn't seen a man wear since his military days. "But even on our best day—she never looked at me the way she does you." He hung his head, a heavy sigh escaping his lips. "It kills me to say this… but you give her something that all my money can't buy."

A warmth, soft and soothing, infiltrated Mace—but he didn't want Kent to know that. He offered a nod of acknowledgment.

"Piece of advice—just don't screw it up like I did." Kent shook his finger at Mace.

"Don't worry, I'm not *stupid*." They left Kent the same way they found him: lying on the massage bed, naked.

In the dim, hush-filled hall outside door number three, Mace leaned against the wall and watched as Scotch zippered his black bag. "Where to now, chief? Should we track down Annie?" the Scotsman asked.

Mace tilted his head back against the hard surface, his shaggy crew cut flattening as it pressed against the plaster, the gears in his mind turning. Something Kent said stirred a portent of discord in the pit of his stomach: determine if they want her life *onscreen* or *offscreen*. Then, it hit him. "I'm so *stupid*," he mumbled, his heart pounding. At once, his razor-sharp sensitivity to threat spiked. He caught Scotch's quizzical expression a split second before he bolted toward the exit, the sound of his mate's heavy boots running to keep pace echoing down the hall.

Chapter Fifty-Eight

Ava basked in the sun's radiating glow; Mother Nature seemed to be feeling generous this morning.

Reed twisted his wrist's timepiece into view. "I'm starving. Feel up to grabbing some lunch?"

Ava tugged at the hem of her satin pajama pants as she hugged her knees against her chest. She glanced at her ruby-encrusted wristwatch, squinting with the sun's reflection. "It's not even eleven."

"I know…" Reed's bottom lip jutted out. "But Steph and I didn't have breakfast."

"We were in such a hurry to check on you this morning." Stephanie stowed her nail file back in her sweatshirt's kangaroo pocket. Then, with the help of a long thumbnail, she addressed her cuticles.

Ava realized she, too, was starving. She remembered the plate of extra crispy potato pancakes that still lay beside her bed. She loved that he tried, but—with the exception of his mouth-watering cranachan—Scotch's culinary skills left a little something to be desired, and, after forcing down one bite, she couldn't bear the thought of a second. She reminded herself to dispose of the evidence before he and Mace returned. "I'd rather stay here, if you don't mind." She stretched her arms above her head. "Though I should probably shower and prepare for the day." As she rose from the deep, slanted chair, a wave of dizziness crawled over her, forcing her to brace herself against the cedar railing.

With concurrent timing, Stephanie and Reed appeared at her side. "Are you okay?" Reed asked, his glacial eyes overflowing with concern.

"I- I'm fine." Ava felt a surge of heat in her cheeks. "I just feel a bit dizzy..."

"Ava, I think you should take it easy. Why don't you sit back down?" Stephanie's palm made vigorous circles over her back.

"I'm fine. My blood sugar is probably just low." Ava twisted free from their supportive embrace. "I'd really like to take a shower."

Reed let out a loud sigh. "I know you well enough not to argue. But can we compromise? How 'bout a bath instead?" He reached for her elbow. "That way, you're already sitting down, should you feel dizzy."

"No, Reed, that's just as dangerous!" Stephanie's fist rammed her hip. "She could pass out in the bath, too."

"I'm fine—really." Ava's hands flew out in front of her, willing them to stop.

Reed pulled her hand to his heart. "Ava—Mace will kill me if you slip and hurt yourself on my watch."

"Look," Stephanie said, flinging her long braid behind her back, "let me at least help you in and out of the bath."

"This is ridiculous!" *All I want to do is take a shower!* "I appreciate your concern, of course, but I'm quite capable of taking—"

"Ava, I love your independent spirit, but now is not the time!" Reed's elevated tone startled her. "I was so scared we might lose you yesterday. Please,"—her onscreen love interest stepped closer, his voice softening to a whisper—"let us help you. Or,"—his forehead puckered—"should I call for Redge? 'Cause I guarantee he'll say the same thing."

Ava didn't feel like being scolded by the retired SEAL. "Fine," she mumbled.

"Great—problem solved!" He ushered her through the open balcony door. "Okay, you enjoy a nice, hot soak, while I go ransack the kitchen," he said with a wink before wandering off.

"All right, my dear, you wait here while I draw up your bath." Reed's girlfriend traipsed into the bathroom, disappearing from her view.

Ava minced toward the ensuite. A quick peek inside the spacious space revealed Stephanie leaning over the whirlpool tub, adjusting the polished-nickel handles as water spurted from the faucet. With Stephanie's back to her, Ava took advantage of the moment and covertly grabbed her towel off the hook attached to the back of the door. Although an industry norm, she'd never gotten comfortable dressing and undressing in front of others—Mace excluded. She slid her pajamas from her frame and secured her long hair in a quick updo with the help of a large claw clip. Wrapping the white Egyptian cotton towel around her body, she locked it in place under her arms before meandering back into the bathroom.

Stephanie swiveled when the sound of her approaching footsteps debuted. "Ava—you were supposed to wait for me to help you!" Her eyes reinforced her scolding tone.

Ava chose not to engage. Instead, she eyed the cells of iridescent bubbles boiling across the surface of the tub, already three-fourths full. Her hands held tight to the dobby border of the towel draped around her.

Stephanie must have sensed her reluctance. "Oh, Ava, there's no need to be shy! I've seen all kinds of female bodies in the studio. And don't even get me started on my nursing assistant days!" Stephanie reached for her hand, then placed the other on Ava's elbow, and guided her closer to the tub. Ava lifted her legs, one at a time, and stepped into the roomy fiberglass enclosure. "I'll close my eyes if it makes you feel better," Stephanie continued, as her grip on Ava's arm held firm.

After a moment's hesitation, Ava tugged on the towel with her free hand, exposing her bare form to Stephanie's shielded eyes. She draped the cotton over the bench next to the tub, then immersed herself in the teetering-on-uncomfortably hot water, with Stephanie blindly assisting. Displaced water threatened to spill over—but provided ample coverage—given the exorbitant amount of bubbles that clouded the top, as Ava leaned her head back against the rim.

"There. All better." Stephanie opened her eyes with a smile. "How's the temp?"

"It's a bit hot, but I'll get used to it," Ava answered.

"Oh, goodness! Let me add a splash of cold water," Stephanie said, reaching for the handle marked with a blue dot.

"It's fine, Stephanie. Truly." Ava offered a gracious smile. "Thank you."

The model relocated Ava's fluffy towel from the bench to the hook on the back of the door. "You sure?" Ava offered a firm nod. "All right… can I get you anything?"

Ava didn't like the thought of being waited on, but appreciated the offer. While bath time often served as her refuge, she felt compelled to have her phone nearby. Especially since she was hoping to hear from Mace. *I hope he isn't being too hard on Kent. Scratch that. I hope Scotch isn't being too hard on Kent.* The guy seemed excessively eager to employ their tactical questioning.

"May I trouble you to bring me my phone?" Ava asked with a guilt-infused tone. "I believe I left it on the nightstand."

"No trouble at all!" Stephanie hurried out of view only to return a moment later carrying Ava's luminous pink device. "Hmm, looks like the battery is about dead. Let me grab your charger, too," she called out as she repeated the circuit.

I bet she made a really great nurse. "Thank you, Stephanie."

A moment later, Stephanie reappeared, dragging a long gray cord. She plugged one end into Ava's phone, the other into the outlet beside the beige quartz counter. "There." Stephanie swiveled to face Ava. "Can I get you—"

"How're my two favorite girls?" Reed's voice echoed through the cracked doorway.

"Reed, don't you dare come in here!" Stephanie ordered.

"I wouldn't dream of it!" His impish tone suggested he was indeed dreaming of it. "I come bearing news!"

Ava's curiosity piqued. "Oh?"

"First, Redge wanted me to tell you that he's going for a quick walk on the trails behind the property."

"Okay..." *Interesting timing.*

"Second," his bassy tone grew serious. "I don't know who's supposed to be on grocery duty, but they should be fired."

Cue the eyeroll. "Very funny."

"Oh, Reed!" Stephanie said with a sophomoric giggle.

"Anyway, I'm going to order some Chinese."

With a whisper of a sigh, Ava closed her eyes. *That sounds so much better than blackened pancakes.* She opened them to discover Reed poking his head around the edge of the door, a huge smile pasted to his face.

"Reed!" Hands planted on her hips, Stephanie imparted a none-too-pleased glare before plopping down on the bamboo bench near the large glass-enclosed shower.

Her co-star waved a dismissive hand. "Oh, calm down. Besides, it's not like I haven't seen Ava in the tub before. Remember *Lavender Love: More Lavender?*" he asked with a waggle of his brow.

"Except that I'm not in character!" Ava countered. She skimmed over her bubble-cloaked body, ensuring any noteworthy sections remained sufficiently veiled.

"*Any*who…I'll order your favorite, Ava, but,"—Reed's head oscillated toward Stephanie—"what can I get you?"

A flicker of irritation vanished from her brown eyes as quickly as it presented, making Ava wonder if she'd imagined it. "I'll take the orange chicken."

"Great!" Reed turned back toward Ava, delivered a wink, saying, "Enjoy the rest of your bath," before vanishing.

Following a concurrent shake of their heads, Ava and Stephanie broke out in a fit of laughter. Their glee soon abated, and silence ensued. Despite the audience and the muted, rhythmic tap of Stephanie's nails as she scrolled through her phone, Ava found the refuge she sought. With the water temperature now perfect, Ava closed her eyes and tried to shut out the worrisome threat that plagued her. Part of her wondered if, in fact, the champagne flute—from years of improper storage—held trace amounts of penicillium spores. *It's not that far-fetched.* But then the memory of her zipline accident and ransacked room overshadowed her optimism. Poking her lustrous painted toes from the water, Ava peeked through half-lidded eyes. Stephanie remained seated on the bamboo bench at the opposite end of the room, staring at her phone. Gravity took hold, and her eyes again shuttered. Besides the incident last fall, which her trio of titans eliminated, she just couldn't imagine anyone wanting to kill her. She'd always strived to treat anyone she encountered with kindness. Well… not so much Annie. That woman really tested the limits of her grace. No matter, she was now out of the country and, with any luck, out of their lives forever. *Unless she tried to contact Mace when he went back to London… Would he have the strength to resist her outreach?*

The disturbing thought stole her soothing, and her eyes jolted open. She lowered her chin to her chest, the warm water lapping against her lips. The shroud of iridescence began to dissipate, and portions of her body became visible. She reached for the body wash just as the sound of muffled footsteps emerged.

Reed's gorgeous, thick, soot-black hair again appeared around the side of the door.

"Reed!" Stephanie cried out a moment too late.

Ava wrapped an arm across her chest and palmed the precious spot between her thighs, splashing water over the rim of the tub. If Reed had seen anything prior to her lightning-fast response, his face didn't show it.

"Just wanted to let you lovely ladies know that *apparently* the Chinese place doesn't deliver!" Reed scoffed, as if that was the most outrageous thing he'd heard in all his life. "So, I have to run out and pick it up. I'll be back in a bit." After a swivel, he disappeared, and the pounding of his feet bolting down the steps faded.

Stephanie continued tapping away on her phone. "Ugh! I'm starving!"

"Me, too…" Ava mumbled, her stomach rumbling in agreement. She squeezed her eyes shut and tried to estimate how much longer she could stay in the bath. She decided on eight minutes before her phone came to life with a hushed rattle against the stone countertop.

Stephanie sprang from the bamboo bench. A few long strides later, she peeked at the screen of the vibrating device. "It's a call from someone named Victoria."

It had been weeks since Ava heard from her trusted agent. *Either she was simply calling to check in, or Pierre reached out to inform her of yesterday's incident. Or perhaps she had yet another opportunity to present.* Ava registered Stephanie's expectant stare and realized she hadn't issued a directive. "Victoria's my agent," she explained.

"Oh." Stephanie's honey-hued eyes remained glued to her.

Lifting her arm out of the warm water, Ava gave a gentle shake, providing a sufficient air-dry. "Mind handing it to me?"

"Of course!" Stephanie grabbed the still-charging device and pirouetted around with unnecessary haste, throwing herself off balance. The phone spilled from her hands—and plummeted towards the water.

With catlike reflexes and breath pinched, Ava rescued the diving device mere millimeters from submersion, avoiding yet another encounter with death.

An injured expression crossed Reed's girlfriend's face.

"Stephanie—really, you must be more careful!"

Chapter Fifty-Nine

He'd mastered the art of blending in with his environment—molding to its landscape, unnoticed by all but those with an acute sense of perception. Redge maneuvered soundlessly through the dense woods, approaching the narrow trail that led to the open expanse behind their cabin from the east. He kept a keen eye trained on the subject, alert for any signs that she sensed his presence. None were offered.

Veiled by the bountiful, leaf-filled branches, Redge halted two feet from the woman. She stood still, her eyes locked onto the back of their vacation rental. A red canvas jacket clung awkwardly to her average-sized frame, its sleeves swallowing her arms. Her short dark hair was cut longer in the front, sweeping across her forehead. Redge had seen the woman before but couldn't recall her name.

For a long moment, she just stared, as if seized by some unknown force. Redge half wondered if she had detected his presence, but was too afraid to move—much like a deer frozen in place by headlights. Then, with deliberate movements, she reached into the leather satchel that lounged against her hip.

Her head didn't even complete its turn before Redge's arms were upon her, one large hand covering her petite mouth, the other pinning her arm against her back. Two twists of her shoulders, a pathetic attempt to free herself from his strong grip, then her entire body went limp. Redge loosened his hold over her mouth to test her response—no scream— but he felt the stain of her tears sliding down his skin.

"What are you doing here?" Redge's deep voice whispered into her ear.

Her response came in the form of a sob, her body trembling in his arms. Redge spun her around, relinquishing his hold. He towered a good fifteen inches above her, and she craned her neck skyward to meet his stare. Tears streamed from her dark, riddled-with-fear eyes. She didn't strike him as the deviant type; then again, everyone in this industry fancied themselves a performer.

"What are you doing here?" he asked again, keeping his baritone voice soft.

"I-, um-," she stammered, her chin falling to the earth.

"What's in the bag?" Redge didn't wait for a response. He hooked his fingers over the edge of the single-button pouch and gave it a tug, exposing its contents. A bulky, black camera with a long lens monopolized the space. "How long have you been spying on Ms. Ellis?"

"Not long—I swear!" her voice quivered.

Redge clenched his long fingers around the camera and removed it from her bag. A few high-pitched beeps produced a series of close-up images of the balcony attached to Ava's suite. Save for a few pictures of Ava in her robe and one intimate embrace between the actress and Mace, the other shots featured only a vacant balcony with glimpses of the rocky gully thirty feet below.

"What were you planning to do with these?"

"Well,"—she shoved her dangling bangs behind her right ear—"uh…"

Redge's patience was wearing thin. "The truth—now."

"I've got a lead on a magazine that'll pay top dollar for any shots of her!" she cried.

Redge sized her up with a skeptical glance.

"It's true!" Her dark eyes pleaded for his credence. "She's frustratingly private—not like your typical actors these days who flaunt *everything*. And with her career taking off again, everyone wants a glimpse of her private life!"

Her name finally came back to him: *Jasmine*. "Invading someone's privacy is wrong—no matter how you justify it." Redge scrolled through the pictures, tapping the garbage can icon after each one.

Reed's stylist slammed her arms against her chest. "Oh, come on!"

"Did you download these yet?" No response beyond a sigh. "Did you?" Redge asked again, his drill-sergeant tone making her flinch. An insistent headshake ensued, and he passed the heavy camera back to her. "You'd want me to do the same if the tables were turned," he declared.

Jasmine's shoulders slumped. "I guess..."

Redge ran his hand over his smooth head. "Did you ever encounter anyone else when you were out here?"

Jasmine pursed her lips as she snapped her camera-laden satchel closed. "No... but there was a small SUV parked nearby one day."

"What color was it?"

"I dunno... I remember it being dark, though."

****

The red-stained cedar felt warm against her petite, bare feet. She propped her elbows over the railing, her searching eyes captivated by the green cascading backdrop. She could discern no sign of Redge but knew he wouldn't leave without having a good reason. Ava canvassed the mossy abyss, troubled by thoughts of what may have lured her favorite six-foot-seven titan away.

A *shoosh* of the screen behind her announced Stephanie's return.

"Ava!" The model called out—either failing or making no attempt to hide the irritation in her voice. "You were *supposed* to wait for me to help you!"

Offering a momentary sideways glance, Ava mumbled, "Sorry, but I was confident I could handle myself." *And I did just fine, thank you very much.* She returned her gaze to the horizon; branches laced with leaves waved back with the breeze in random spurts. Still no sign of Redge.

"Well, my dear, you certainly make for a trying patient!" Stephanie chuckled. She carried a mirrored tray in her arms and set it upon the glass-covered wooden table in the center of the Adirondack chairs.

Ava minced across the deck to join Reed's girlfriend, opting for the middle chair, after Stephanie plopped down in the angled wooden seat closest to the bedroom door. Her eyes skimmed the platter before them. A beautiful ceramic kettle adorned with delicate periwinkle flowers, steam billowing from its spout, rested in the center of the reflective tray. Beside it, two coordinating teacups sat upon their saucer counterparts. Below, an array of loose-leaf tea bags, a medium-sized lemon, and a serrated paring knife completed the picture-perfect presentation. "This looks beautiful, Stephanie." Ava cast an appreciative smile. "Thank you."

"Of course!" Stephanie slid her chair closer to the platter and sifted through the assortment of tea bags. "There's green, rooibos, earl grey, and hibiscus."

"Green, please." The breeze brought a chill her way, and Ava zipped her turquoise hoodie over her matching sports tank.

A glimmer of satisfaction shone in Stephanie's eyes. "I figured… that's why I brought the lemon."

"Let me help you," Ava said, reaching her long nails out towards the kettle.

With a gentle touch, Stephanie propped her hand against Ava's forearm, offering a nonverbal, *Stop*. "No, please let me. If you won't let me help you from the tub, you can at least let me help you with your tea."

"I really don't want you to feel like you have to wait on me, Stephanie." Ava leaned her head back against the chair.

"I know, but it's the least I can do. Besides, Reed promised your monstrous bodyguard slash lover we'd take care of you."

Ava crossed a lean leg over the other. "That may be, but there's a difference between helping me and waiting on me…"

Stephanie shrugged. "I suppose." Hand shaking with its weight, she lifted the kettle from the mirrored tray. She tipped the dainty flower-covered spout into both cups, filling them with steaming, clear liquid.

Ava again peeked out at the horizon. *Maybe Redge simply wanted to go for a run.* She slid her pendant back and forth across the gold chain that hung from her neck, her gaze falling to Stephanie as she prepared their tea.

Stephanie bobbed the tea bag in and out of the hot water, then let it sink to the bottom. Then, she reached for the yellow-hued fruit and serrated blade. Holding the lemon between her thumb and forefinger, she brought the blade to its rind and sliced into its flesh, sending traces of juice spraying north and south. She removed the wedge, gave it a squeeze, and dropped it into one teacup, then repeated the process. "Seriously, Ava," Stephanie's tone turned serious, "you should have let me help you from the tub."

Ava quelled her irritation as she veered out at the horizon. "Well, I obviously survived, so no harm done." *Honestly, what was her hang-up with me and the tub?*

"Perhaps," Stephanie said with a smile. "But I had your outfit picked out and everything."

Ava craned her neck toward Reed's girlfriend. "Excuse me?"

"Oh, yeah. I mean, I like the black leggings you're wearing and your sports tank, but I had a different shirt picked out."

Ava's stomach grumbled. *Where the hell was Reed?* "Which one?"

"I love that teal cardigan you have." Stephanie passed her a teacup, floating lemon and all.

"Thanks." She raised the cup to her lips, took a test sip, and worried her esophagus might never recover.

Stephanie leaned forward in her chair, elbows poised over her knees, her hands wrapped around the teacup. "I even had your bra and panties picked out."

"What?" Ava's eyes tightened; the upper half of her body instinctively pulled away from the model as she stared at her.

Stephanie set her cup on the glass-covered bistro table. "I thought the sage green polka dot thong would be cute, along with the matching push-up bra."

Chapter Sixty

Ava swallowed the lump in her throat. *There's only one way she would know about those garments*. She sat still, studying the model's face; its transformation shocking as an emerging evil shed its typical youthful expression. Her honey eyes glazed with molasses, and her pink lips stretched tight over her teeth—the canines becoming more pronounced.

Dread stemmed from every nerve in Ava's body as the realization sank in. "How long have you been planning to kill me?" she murmured.

Thin lips upturned at their corners. "Let's see… since Reed enjoyed your kissing scene in *Lavender Love: More Lavender* a little *too* much."

"Stephanie," Ava whispered. Her hands gripped the arms of the wooden chair so tight her skin blanched. "Reed loves you. There's no reason to be jeal—"

"Oh, please! I'm not *jealous* of you—I *loathe* you." Her expression remained ghastly as she continued, "You've been a dark cloud hanging over my head since we met—a constant reminder of how I don't measure up."

A fear crawled up Ava's spine as Stephanie's hatred grew palpable. Her mind raced while Stephanie continued to voice her abhorrence.

"…Even if I were to break up with Reed, I'll save the next girl from a world of pain…"

Ava inspected her surroundings for options. Could she survive a thirty-plus-foot fall? She did the other day, but only because she found a branch to cling to; the balcony led straight down into a rock-filled gully—there would be nothing to help break her fall. A narrow ledge of earth lay to the side of the cabin. If she could get there quickly enough, maybe she could jump and—with any luck—reach solid ground. But that was a big if. She was fast, with two fully functioning ankles anyway, but she knew her still-recovering joint would hinder her speed. Could she outrun Stephanie? Ava eyed the model's footwear—high-end athletic shoes. Ava wore only her bare feet. Still, the north side of the balcony lay only twenty or so feet away.

"…I wasn't even *invited* to the Mystery and Mayhem reception!…"

Fearing a sudden move would provoke Stephanie, Ava, with measured movements, rose from the chair, maintaining her terror-filled expression for two reasons: one, because it was genuine; two, because it was necessary to convey that her fear incapacitated her. Slowly, Ava backed herself against the cedar railing; the feel of the smooth wood against her palm grounded her. Stephanie would expect her to run toward the door—at least that seemed like a logical assumption. She wouldn't, however, expect her to dash toward the side of the railing twenty feet away. The unexpected action could buy her precious time.

"...of feeling like a second-rate citizen *every* second of *every* day." Stephanie followed suit, rising from her Adirondack chair. "Peace has escaped my mind since you came into my life. *Ava did this today! You should have seen Ava on set! The queen of the first take! She was incredible!*" Stephanie, in a pathetic attempt to mimic Reed's bassy voice, flopped her arms wildly like a toddler throwing a tantrum. "Oh, *please*. If I had a dime for every time I threw up in my mouth, I'd be as rich as your ex, Kent!"

Ava worried her opportunity might slip away as Stephanie inched closer. She set her sights on the side railing as she worked up the nerve to bolt. She lifted her foot, but it seemed to grow heavy, so very heavy—fear weighed her down like concrete. Stephanie inched closer, and the realization that the opportunity had passed by seeped in.

Dread again spiked throughout her body; tears threatening to burst at any second. If she could no longer outrun Stephanie, she had to figure out a way to dissuade her. She channeled every de-escalation strategy she could muster. "Stephanie, listen to me, please,"—a deluge of tears escaped her eyes—"I pose no threat to you! I'm planning to retire from acting, for crying out loud!" Her heart clenched in desperation. "You and Reed never have to see me again!"

Ava felt certain Stephanie's pupils contained hidden lasers; their pointed heat searing her from four feet away. "Till the screenwriting starts?" Stephanie's chin dropped to her clavicle. "Nope. I need you gone—permanently." Stephanie took another small step towards Ava, her eyes wild as she flung her thick braid over her shoulder. She angled left for two steps, then back to the right for three before repeating the horizontal circuit. "Six months we've been together! Six months,"—she threw her hands up— "and he still can't remember what my favorite Chinese dish is! Oh, but he *knows* yours. Wouldn't *dare* forget that!"

Ava's head throbbed as her blood pounded through her veins, dulling her sense of sound. "Then why ransack my room? Why bother trying to scare me into leaving for California?" Ava kept her tone as soft as possible.

Stephanie jammed her hands into her sweatshirt's kangaroo pocket. "I was hoping you'd simply leave after my first threat, but nooo,"—craze-filled eyes rounded their lids—"You had to stay and bring on more security." She continued with her pacing sidestep.

With her feet still cemented in place, Ava's knees grew wobbly. "But how did you know about my penicillin allergy?" her voice trembled.

A loud snicker sounded. "You can thank your gorgeous ex for that juicy tidbit! And the fact that the resort's joke of a medical center has, like, zero security."

Ava added nausea to her growing list of current ailments following Stephanie's admission. *How could I be so blinded by this woman?* "Stephanie, please," Ava pleaded through quivering lips, "I know you don't really want to hurt anyone. You couldn't live with that on your conscience!"

"Then the zipline! How the *fuck* did you manage to survive that?! That man of yours! I swear, he's like your guardian angel or something."

By the grace of God.

"Oh,"—reappearing hands clapped in front of her—"how my luck changed when Redge and Reed took off! Of course, you and your amazing reflexes had to foil my little electrocution attempt." Stephanie rendered a shake of her head, her pouty lips pursed. "That would have been *so* perfect."

Ava's grip tightened on the railing, as if the inanimate wood could somehow be convinced to help her.

"… So, either I dunk you back in the tub, or you have an unfortunate fall from the balcony." She crossed her arms over her chest and issued a menacing smile. "Which would you prefer?"

She stared into the expanding void of Stephanie's wrathful eyes, expecting another wave of paralyzing fear to roll over her. Instead, her knees felt steadier, her feet lighter.

"Stephanie—this is pure insanity! No one will believe either scenario!"

"Um, I don't know, I'm a pretty convincing… She thrust her nose in the air. "After all, you had no idea it was me behind all of this."

Ever so slowly, the fear abated from Ava's bones—at once replaced by a suppressed strength she didn't know she possessed. "So what? You off me—then hope to take over my roles with Homepoint?"

"Well, that only seems logical." Stephanie shrugged. "After all, Reed and I have great chemistry, too, you know."

"But what happens if they offer it to someone else? Are you going to make sure she has an"—Ava's fingers quoted the air—"accident, too?"

"Oh, please, they'll be desperate to fill your void, and Reed will advocate for me. She dispensed a conceited smile. "In case you haven't noticed—I'm a pretty amazing actress, too."

"Says the department-store model who can't seem to land an acting gig." Ava arched an eyebrow. "Even with Reed's connections."

A shock-filled gasp fled Stephanie's mouth. "You spoiled little bitch—how dare you!" In one seamless movement, Stephanie scooped the wooden handle of the knife from the platter—and lunged toward Ava.

Ava abandoned her thoughts to instinct. She raised her knee high, then chambered an explosive front kick to

Stephanie's midsection, her shin narrowly avoiding the knife's trajectory. Reed's girlfriend went flying backward, dropping to the deck with a loud *thunk*, the knife spilling from her hand.

A split-second decision had Ava sprinting toward the bedroom door instead of attempting the jump from the side railing; the pain in her right ankle numbed by the adrenaline spiking through her body. She leapt over Stephanie's horizontal body, her fingertips brushing against the handle of the screen door, before a fierce tug on her good ankle threw her off balance. She came down hard—all of her weight shifting to her injured joint. She remained upright for a moment before buckling at the knees, the door's handle slipping from her grasp.

The opportunity to catch her breath did not come. An excruciating pain radiated across her scalp as Stephanie yanked on her long hair, jerking her onto her back. Her head slammed against the cedar with a *thud*, and she squeezed her eyes shut momentarily before an unexpected weight over her torso triggered them back open. Ava stared into Stephanie's once-beautiful-brown-now-bulging eyes. With crushing force, the model cupped her hands around Ava's delicate neck.

Chapter Sixty-One

His phone continued to chime every thirty seconds from his chest pocket, alerting him to ongoing motion, as he ventured back toward the cabin. He'd checked it twice just to make sure it wasn't the front doorbell camera, but the activity came from the camera he'd mounted on the large oak tree next to the rear balcony. Redge had taken great care to conceal it amongst the wide, lobed leaves—its viewing angle wide enough to pick up anyone approaching from the back, which was his first priority; the balcony view—a bothersome byproduct—as the damn thing had been chiming all morning with the arrival of Ava's guests. He had to admit, it was nice to see Stephanie taking such good care of Ava... bringing her tea and keeping her company. Though he was surprised Reed hadn't joined them. It was obvious the guy was infatuated with Ava. Stephanie was a patient, confident woman, for sure. Initially, she'd rubbed him the wrong way—nothing he could put his finger on—but she seemed... superficial. Anyway, every once in a blue moon, he got it wrong, and he felt guilty for his lukewarm reception of her when Ava had first introduced them. With any luck, she'd become a great, loyal friend to Ava. After all, the actress could use it. She'd lost so many friends during the Hollywood fiasco a few years ago, and he knew it was difficult for her to trust anyone. He wished Angie could have accompanied him on this trip; she'd love it up here. Plus, he'd love for her and Ava to cultivate a friendship. Nonetheless, it granted him some much-needed space from her drama-laden sisters.

Another chime sounded at a predictable interval. *Kinda wish they'd go sit inside.* With a loud sigh, Redge slid his hand into the pocket hidden inside the chest of his fleece vest and extracted his military-grade phone. He swiped to unlock, then opened the app that controlled the cameras. He bypassed the live feed icon and went straight to the settings, tapping the *disable notifications* symbol. The action brought him to the main screen. *One more peek at the live feed because my gut is telling me to. Holy shit.* Then the former track-and-field state champion broke into a sprint.

****

Ava slammed her palm against the back of Stephanie's elbow, sending her toppling to her side like a table losing one of its legs. Ava took advantage of the momentum and drove her elbow hard into Stephanie's ribcage, eliciting a loud *oompf.* Ava rolled to the side, then sprang to her feet and aimed for the door. She kept her steps light as she maneuvered around Stephanie's body—whose hands were desperately patting the deck boards—fully anticipating another ankle tug.

Her anticipation was on point, but it wasn't a tug on her ankle that brought her to her knees—it was a stabbing pain in the side of her right thigh. A primal scream escaped her lips, her palms breaking her fall as she crashed down on all fours. Warm liquid trailed down the inside of her leggings as an unbearable pain invaded her body. For a moment, as a wave of dizziness washed over her, she feared she might pass out. Chest heaving, Ava stared at her reflection in the glass door—her expression steely—congruent with the emotion coursing through her.

In the reflective surface, a dark form took shape behind her. Stephanie, with one arm wrapped around her ribs, closed in. Ava waited for the opportune moment, then kicked her knife-free leg out sideways and, with as much force as she could muster—swept it back in a wide arc—colliding with Stephanie's ankles. Stephanie's legs swung out from under her, sending the model crashing to the deck with a resounding *thwomp*.

It took all of her strength, but Ava lifted herself onto her good ankle. She wrapped her trembling hand around the handle of the knife protruding from her right thigh, searching her mind for the best approach. *Am I supposed to leave it in? No, that's only for a gut or head piercing. At least, I think.* Fighting to keep her hand steady, with a calculated pace, Ava slid the knife from her flesh. The tip broke free, followed by a gush of blood, and Ava grew weak, her vision fading. She braced herself against the cedar siding and spied the blurry form of Sephanie lying flat against the deck, her hands clutching her head.

Blood began to pool at her feet, and she feared removing the knife had been a horrible mistake. A cold washed over her; her vision eclipsed, and she stumbled backward—right into a pair of dark, strong arms. The feel of Redge's solid chest against her back, his warm breath upon her cheek, brought her back to the light. He tore the ripped half of her leggings free, bunched it up, and pressed it hard against her thigh as she rested in his arms.

She'd never been so happy to see the retired SEAL. She clung to his arms, absorbing his strength. Tears flew down her cheeks as she stared into his beautiful sable eyes—her own casting her gratitude. Movement out of the corner of her eye lured her gaze. A wheezing Stephanie had propped herself up on her elbows, then slowly lifted herself upright; her hunched form landing several feet away.

Redge glared at the cunning model. "Jig's up, Stephanie."

Stephanie scoffed before a duplicitous smile broke across her lips. "Whatever do you *mean*? She attacked *me*!"

Redge shook his head, his expression phlegmatic. "You're not fooling anybody."

"Yeah," Ava panted. "You're *definitely* not that good of an actress."

Stephanie imparted a one-shouldered shrug. "It's your word against mine."

The throbbing pain in Ava's thigh intensified, causing her to wince. "What..."—she struggled to find her breath—"would be your angle?"

"You're in love with Reed. Always have been."

"Except that anyone who knows her knows she's crazy about Mace."

"She was just using Mace to try to make Reed jealous." Stephanie shifted her look to Ava. "*You* attacked *me*—and I simply fought back."

Redge bobbed his head. "That's plausible. Aside from the fact that all of this was recorded."

Ava's mouth fell open as she studied Redge, trying to discern whether he spoke the truth or employed a brilliant ruse.

The color drained from Stephanie's face. "You're lying," she mumbled, uncertainty creeping into her tone.

Redge jerked his head toward the large oak tree behind them. "See for yourself."

Ava's gaze followed Stephanie as the model hobbled over to the tree for a closer look. Sure enough, Ava could make out a distinct, telling red light.

A panicked expression seized Stephanie's face; her dilated eyes darted between Redge and the railing.

"There's only one way outta here—and that's through me," Redge stated.

A disconcerting stillness descended as Stephanie stood motionless before them. Defeat dusted her downcast expression. Then, she rendered a slight, fleeting smile before wrapping her arms around herself. Her stare shifted to the deck railing. Canting her head toward Ava, she murmured, "You're not worth going to prison for."

"Stephanie?" Ava asked, before releasing a gasp as Redge put more pressure on her thigh.

Tears navigated her cheeks as she gripped the railing. "Tell Reed I really do love him."

"Stephanie, no! Don't do this!" Ava pleaded, freeing herself from Redge's arms.

Redge jumped up and leapt across the deck—stretching his long arms out to reach her. He was a second too late.

A newfound pain swept through Ava's body as a gut-wrenching *thunk* sounded a few moments later.

Chapter Sixty-Two

Redge and Scotch bolted through the doors of the *Medical Centre*, clearing the way for Mace. Blood seeped through the makeshift tourniquet as her legs dangled over one strong arm, her neck over the other. Her cheek rubbed against the soft-spun cotton of his fitted shirt; the thunderous pounding of his heart mixed with his musky scent lulled her.

Mace paused in the center of the lobby, his head oscillating right to left. Ava buried her shivering body further into his chest, desperate for every ounce of his thermal touch. Should death come for her at this very moment—in the arms of her warrior—she didn't fear its sting. The sound of running footsteps coming closer, then the handsome face of Dr. Levasque appeared in her field of vision.

"Ms. Ellis," Dr. Levasque started, his smooth voice serious, "I strongly suggest you consider another career."

"Duly noted, doctor," Ava whispered, managing a slight smile.

A minute later, she found herself lowered into the very same hospital bed she had lain upon less than twenty-four hours ago. Dr. Levasque and his assistant, after corralling Mace to the corner, went straight to work. The light centered above drew her gaze, its brightness ebbing and flowing as Ava combated spells of unconsciousness.

The authoritative sound of Dr. Levasque's voice echoed in her mind's dream-like state. The words *possible blood transfusion* seeped in before she succumbed to sleep. There was no way for her to tell how much time had passed before she awakened to the sound of his voice once again; her eyelids too heavy to lift. "Given the depth," he announced, whether for her benefit, or his assistant's, she wasn't sure, "I'm afraid this will require stitches." She felt the poke of a needle as it buried into her thigh, then nothing but a few slight tugs.

An unintended groan escaped her lips as her eyes flitted. "Don't worry, my dear." She heard Dr. Levasque's muffled voice. "I took care to ensure the scar would be minimal."

Ava drew in a deep breath before finding the strength to open her eyes—discovering Mace again confined to the corner. A split second later, he emerged beside her.

Dr. Levasque lifted her hand and gave it a big squeeze. "Two things, my dear. One, you have the most fascinating luck of anyone I've ever known." He issued a beautiful smile, and Ava couldn't resist responding with her own. "Two, that boyfriend of yours,"—he kept his eyes locked onto her as he gestured to the six-foot-five-inch titan standing next to her—"has a terrible time following directions." Following another gentle squeeze, he cast a playful wink and whispered, "I'll let you two have a minute."

Mace clasped his rugged hand over hers, then pressed it against his heart as he crouched down beside the bed. Ava studied his handsome face, worn from the trauma of the day, as he closed his damp eyes and allowed his beating heart to communicate on his behalf. For a long moment, Ava simply cherished the profound message it conveyed.

Mace's lids lifted at a snail's pace, and tears sailed down his stubbled cheek. "There's something I have to get off my chest—" he whispered.

Ava felt her forehead pucker. "Oh?"

Mace drew in a sharp breath. "I—"

The door slammed open with a loud *bang,* and Reed burst into the room, sobbing. "Oh, Ava!" He ran to her side and fell to his knees, his torso collapsing over hers.

Mace shoveled his fingers through his hair, his eyes growing wide. Ava patted the top of Reed's shiny, jet-black hair. "I'm okay," she murmured.

"If only I hadn't left to pick up lunch!" he cried. "This would never have happened!"

"Stephanie would have found another way," Mace assured. "No doubt with a worse outcome."

Ava continued to pet his head in motherly fashion. "Maybe your leaving was a blessing in disguise."

Reed lifted his chin, revealing bloodshot eyes. "I had no idea, Ava, I swear!"

Mace flashed a look of doubt as he crossed his arms over his chest, his biceps bulging with the motion.

"Reed, it's okay, none of us did," Ava murmured.

"I just can't believe that she would try to do something like this! I'm devastated on so many levels!"

Mace stood with a jolt. "I'll give you two some space." He marched out of the room, looking none too pleased.

Reed at last straightened his back but remained on his knees. "Here's what's ironic,"—Reed wiped his misty silvery-blue-now-tinted red eyes with his sleeve—"I was planning on breaking up with her after this film."

"What?"

"Yeah, I even thought about doing it before coming to Canada, but she so badly wanted to join me on this trip." His chin fell to his chest. "Now, I'm afraid I know why."

A numbness pervaded her body. "Reed—weren't there signs of her… feelings… beforehand?"

"Nothing I noted… I know, I feel like a complete failure!" His tears were back in full force. "Like I should've somehow known. She just wasn't the biggest priority in my life." His shoulders rolled forward as he continued, "I didn't pay as much attention to her as she deserved… But she never really bonded with my kiddos—you know how important that is to me…" Reed's guilt-ridden eyes searched hers in need of affirmation.

"I know," Ava whispered. She offered a reassuring smile despite the sick feeling growing in the pit of her stomach. The thought of such jealousy brewing in Stephanie over the past few months devastated her. She wondered how many others on the sidelines of her life might harbor a similar sentiment. Given Stephanie's actions, Ava craved justice, but the thought of her receiving judgment so soon filled her with anguish. The hopeless expression on the model's face before she leapt over the side of the balcony, coupled with the sickening thud moments later, would haunt her for the rest of her days.

"Reed, I think—"

"I just want to find what you have with Mace, ya know?" *Yeah, I do know.*

"A woman who will have my back and rescue me when I need to be saved."

Ava's brows shot up, just as the door burst open with a slam yet again.

"Oh, my precious child!" Pierre darted into her room, gasping for air. He paused beside her bed and captured her hand, planting several kisses along the top.

"I'm okay, Pierre, really."

"Reed—I'm personally going to vet any and all of your future girlfriends!" The director raised a fist in the air. "Now, my sweet darling, what do you need? Anything? How long do you think you need to fully recover?"

"I'm not sure… I was hoping to talk with Dr. Levasque… maybe a few days?" Ava offered, her bottom lip finding its way into her mouth.

"*Oui, oui*, of course." As he patted her hand, his head, with turtle speed, angled up at a forty-five-degree projection, his eyes lost in thought. "Unless…"

Ava glanced at Reed—offered a nonverbal, *Here we go again*, to which Reed stifled a laugh.

"Picture this!" The director shouted, drawing his arms out wide. "Instead of an ambulance scene—which is so overdone these days—Reed—disguised as a doctor—sneaks into your hospital room and declares his undying love for you!"

"That's the big end scene?"

"It's *parfait*! We can film it right now! Ava—despite your recent stabbing, you look incredible!"

"Pierre, I'm not sure that's the best—"

"It'll be perfect!" The director brought his fingertips to his lips and made a loud smooch sound. "We'll need one, maybe two hours tops!"

Ava met Reed's stare; the bright gleam in his eye told her all she needed to know. With a smile, she rendered a gentle shake of her head. *Only in show business.*

Chapter Sixty-Three

With the words, "That's a wrap!" still echoing in her ear, Ava rested her head against the cruelly thin hospital pillow. She missed her down pillows at home. She missed *everything* at home. She closed her eyes, in desperate need of a moment's silence. But the action manifested Stephanie's injured face, and her eyes opened with a jolt.

She observed Mace as he wandered into the room. He pried the small vegan armchair from the corner and pushed it next to her bed with ease, then plopped down in it, the cushion releasing a *whoosh* under his weight.

He brushed the hair from her cheeks; the feel of his strong hand against her face left her entire body yearning for his touch. Tears welled in her eyes as she gazed into the steel-blue of his; the fine lines stemming from the corners became more beautiful to her with each day.

He planted a tender kiss on her forehead. "Doc said you might be able to go home tonight."

"Oh, Mason!" A shake of her head sent the welling tears gushing down her cheeks. "I can't step foot in that cabin again after what happened!"

He lifted her hand to his lips. "Don't worry, it's already been taken care of."

She made no attempt to conceal her inquisitive expression while, following a prefacing squeak, the door swung open a moment before it slammed against the adjacent wall.

Scotch strode into the room wearing a broad smile. "Ava, my bonnie lass, just when I think I'm destined for another boring assignment, no offense,"—he inclined his head; an impish gleam in his eye—"you go ahead and deliver. Big time."

Redge followed behind, his customary impassive expression soft. Eyes coated with silent praise, Ava cast her gaze in the retired SEAL's direction. His beautiful, sable eyes met her stare and reflected a glimmer of appreciation.

Ava traced the outline of gauze adhered to her thigh, then her fingertips traveled to her neck, where, with a delicate touch, she patted the tiny scab that covered her carotid artery. Had it not been for the three men standing before her, she wouldn't even be alive. Her trio of titans weren't simply gorgeous men with muscle for days, and a unique, honed-to-a-point skillset that suited her needs perfectly—they were her family.

Another swing of the door had Mace tossing a glare that said, *I'm ready to tear that damn thing off the hinges*. Dr. Levasque appeared, followed by a beautiful dark-haired woman wearing a sleek, form-fitting pencil skirt and collared blouse. Ava caught Scotch's gaze drop to the floor as they approached the center of the room.

"Ms. Ellis," Dr. Levasque cocked his head toward the woman beside him. "My sister and I offer our sincerest sympathies for the unfortunate incidents you experienced while staying at our resort."

"None of what happened is a reflection of your beautiful resort," Ava whispered, desperate to put their minds at ease. *I'm not planning to sue, if that's what you're thinking.*

"Regardless," Julietta placed a hand on Ava's sheet-covered shin. "We'd like to offer you and your guests our Presidential Suite for the remainder of your stay."

With an incline of her head, Ava offered a gracious smile. "That's very kind of you."

"I trust it has a mini bar?"

Julietta whirled around to face the Scotsman as he stroked his unruly beard into a point.

"*Oui*. And there's nothing *mini* about it."

Scotch fixed his jade eyes, sans their usual mischievous gleam, onto her. "Thanks."

"*Non, Monsieur* Scotchfeld… Thank *you*."

With that, she pivoted and sauntered out of the cozy room, the *click-clack* of her stilettos fading into the distance.

The doctor imparted a subtle shake of his head. "Anyway, we'll have our bellhops gather all of your belongings, so you won't have to set foot on the property. I imagine it would be… difficult for you to see…"

Mace nodded. "Much appreciated."

"I'd like to monitor you for a bit longer," the doctor continued. "Then, provided your progress continues, I'll send you on your way with an antibiotic."

Mace's eyes popped out of his head. "No penicill—"

"Don't worry," Dr. Levasque put up his hands. With a wink at Ava, he did an about-face and marched from the room.

Mace expelled the air from his lungs. A light chuckle escaped Ava's lips as an expression of relief appeared on his handsome face. Then, her tone turned serious as she set her sights on Redge and Scotch. "How'd it go with the police?" she whispered.

"Just fine," Redge said.

Ava studied his expression for signs he may be downplaying any concern—found none. "Really?"

Redge nodded. "They'll need you to give an official statement, of course, but they have everything they need to officially rule it a suicide."

"Thanks to our brilliant videographer," Scotch grinned, patting Redge between his wide shoulder blades.

"Dude, you brought me on for extra security. The fact that you thought I'd only install one camera is insulting. Plus,"—Redge folded his massive arms across his chest, projecting a sideways glare at Scotch—"it's time you pay up."

"The bloody hell it is," Scotch grumbled.

With a nonchalant shrug, Mace eyed his Scottish friend. "A deal's a deal, mate,"

"Fine, whatev." Scotch glared at Redge, then mumbled, "A SEAL's way saves the day," under his breath.

Ava palmed her mouth to conceal her laugh.

Redge cupped his hand behind his ear. "What's that? I couldn't quite hear you?"

"Mate, don't push it," Scotch yelled, shoving a palm into Redge's bicep.

Ava gripped Mace's hand tighter, her eyes skimming over her trio. "Ahem." Three sets of beautiful, devoted eyes turned to her. "Gentlemen," Ava fought back tears, "I once again find myself forever in your debt."

"From what I saw on camera, sweet lass, you handled yourself just fine," Scotch said, bobbing his head.

"Yeah, Ava, remind me never to piss you off," Redge added.

Mace nuzzled her cheek, then whispered, "I had no idea my girlfriend was such a badass," into her ear.

Ava reached her hands out to Scotch and Redge, summoning them to her bedside. Overcome with gratitude, she clasped their large hands in hers and whispered, "I love the three of you—so very much."

Scotch kissed her left hand. Redge kissed her right hand. Mace kissed her forehead. Then—in unison—her trio of titans replied, "We love you, too."

Chapter Sixty-Four

ONE MONTH LATER

Late morning light trickled in from the crack between the venetian blind and the window frame, casting a spade of illumination over the soapstone counter. Mace crept across the vinyl floor, as if the sound of his heavy boots might disrupt the structure's quiescence. He reached the threshold of the living room and paused, scanning the environment to ensure everything remained the way in which it had been left. Although all appeared well, a strange feeling came over him. This condo had been his home for the past three years, but it no longer felt like home. Perhaps it never did.

He traversed the long, narrow hall between the kitchen and his bedroom and was greeted by the gloomy darkness of the shade-drawn room. He slid the bifold closet doors wide, then pushed the mostly black—offset with an occasional gray—garments that hung from the rod to one side, exposing the elongated safe he'd installed upon purchasing the unit. Following a series of rapid *ticks*, the metal door swung open. After a quick inventory, he extracted a crimson envelope—along with a small, square velvet box.

He slid the crimson envelope into the front pocket of his tactical bag before lifting the hinged lid of the velour box. A wave of emotion almost capsized him. *It was good enough once; I hope it's good enough now.* He closed his eyes and took a deep, calming breath, allowing the stillness of his environment to wash over him. After a long moment, he glanced at his titanium diver watch. *She should be here any minute.*

He secured the small box inside his tactical bag before retreating through his condo. Outside, he leaned against the wrought iron railing that lined the concrete steps and watched as a compact sedan approached. *Right on time.* She was always right on time; it had been one of the reasons he'd fallen in love with her.

The car rolled to a stop with an ear-piercing squeal, and a moment later, a woman stepped from the passenger seat. She strolled towards Mace, her dark, shoulder-length locks swaying with the movement. Other than a few new creases along her forehead and on either side of her lips, she looked just as he remembered.

"You cut your hair."

"You didn't." She climbed the steps and stood in front of him.

Mace's thin lips spread wide for a fleeting moment. "That's fair."

She bestowed a pleasant smile… a hint of warmth glimmered in her bronze eyes. "You look good."

"So do you," Mace mumbled.

She reached into her apricot satchel, removed a folded document, and passed it to him. "I trust you don't intend to rip this one in two?"

Mace felt his cheeks grow warm. "No," he said with a shake of his head.

"Good." She placed a hand over his, gave it a light squeeze. "And I'm glad to hear you've found happiness. This actress of yours sounds pretty incredible."

Mace's brows snapped together. "How—?"

"Mrs. Scotchfeld can't stop talking about her. Tells *everyone*." She flashed a dimpled smile. "The whole town knows."

Mace couldn't help but laugh. "Of course she does." *And that's where Scotch gets it.* "Thanks for bringing this by. It saves me a huge headache."

Shay shrugged. "No problem." She turned and started down the steps towards the car. With a glance over her shoulder, she paused as she called out, "I wish you well, Mace."

He offered a nod. "You, too." Then, following a wave to the man who rested in the driver's seat, he locked his condo and marched over to his SUV.

****

"*Every* Thursday?" Ava recoiled against the passenger door, her eyes frozen wide.

Mace bobbed his head. "Yep." A roguish gleam speckled his gorgeous eyes as he glanced sideways at her.

"I mean—I recall your mentioning it a few times, but didn't realize it was *every* week." Ava tucked a stray lock of her golden hair behind her ear.

"Well, when you only have five minutes to chat, one has to be concise." A waggish grin debuted.

"Touche… Still, it just seems like a lot of time to spend with my mom. I hope you didn't feel obligated." Ava smoothed the hem of her lavender bell-sleeves over her wrists. The flowing fabric was cut a tad long, just the way she preferred.

"Are you kidding? I adore your mum—she made for a wonderful lunch date. Plus…" his voice dropped to a whisper.

Ava arched an inquisitive eyebrow. "Yes?"

"It made me feel connected to you." He traded her hand for a place on her thigh.

Ava leaned over the center console of his SUV and planted a tender kiss on his cheek. "I'm glad you two have grown so close."

Mace slowed to a stop as he approached his turn. Locking his gaze onto her, he said, "I figured if I couldn't be with the most beautiful woman in the world,"—he brushed his lips across hers—"I'd have to settle for the most beautiful woman in England."

Ava let out a light laugh as she shifted back into her seat. "Oh, that's smooth."

"Not trying to be smooth—just honest." Mace gave a waggle of his brow before engaging the accelerator; the older model SUV was sluggish to respond. Despite its age, the vehicle was immaculately maintained, which came as no surprise to her. He was the kind of man who took great care of everything that belonged to him.

"Sorry, it's not exactly the twelve-cylinder engine you're used to…"

"I didn't always drive a V12, you know."

Mace tilted his head in her direction, his forehead puckering. "Really?"

"No—my first car was only a four-cylinder."

"Ah." He bobbed his head. "Supercharged?"

"No." Ava flashed a coquettish smile. "Turbo."

"Of course it was…" Another squeeze of her thigh had her hoping that wherever it was they were going, a king-size bed awaited them. With the arrival of Grayson's in-laws, guest space at the Embassy property had become sparse, and Ava found herself sharing her mother's quarters, while Mace bunked with Brody while his wife was out of town. The time with her mother, although cherished, didn't exactly offer opportunities to spend her nights wrapped in his arms, and every ounce of her body coveted his therapeutic touch.

When Mace suggested they plan a weekend holiday, she was thrilled.

A series of curves lined their path, and Mace maneuvered around them expertly, despite one hand being glued to her toned thigh. She laced her bell-sleeved fingers over his as they rested upon her, just to the side of the two-inch-long scar that now marred her right thigh. She pulled the lever attached to the side of her seat and reclined. Fatigue seemed to come and go ever since leaving Canada, and she found herself feeling particularly tired this afternoon. She basked in the filtered sunlight that trickled through the sunroof and windows as the SUV traveled at a smooth, steady pace. Soon, her eyelids grew heavy, and thoughts of the past few weeks occupied her mind.

A silhouette took shape behind her closed eyes—a woman with long, dark hair and ivory skin. Weeks prior, Mace confided that he had called his ex-wife instead of the Embassy the morning following her zipline accident. His admission had made her feel sick.

"I don't understand—why would you feel like you needed to lie to me?" she'd asked.

His beautiful, but guilt-ridden eyes had searched hers. "I justified it by telling myself it fell within the parameters of a white lie."

"How could sneaking a call to your ex *possibly* be considered a white lie?" She had struggled to keep her tone even. Mace had kissed her forehead—reassured her that he had a good reason—and promised to tell her, "Soon enough."

Although she believed him, it gnawed at her from time to time. Lounging in the very seat his ex-wife once did happened to be one of those occasions. She canted her neck to study his face as they drove along in silence. His eyes held a particularly joyful, almost childlike gleam today, which simultaneously entertained and intrigued her; however, thoughts of his ex-wife threatened to temper her buoyant mood.

Ava removed her hand from his, choosing instead to squeeze the chest portion of her seatbelt—it offered little comfort. "Do you miss her?" she blurted, her voice smooth and hushed.

Mace cast a sideways glance, his face scrunched up, as he navigated the windy, traffic-free path. "Huh?"

"Your ex," Ava maintained her whisper. "Is that why you called her from the cabin that morning?"

Mace jerked his head from left to right. "No—not at all."

Relief coursed through her veins. She pressed her head against the seat, then clasped her hands together in her lap.

With a yank of the wheel, Mace whipped his SUV onto the shoulder, slowed to a stop, then threw it in park—the vehicle lurching with the command. Gripping the leather steering wheel at the twelve o'clock position, he rested his forehead against his hands before craning his neck toward her. His steel-blue eyes held an undeniable authenticity. "I needed a legal document from her. That's the only reason I reached out."

"For your Visa?"

With the slightest of movements, the corners of his lips upturned. "Yeah, something like that."

Chapter Sixty-Five

Clouds of cotton hung over the horizon, mingling with the green peaks of deciduous trees that outlined the captivating navy-hued inland lake. Hand in hand, Ava and Mace strolled along the lush, lined stone path that led toward their private room.

"This place is beautiful," Ava murmured. Her eyes skated across the expansive lake, then noted the charming, individual cottages in the distance that lay along the shoreline.

Mace's pace slowed, and he pulled her to him, his solid chest pressing against her petite form. He cupped her chin in his hands. "I was hoping you'd like it."

Ava lifted herself on the tips of her beige high heels. "I do—very much." She planted a tender kiss on his clean-shaven cheek; his musky scent excited her senses. "And I'm not just referring to the resort," she said with a repetitive arch of her brow.

With an irresistible grin, Mace locked his hands at the small of her back and pulled her tighter, before grazing her lips with his. "Let's get settled." After passing by several small, identical white bungalows, Mace paused in front of the remaining unit—the number seven carved into a waist-high post at the end of the path. Surrounded by lush perennials, the charming structure appeared comparable in size to the others, but featured a five-lite rounded bow window across the front, setting it apart from the other units. Removing the metal key from the pocket of his cargo shorts, Mace inserted it into the lock. Following a flick of his wrist, the door swung inward.

Received by the curved wall of the white grille-trimmed window, which afforded a spectacular view of Lake Windermere, the cozy room—much to Ava's relief—offered a king-size bed, wrapped in crisp white linen. Two smoky-gray fabric accent chairs rested opposite the bed, with a round glass table between them, which bestowed a fresh arrangement of white orchids, along with a bottle of champagne.

Ava flashed a beautiful smile as she took in the details of the light, breezy space. "This is lovely," she proclaimed as she smoothed the bottom half of her minidress before stepping out of her heels.

An impassive expression crossed Mace's face as he inspected the space, seemingly assessing its worth. "You sure this is okay?"

Ava moved in close and, with a stroke of his jawline, directed his head toward the vast window. "Of course—just look at that view."

He enveloped her in his arms; rapture-filled eyes lingered over the crease of her breasts as they peeked from the hem of her décolletage before ascending to her eyes. "I'm much more interested in *this* view."

Her whole body ached with yearning as she anchored her lips to his, teasing the tip of his tongue with hers. She ran her hands over his fitted shirt—cherishing the rock-hard flesh beneath—before landing at the row of buttons that obstructed her path. With a gentle nudge, she encouraged him to retreat to the bed, her fingers feverishly working toward the button at his waist.

"No," Mace mumbled, parting from her lips.

Ava recoiled, "No?"

Mace threaded a hand through his hair, a sigh fleeing his lips. "I just mean,"—a scarlet hue splashed across his cheeks—"not right now."

Ava opened her mouth to speak, but confusion stole her words, and nothing came out. She couldn't recall a time when a man had ever shunned her affection.

Mace took her hands in his and kissed the top of both. "I just really want to show you the grounds before sunset."

Ava felt her brow furrow. "You do realize we have all day tomorrow?"

"Yeah, but,"—his broad shoulders shrugged—"the weather might not be as nice."

Ava shook off her shock. "All right…" she murmured before marching toward the door and slipping back into her high-heel mules. *He must really love this lake.*

Chapter Sixty-Six

B rilliant!" Mace procured his black tactical bag from the pile of luggage the porter delivered while they checked in. A minute later, again hand in hand, they traversed the slate stone path that curved along the beautiful lakeshore. They encountered several other couples as they roamed the grounds. Most offered a polite gesture; others stared, eyes gleaming with adoration. Two months ago, that would have made his blood pressure spike, but he seemed to be acclimating to her admiring leers. Not that he could blame them; her beauty was transcendent. And today proved to be no exception. She wore a lavender dress that hugged her voluptuous frame, with sheer bell sleeves that flowed to her fingertips. Loose, golden curls heaped high—his favorite style—and rosebud lips—devoid of their usual sparkle because he suspected he now wore the shade after she bombarded him with kisses moments ago—made at least two of his organs swell.

He scanned the horizon for his target; found it positioned about two hundred meters ahead: an elegant white gazebo perched on a mound overlooking the picturesque lake. Spears of pink and purple pierced the gilded sky as sunset drew near, prompting Mace to increase his stride. His rushed pace was hindered by those adorable but impractical patent beige heels. He glanced at his titanium diver as he wrapped an arm around her waist.

"I guess I should've brought my running shoes…" Ava mumbled as he peeked at his watch a second time.

He cast a sheepish grin. "Sorry." He wiped the sweat from his hands against his cargo shorts, then clasped her delicate fingers, slowing his pace to match her comfort. His heart thundered inside his chest. *Why am I so bloody nervous? I wasn't this nervous with Shay.* Years ago, he had *wanted* to be with Shay. But now, he *needed* to be with Ava; his very subsistence depended on it. And the thought of rejection was crippling to him.

Shrouds of green vines, pink roses playing peek-a-boo, climbed an indiscriminate route across the posts of the gazebo. The stone path continued along the lakeshore, leaving anyone interested in the octagonal structure to walk along the well-manicured grass. A few steps in, Ava's heels sank into the soft soil, slowing their progress further.

She looked at him with a stunning smile, whispered, "Sorry," then started to slip her heels from her petite feet.

"It's okay—I've got you," Mace said as he swooped her into his arms. With no heels to impede his movement, they reached the gazebo in no time. Reluctant to release her from his grasp—her tender kisses along his neckline didn't help—he held her for a moment in the center of the wooden structure, before setting her down. She twirled toward the lake and released a whimper of appreciation as his hands locked onto her hips from behind. She rested her head against his chest, her curls tickling his chin; their fresh scent pleasing his nostrils. His pounding heart transitioned to its resting rate. She was nothing short of divine, and her pacifying effect evaded his comprehension.

Angled benches lined the inside perimeter of the gazebo; their wood painted to seamlessly coordinate with the covered structure. Wanting to preserve as much of the tranquil view as possible, Mace gestured towards the bench directly opposite the lake. His heart resumed racing speed as he sat down beside Ava. The hem of her lavender dress came to a rest several inches above her knees, exposing lustrous thighs. Temptation proved too much, and he slid his hand over her soft skin, his fingers following their natural curve.

His eyes ascended to discover hers locked onto him. She cupped his jaw and lifted her lips to his, brushing across their surface before imparting a series of tender kisses. This woman fueled his soul.

"Ava," Mace whispered, following her loving pecks. "There's something I want to show you." He reached into his tactical bag, unzipped an inside pocket, and extracted a thin crimson envelope. Sapphire eyes filled with curiosity as Ava studied his movements. He lifted the top flap and gingerly removed a glossy, four-by-six-inch print. A mixture of admiration and sadness brewed in her expression as recognition set in. The photo depicted a middle-aged man who bore a striking resemblance to Mace, with piercing blue eyes and a broad chest. Wrapped in his arms was a beautiful woman with silvery eyes and blonde hair that fell in waves past her shoulder. Beaming smiles conveyed a rare, profound affection as they rested on a white bench, vines of green and pink climbing the post behind them.

A long, raspberry-colored nail traced the edge of the photo. "Of all the pictures you've ever shown me of your parents, this is by far my favorite," Ava whispered.

"This picture," Mace cleared his throat, "was taken twenty years ago today—in this very spot." Ava flashed an inquisitive expression as he turned the photo over. The label on the back read: *Nora and Murphy—20th wedding anniversary. Lake Windermere.*

"Now I understand why you were in such a hurry to show me this place." Ava planted a kiss on his cheek. "I'm so sorry that they're not here to celebrate."

"Oh, they're celebrating somewhere, I suppose."

Ava continued to study the beautiful print. "I really wish I could have met them."

"Yeah, me, too." Mace offered a fleeting smile. "They would've adored you."

"And likewise, I'm certain." Ava squeezed his hand and gazed into his eyes. "I have no doubt they would be very proud of the man they raised."

Mace brought a hand to his jaw and applied slow, gentle strokes; the movement allowed him to choke back his emotions. He cleared his throat a second time, then again reached into the crimson envelope to remove the remaining print. Placing it in Ava's lap, he followed up by pulling her close.

"Oh my gosh..." Her words came out with a breathy whisper.

Mace's eyes hovered over her as she stared, her jaw slack, at the picture of Susan and Charles Ellis embraced by each other's loving arms, as they rested on a white bench—a curtain of green and pink behind them. With a turn of her wrist, she rotated the picture to reveal: *Susan and Charles— Lake Windermere.* It was dated fifteen years ago.

Mace made no effort to curb his wide grin. "They sat upon this very bench."

Ava's head shook in disbelief. "I vaguely recall this photo... This had to be from their first trip to England..."

"Second, actually." He brushed a wisp of gold from her shoulder. "According to your mum, anyway."

Semi-cloaked lavender shoulders slumped, coinciding with a hushed, humbled sigh. "I can't believe our parents sat in this very same spot."

"Either could I."

"What else did you discover during your Thursday lunch *dates?*"

A roguish gleam penetrated his eyes. "I'm sworn to secrecy." Ava rendered a playful elbow nudge to his obliques. "Okay, okay…" *Let's see… you're without a doubt the woman of my dreams, and I'm one hundred percent certain my heart will wither and die without you by my side.*

Swallowing the lump in his throat, Mace reached into his tactical bag once again and removed the small velour box. "I discovered the courage to do this." He slid off the bench and positioned himself on one knee in front of her. He clasped his trembling hands over hers, then raised them to his chest. "Ava, my sweet angel." He struggled to keep his voice steady. "You captured my heart the second you appeared in the kitchen of your Connecticut house." He fixed his gaze upon her. "What we've created is sacred to me—and I promise to fight every day to protect it." Tears welled in his eyes as he watched Ava's stream down her porcelain cheeks. He took a deep, calming breath, then lifted the lid of the hinged box. "Ava Rosemary Ellis, will you please be my wife?"

No words traveled to his ears, only the sound of joyful whimpers—and the sight of her angelic, albeit tear-stained, face as her head bounced up and down with fervor.

Chapter Sixty-Seven

Gilded rays of morning sun, signaling the promise of a new day, permeated the glass of the bow window. Ava stifled a yawn, then took a moment to appreciate the slumbering, colossal presence that cradled her. In his arms, she felt weightless, unhindered by the threats of the world, as if she could ride out any storm on the horizon.

Mother Nature's light reflected off the diamond attached to her favorite finger—casting a dazzling, dancing circle on the ceiling—as she stretched it out at arm's length. Her previous one, a princess cut and *several* carats large, had garnered impressed and envious stares alike, much to Kent's satisfaction. Despite its decadent beauty, the ring had never *felt* right; it remained a piece of jewelry, an accessory that drew admiring eyes, but failed to transition to a greater sentiment. Although far simpler than her first engagement ring, the thin gold band seemed to fuse with her finger—as if destined for her hand. And the round, half-carat diamond—simple but timeless—captured her venerating heart.

She smoothed the cool cotton sheet over her chest and felt the stirring of Mace behind her. "'Morning," she whispered, as his lips grazed the crease of her neck.

"I'll get you a bigger diamond," his gruff morning voice mumbled.

Ava rotated her body to face him, her breasts threshing against his sculpted chest. "Don't you dare." She arched her brow. "This one is perfect."

Mace cast a doubtful expression. "My mum won't mind if we replace her diamond." He draped her bare thigh over his. "It's the ring itself that I wanted you to have."

Ava placed a delicate kiss upon his lips, then whispered, "I'm honored to wear this ring," followed by a second kiss. "And it's perfect—truly—in its existing condition."

Mace stroked her cheek, then traced her lips with his thumb. "Well, the offer stands if you ever change your mind."

Ava flashed a demure smile. "I won't, but thank you." She pressed her head to his chest; his soft, resting heartbeat pacifying. *There's something I need to tell you.*

With long, delicate strokes, Mace caressed her thigh as it lay atop his; his full mast pressing against her. "Maybe we should make plans before you start filming *Candy Cane Calamity*…"

"Mason," Ava began, fixing her gaze upon him. His steel-blue eyes appeared opalescent in the morning light, and, after taking a moment to appreciate their beauty, she whispered, "I've decided to retire from acting—officially."

"Ava…" Mace's voice grew taut, and he pulled her tighter against his chest. "I would never ask you to give up your dream."

"I know," she whispered. "Acting may have been a *passion*, but it was never my *dream*." She planted a tender kiss on his lips. "You are."

His eyes searched hers. "But I don't want you to have any regrets," he murmured, stroking her cheek.

"Mason—I almost died three times inside of a week." Her eyebrows rose. "I think it's time to throw in the towel and give another aspiring actress an opportunity."

Delight danced across his face for a moment before fading into his signature impassive expression, and Ava knew him well enough to know he tried to mask his elation. "In that case,"—he cleared his throat—"have you given any thought as to a date?"

Ava bobbed her head, the slightest unease brewing inside her. "The sooner the better."

"Oh yeah?" A roguish gleam appeared in his gorgeous eyes. "Can't wait to be Mrs. Storm, huh?" he said with a waggle of his brows.

Ava nibbled her bottom lip. "That…" she laced her fingers with his, needing to feel the strength of them. "Combined with the fact that I'm pregnant."

Mace's jaw fell open as his eyes veiled with a weighty glaze. Then, ever so slowly, his lips spread into a wide, crooked grin.

The end

Their adventure continues in Weathered the Storm... coming soon!

About the Author

Hailing from the picturesque landscapes of northern Michigan, author Josephine Jordin's literary passion embodies her craving for all things sweet and spicy. Armed with a degree in Criminology from Portland State University, and drawing inspiration from the likes of C.S. Lewis, Dean Koontz, and the dynamic duo of Douglas Preston and Lincoln Child, Josephine weaves tales that blend romantic depth, suspense, and humor. She invites you to experience her debut novel, *Ready for a Storm*, the first in a continuous three-part series, and recipient of both the Readers' Favorite and NN Light Book Heaven Five-Star Seals.

Please visit her website at www.josephinejordin.com or follow her on social media to stay up to date on current projects.